ANGEL'S LIGHT

A PARANORMAL ANGEL ROMANCE

ELEMENTAL ANGELS

AIMEE ROBINSON

AMR PUBLISHING LLC

Angel's Light

Copyright © 2023 by Aimee Robinson

Cover by Angela Haddon Book Cover Design

Edited by Sara Burgess at Telltail Editing

All rights reserved.

*To Cynthia St. Aubin, who makes me smile with my whole face and
loves cheese just as much as I do.*

ELEMENTAL ANGELS

Angel's Target

Angel's Duty

Angel's Devotion

Angel's Light

Angel's Temper

CHAPTER 1

Heaven was on fire, and there wasn't a fucking thing Tyrus could do about it.

For the past four days, he'd dispatched his seraphim scouts to the demon charmers' advancing line. Every time, his scouts returned in pieces. At first, he sent them out alone into the shadowy landscape that stretched beyond the Empyrean's gates. Once they reached the edge of the dark realm, however, communication had been lost, only to return hours later in the form of mangled wings and severed limbs dropped from the sky. The gruesome message was received loud and clear: there would be no survivors.

His most trusted spies had been reduced to carrion. Spies he'd saw off his limbs for. Spies who'd begged, then *demanded* to be sent into the field.

Since then, he'd ordered the seraphim to travel in pairs,

though it had been little more than a death order. No pair ever returned with both scouts alive. The singular spies who crawled back, however, brought news far more terrifying than the mere promise of death.

Cyro was coming. The demon ruler and sire of charmers in the dark realm hadn't just inched his presence closer to heaven and its defenses but steamrolled through them. The Veil, which had cocooned the Empyrean—heaven's highest realm—and its inhabitants since the Eternal Flame flared to life, had fallen. Not just fallen but disintegrated into a fragile mess of stardust and shattered hope. All from a single blow of dark magic Tyrus and the other sentinels had not known Cyro capable of.

It had been a crucial lack of intel. Intel he alone should have discovered.

The view from his outpost in the soul repository was bleak despite its vibrancy. Or perhaps because of it. Bleary eyes scanned through list after list of cataloged souls secured behind the gates. Every blinking orb on the celestial map overhead was one more creature that would be lost to time once Cyro and his charmers breached the celestial mages' hastily erected wards. The wards would hold, they had assured him.

Yeah, until they don't. Then what?

That question was just the tip of the mountain. There had been so much more he demanded to know, so much more the mages weren't sharing. Before he could bark out any more of his frustrations, however, his prime sentinel, Beltar, booted his ass from the chamber.

That was the last he'd seen of the mages before they squirreled themselves away to comb through their texts and magic stores once more. As if the magical kernel of hope that would save them all had simply been misfiled.

Tyrus picked at the collar of his armor and did his best to roll out a newly forming kink in his neck. Skin long irritated by sweat and facial hair that had blown past shadow beard two days ago begged for fresh air he couldn't afford to indulge in. How long had it been since he'd donned anything other than his battle skin? A week? A month? Did any of it matter when he and the sentinels stood on the precipice of a war for not just light and dark but existence itself?

He'd left Malthoran, Beltar's second-in-command, no more than an hour ago so the sentinel could gather the legions for their final campaign. Tyrus could no longer stomach his brother's rousing words of determination. Though the bastard could be just as brutal as the rest of them, Mal had the lamentable ability to hope for the best.

Tyrus's shoulders lifted with a dark chuckle at the sardonic memory. Hope. He never had much use for the stuff and saw no reason to invest in it now. The approaching nightmare was a far more useful motivator, and Tyrus was nothing if not efficient.

Heavy shoulders peeled away from his ears as he scanned the lists once more. Counting. Cataloging. Memorizing. All souls he and his brothers were bound to protect.

And he didn't have a fucking clue how to do it.

A crash broke through his melancholy. Tyrus's wings moved before the rest of him did. Pearlescent energy flared from his back, stretching and bending around his frame until it glowed in sync with his armor. Fucking hell, he wasn't in the mood. His shield pulsed in intuitive warning to the intruder: *get gone or get dead.*

A sigh released from deep in his chest. "Shouldn't you be working on your pretty game-day speech, Mal?" Tyrus didn't bother to look away from the map as he lifted his third—fourth?—glass of amber ether and took a swig.

Silence greeted his query, followed by the hesitant shuffle of slippers and satin, not boots and leather. "I'm so sorry, Sentinel Tyrus! I had no idea anyone would be here at this hour. Forgive me."

The smoky feminine voice instantly pulled all relaxed parts

of him to attention. The deep resonance punched him square in the chest, then vibrated down his back before landing between his legs. He'd only just managed to place his glass down before his fingers threatened to shatter the damn thing. After an embarrassingly delayed attempt, he finally managed to lower his shield and relax his wings enough to take in his intruder.

A riotous flounce of lavender skirts and long blonde hair melted to the floor. A hand frantically grasped at scrolls rolling this way and that while the other clutched a bevy of those already caught close to her chest.

A chest that, from his higher vantage point, heaved with no small amount of exertion. Had she been running? From what?

"No need. Here, allow me." Tyrus dropped to his knees and corralled the remaining scrolls, then gently lifted the burden from her arms and placed them on the side counter. He'd kept the repository's lighting dim, as was his preference, but the faint glow from the celestial map was enough to highlight the honey-hued tresses that had worked themselves free of her plait. Violet eyes far too wide for her face danced around the space, as if she were uncertain how to proceed.

Then she stood. The fluid sensuality with which she rose gripped him almost as much as her voice had. He only let out a breath when her knees finally locked into place and her full stature met his. Met, he should say, because the female was so tall and captivating, she could hold court at any council in the Empyrean and have a body count of drooling mages at her feet yes-ma'am-ing her desires before the meeting's opening chime had even sounded.

Tyrus thought he knew every mage in the Empyrean, but as he studied her face, his brain bank came up empty.

"Thank you. You didn't have to do that," she said.

"I do what I like." The words came out gruffer than he'd intended, a habit born from giving orders to seraphim scouts, and he regretted it instantly.

"Yes, of course, Sentinel." Her head dipped in a slight bow common among the laboring classes of mages. The gesture, intended to be one of respect, grated. Males should be bowing to *her*.

"There's no need for that. Given the circumstances, I wouldn't advise wasting time with curtsies and formalities." Perhaps honesty wasn't the best policy, but it wasn't like the approaching army was a well-guarded secret.

Not like the intel you'd sworn to uncover and hadn't.

Instead of scurrying away and leaving him to a good brooding session, as most mages tended to do, the female didn't move. Her eyes swept the repository. Once they alighted on the celestial map still up, she released a breath and buried her fingers into the folds of the royal-blue sash banded across her midsection. Slippered steps carried her forward, until the map's glow revealed the sunken shadows beneath her amethyst irises. "It's really happening."

Tyrus made a noncommittal noise, then joined her at the console. Fine, he'd deal with the company.

She bobbed her chin. "Then I am not too late."

"You're the only being in the Empyrean who would say such a thing." Darkness coated the sentiment before he could temper the disdain.

"As you said, it is best not to waste time. I have a soul to catalog. I've already entered my run's pertinent details in the scrolls, but the soul itself must be recorded."

That confounded him. "Really? Now?" Had she not heard the chaos in the streets of the Empyrean? The war gongs urging everyone to safety?

"It cannot wait. She's already settled, poor dear, but I must log her arrival while I can."

Every soul that had ever existed was about to be extinguished with the approaching morning, and she was worried about fucking paperwork?

Not your burden. You have enough to worry about.

He sighed and swept his hand toward the map's display. "Far be it from me to force a day off on a workaholic—" Tyrus jumped back, narrowly avoiding her flailing arm, which had begun animatedly waving in time to her words. His boots barely cleared her path before she hurried past him.

"That's just it!" The air around her fingers rippled, and a stylus appeared. Snatching the thing, she ducked her head over the console and worked feverishly. "If there's only tonight, I've got to make it count. I promised Iona I'd see her passage secured, and that's exactly what I'm going to do. I've never lost a soul yet, you know. Even those times when the Veil's mist was particularly thick, I still managed to get the souls settled. The other messengers always used it as an excuse, you know. But not me. Nope. Of course, I always offered to show them my navigation tricks for getting through the mist when it turned soupy like that, but the other messenger mages weren't interested. How absurd. Can you imagine not being interested in learning a technique that could save a soul?" The uneasy chuckle matched the ferocity of her frantic scribbles. With a final *swoosh*, her stylus disappeared, and she released the common and weighty breath of the overworked and underappreciated.

A bit of Tyrus's own tension fled his shoulders as the air left her pursed lips. Again, her hands returned to her blue sash where her fingers nervously carded through the fabric's pleats. The sash's color and significance, along with the rest of her uniform, finally slammed into his skull.

She was a messenger mage. That was why he didn't know her. Messengers rarely spent time in the Empyrean once a soul was delivered. They largely worked in the field, shuttling souls from all the different worlds into heaven. Many of the spiritual and governing mages thought of it as grunt work, though Tyrus never subscribed to that philosophy. If work needed to be done, it needed to be done.

But why was she still going into the mist? The Veil was down. It wasn't safe anymore. She should be secured behind the gates with the rest of the mages.

He opened his mouth to say as much, but her smoky voice robbed him of speech.

"I think I'm going to miss the water worlds the most."

If despair was a weapon, he'd be speared through and strung up on the Empyrean's gates waiting for Cyro's boys to make him go lights out for good. The female mage's arms banded more tightly around her middle, as if she could hug the misery out of her system.

"Iona was a sea nymph who had just entered her final ripple of life. Her family were other nymphs and naiads who lived on the surrounding cluster of water worlds. I was with her when the Veil fell, and she was so worried about getting to heaven. Not for her, mind you, but for them." She swallowed past emotion that had grown thick and stifling in the small repository. "I swore to her that I'd get her through, and when I was able to and it was their time, I'd come back for her family, too."

Tyrus shifted his wings. "You shouldn't have promised that."

"I shouldn't do a lot of things. At least, that's what my mentoring mage tells me." Misted pools of violet lifted to his stony mug and pinned him with sincerity so brutal it shattered his hardened defenses. "But if I don't, who will?"

By the mages, who was this female? Who, in all of the Empyrean, had granted this messenger the power to dismantle a sentinel on the eve of his army's last stand?

Outside, faint noises grew in ominous crescendos. Cries turned to sobs, and moans turned to muffled moments behind closed doors. Buildings either emptied out or filled up, depending on the proclivities of the establishment and its patrons. Every soul and creature in heaven was responding in their own way to the Empyrean's final rallying cry: smoke 'em if you got 'em.

He was a sentinel. A guardian of the Empyrean. He should have ignored it all and thrown in with his brothers' harried storm of training, intelligence briefings, and what little rest any of them could manage before hell descended on them.

He shouldn't be here, wasting time counting up all the chips he was going to lose. Or marking the golden flecks dappling violet irises he couldn't look away from.

"I shouldn't do a lot of things, either," he admitted.

A shy smile brightened the repository's gloom, adding to the glow shimmering from the souls on the map. Something about the female before him dragged him out of the hole he had been happy to wallow in. Well, maybe not *happy* but was certainly resigned to. This female, though, with her husky-voiced urgency and electric charge that, for one blessed moment, pulled his thoughts away from the horizon . . .

"What's your name?" he whispered. When the hell did he ever whisper?

"My mentors call me Dee."

That voice crept beneath his skin, tightening everything from his chest to his cock. "Is that what you'd like me to call you?"

He didn't miss the quiver in her words or how she lowered those lashes to avert her gaze. "You may call me what you wish, Sentinel."

"What I wish"—his hand lifted before he realized it and brushed the high curve of her cheek—"is to forget for one night."

"Pardon?"

"I wish to forget my position, to forget the weight of it, everything I can't predict, and all who rely on me. For one blessed night, I wish to just . . . be."

Familiar agony and blatant foolishness pulled his hand away

from her, until she secured it in hers. Smooth skin cocooned his hand's rough hide, and he couldn't remember the last time he'd noticed the contrast. The last time he'd *craved* a gentle touch or the last time his muscles twitched with anticipation of protecting and basking in such a caress. The connection was simple, borderline chaste, nothing more than fingers curled around fingers, but he couldn't stop the defensive fist that formed.

Brawn that responded in defense of her, *for* her. He'd never been above using his size in any manner that suited him, but never had he wanted to use it in such a singular service for another. Never had he been more grateful for the bulk on his frame if it meant she'd touch him like that again.

Then she brought her lips to his knuckles. "If there's one thing I recognize with all my being, it's a soul in need of saving."

He snatched his hand away before other parts of him developed different ideas. "I'm no gentle soul in need of guidance."

Her resolute chin lifted. Not a hint of fear or trepidation. A warrior in her own right. "Aren't you?"

He followed her gaze to the map, where rows upon rows of star-lit clusters blinked back at them. Some clusters, he'd just realized, blinked more brightly than others, nearly outshining the single souls' lights in some areas. And then the reason dawned on him. They were *pairs* of souls. Those who had found each other in eternity. *They* glowed the brightest.

The awakening hunger and promise of blissful ignorance constructed Tyrus's desire before logic could tamp it back down.

He took a step forward. "If you had one night left, would you want your soul's light to be a single blip on the map?"

He couldn't bring himself to look at her. He wasn't even sure what he was asking. What he *did* know was the clawing pain that flared behind his ribs whenever he allowed himself to sit in the suck of solitude. If tonight was truly all they had, would he be content with his duty, knowing he did what was asked of him?

He didn't know which question she answered or whether he'd spoken his thoughts out loud, but the warm steadiness in her voice told him it didn't matter.

"No."

CHAPTER 2

The allée of trees sheltering their path was way more of an omen than an angel like Tyrus needed. Flora stretching toward the messenger mages' dormitory may as well have been death march decorations. In the Empyrean, celestial sun cycles existed and mimicked what the souls were accustomed to in the mortal worlds. It made for an easier transition all around, both for the souls and the mages who frequented the worlds. Didn't mean Tyrus had to like all the growth that came along with it, though, or what it meant when the darkness finally emerged.

With every depression Tyrus's boots left in the compacted white sand along the Empyrean's main thoroughfare, the jewel-toned branches arching overhead seemed to droop in weighty response.

A million other tasks piled up in his mind, all among the protect and serve variety. Protect against the demon invasion that'd be there before breakfast, serve the celestial mages in whatever final tasks they commanded of him.

All of that could dissolve into the once-Veiled mist and choke out a charmer or two thousand to boot, for all he cared.

Only one thought propelled him forward through the abandoned streets and his even more abandoned mind: what if he missed his chance?

But because he was a fucking sentinel and there were codes of honor even his debased ass couldn't ignore, he'd talked himself out of any chance beyond seeing her home safely.

For whatever hours any of them had left.

"This is me." Dee's whiskey voice pulled him out of his sulk fest and tugged him up the ramp to an arched door. She placed her hand on the center of the pane. After a quick pulse of magic, the seal released and the door fell open with a moan of invitation, as if even the buildings were conspiring to test him.

A hitch in his side reminded him of the armor he still wore and why. Before Tyrus's boots carried him closer to a female he had no business getting close to, he flared his wings and executed the sentinel's bow. The gesture was instinctual and often used in deference to the celestial mages. *My power bends only to that which serves the Empyrean.* Perhaps it'd keep him good and planted on the right (or wrong, as his instincts insisted) side of the door.

The moment his gaze dropped low enough to take in the space beyond the threshold, however, all thoughts of honor fucked right off. He was up and moving. Gently nudging her out of the way, he entered her apartment and wasn't at all prepared for the sparsity, the enormity of which hit him in the miserable organ panting behind his solar plexus.

Nothing.

Tyrus stood before two-hundred-and-twenty square feet of empty walls and even emptier emotions. Empyrean-issued white paint coated the bones of the cell, for that was all he could equate the small space to, and no furniture or belongings existed beyond a simple scribe's desk and chair, a scroll or two atop it, and a single rod affixed into a small alcove from which three uniforms hung. There wasn't even a bed, which Tyrus sure as shit knew was standard-issue even for labor-class Empyreans. Instead, a fern-green bedroll with stuffing better suited for tinder than cushioning an actual body lay unfurled on the floor in all its lumpy glory.

"What the fuck is this?" Tyrus tried his best—okay, not really —to keep the outrage out of his voice, but if all they had was one more night, he sure as shit didn't just walk her back home so she could spend it on a cold mound of threadbare fabric on the floor.

Dee quickly shut the door. "It's my bedroll."

"Yeah, I got that. Why do you have one? Why not a bed? And why not, I don't know, decorations or trunks or, hell, a hanging plant or two?"

Those fingers that had been wrapped around his moments ago once again picked through the pleats of her sash. The nervous gesture gutted him, and he mentally tore into his beast for unsettling her.

"I'm not here much."

"Doesn't mean you don't sleep in a bed."

A slim shoulder bobbed in answer. "It's not important."

"The fuck it isn't." Tyrus surged toward her, though he was well aware of what his swelling size could do to a being in such confined quarters. To his surprise, she didn't flinch or even cower. Like she was used to intimidation and either already had a practiced fuck-you ready on her lips or . . .

She'd learned to protect herself in other less obvious ways.

Rage unraveled quickly, but he tamped it back down and threw every ounce of gentleness he could muster into his words. "Dee, I know you're not here often, but all the dormitories have standard-issued equipment. Why is your room different?"

Pain twisted her features, though her proud stature quickly course corrected away from any hint of vulnerability that had escaped through the cracks. "As I said, I'm not here often. In truth, I spend more time with the souls on other worlds than the mages here. My absences have not always been looked on fondly. Many of my compatriots don't share my curiosities, nor the desire to travel as I do."

"Through the mist."

She lowered her head and busied herself with the two scrolls on the desk. "Yes. I take unsavory risks, I've been told. Careless, reckless, even, as my mentors continue to phrase it. Some worlds are harder to get to than others, and we're told those should be left to the more experienced messenger mages." A pale orange glow from the tiny window highlighted the dimness of the space and the gloom of her emotions. "But those mages only make it to those worlds a handful of times a year."

The terrible truth hung heavily in the air around them. If a soul wasn't escorted to heaven, it would evaporate into nothing, and the spark gifted to that soul from the Eternal Flame, the source of all light and life, would extinguish along with it.

The brutal realization coated his throat in bile. They'd all had to make sacrifices, lost good beings to insurmountable circumstances, but never willingly. If there was a way, Tyrus and his brothers had fucking found it. He'd never considered the other lines of work that kept the Empyrean running.

He'd never thought another celestial being's morals would run counter to his own, for that matter.

And here Dee was, fighting the good fight with no weapons other than an iron will and a flawless ethical compass.

"The bed is some hazing bullshit. A statement of disapproval. Punishment." Tyrus's tone didn't ask for confirmation, but the dip of her elegant chin supported it anyway.

Pent-up fury lashed through his shield. Pulsing white power lanced over his wings, splaying them wide in battle instinct. Except he wasn't on a battlefield. He was cooped up in a dormitory no bigger than the size of some of the closets he stored his weapons in. Nor was he alone. Before he could call his wings home, his far-reaching flight feathers whipped out, catching Dee square in the jaw. Stunned, she cried out and stumbled backward.

Tyrus's wings wrapped around her before her head hit the corner of the desk. He caught her and quickly lowered her to the floor, cushioning her with the fan of his wings.

"Shit! Let me see." A slim red gash etched a line around the curve of her jaw.

"No, it's fine. I can heal it, Sentinel. Please, it was my—"

"Do not even think about saying this was your fault. I'm not your peer, nor some spoiled mentor who gets off at the expense of others. Now, hold still." Her features stilled into quiet resolve and the bow of her upper lip flattened out into a line of reluctant submission. "I won't hurt you," he rushed out. "Never. Never again." The vow stung with an impenetrable truth that shocked even his own senses, but when he tried it on for size in his mind, nothing but absolute sincerity rang back at him.

Tyrus had healed more injuries than any angel had a right to heal, under conditions that would make the muck of the water worlds seem sterile. Usually, they were quick and dirty affairs. Minor patch jobs that could wait until the healers arrived. With Dee, however, he held her as one would a precious relic and gently cupped her cheek. It was more touch than strictly necessary, given the size of the wound. And c'mon, who was he kidding? The thing was little more than a scrape. But he simply couldn't resist. Especially not when an inflamed hunger threatened to rip out of him the longer she lay beneath him. A heartbeat later, white light glowed from his palm nestled against her face. Frosted lashes flitted down to rest on the crests of her cheeks. That full upper lip, which had been thinned and tense a moment ago, relaxed away from the prison of her teeth.

The berry-kissed lips that sprang free would have been his undoing. That was why, as soon as her body slackened in his hold and his palm revealed newly healed skin, he pulled away.

Or, at least, he tried to, until Dee lifted that tempting mouth and planted a kiss on his.

Tyrus reared back. "You don't—"

It wasn't until her voice, once so commanding, broke through his objection, sounding as little as the hours left before morning, that he stilled.

What would she ask of him? To stay? To leave? To demand a strike in retribution for the mark he'd made on her, as she was within her rights to do? Or, worse, ask to kiss her again?

Even under the mountainous burdens he'd been hauling around, nothing compared to the tension in his lower abs as he waited for her next words. Words that could damn him tonight or send him to his death with the dawn.

"They're really coming for the Empyrean tomorrow, aren't they?"

His arms flexed around her, instinctively hauling her closer against the wall of his chest. "Yes."

Violet eyes shuttered in resignation. Tyrus cursed every sort of bullshit fate had thrown at him, if for no other reason than to have to witness the anguish painted on her face. Perhaps it was a good thing that he was walking into hell tomorrow, because he'd never be able to live another day knowing he couldn't keep that pain off her fine features.

His lids slammed down in anguish, but not before her consuming kiss captured his mouth with all the passion of a star that would never be given a chance to burn again.

Chances. He was so fucking tired of not taking chances. No more.

Damnation it is.

Once the cord snapped, his fate had been sealed. Instinct took over. Hands bracketed her impossibly tighter while he devoured every flavor that washed over him. The sweet smoke of her tongue invaded senses long deadened by battle and ambivalence. If he had known one kiss from her would make him *feel* again . . .

Feel. Yes, he needed to feel. More. Endlessly more.

He rolled them in a cocoon of his wings' protection until her eternally long legs bracketed his hips. A brief prayer left his lips for whichever female had the good sense to create side slits on messenger uniforms before he traced the smooth skin that greeted his questing hands.

Dee was no less eager, which only increased the painful pleasure begging to break free behind his pants. In answering kind, she rocked her perfect ass right along his cock, and it was all he could do not to sink his teeth into the cleft of her shoulder.

Armor fell away as quickly as bolts of satin. Fingers and teeth tore at each other with an intensity that neither of them was coming back from. That much he knew. She barely let him take his mouth from hers to rip his clothes away. Good. Tyrus would rather incinerate the shit off his body than stop kissing her for even half a second.

Not kiss. Imprint.

The female in his arms wasn't just a mage but a goddess. Some holy entity not merely responsible for creation but devotion. When he reached up to free her honey-blonde hair from its plait, the soft sigh that escaped her was a hymn he'd stamp on his heart for as long as he had beats left in it.

Tyrus dragged his hands up her ribs and silently ticked off every dip and divot, committing them to memory. Every caress needed to last as long as possible, as long as it would take before he had to fly into the approaching inferno and give every last ounce of himself in service to the Empyrean.

In service to *her*, he'd decided.

The underside of her breasts bumped his knuckles, and he savored the feel of the delicate skin there before gently cupping her. He broke away from her mouth only long enough to place a kiss against the wall of her chest. Then another on the crest of her right breast, then her left. Three silent reverent prayers.

She answered with the warm press of her lips against his forehead, perhaps a prayer of her own, if he had the gall to believe in such things.

Fucking hell, if he'd known a simple kiss could be his undoing, he'd have hunted this female down and claimed her mouth lifetimes ago. Searched for her through any mist or sludge or whatever else might have been thrown his way just to bask in the calm that came with her kiss.

It would never be enough, and yet it had to be. They had no lifetimes left, only tonight.

Harried strength and dwindling time spurred them both on. He slipped his fingers between her legs and licked a tantalizing trail along her lower lip once it fell open. When he turned to take her mouth from a different angle, a shadowed image on her arm caught his eye. With his other hand, he gripped her wrist, smiled at the dark ivy-like tattoo painted there, and kissed it fervently. Her long neck, endless curves, and unbound hair were all taunts he cursed himself over. If they had been granted life in another time, one where eons stretched before them, he'd have spent days learning each part of her with each part of him. But now, he'd settle for whatever time she'd give him.

Whatever parts of her she offered.

The powerful thighs bracketing him tensed as she lifted off his questing hand. With a repositioned angle and an unspoken sense of urgency, she sheathed him fully. Tyrus hardly had time to bask in the warmth enveloping him before he gripped her firmly and lifted her with his hips in response. Gasping moans filled the small apartment as they met in a frenzy of unbridled passion. Hands dug into his shoulders. Tongues dragged along skin. A frantic rhythm tore through him with each thrust her body answered. A spiraling connection sang amid an indescribable collision of souls. Climax was too simple a word, even for a warrior's brain like his, but it was the best he could scrounge up. Phonetic language dissolved into one of explosions. Arched backs, tightened muscles, and desperate yearning were all that remained to describe the indescribable, until they both cried out in the language of their souls.

Damnation was right. He'd found his hell sooner than expected. It was in this female's arms, with the promise of never feeling them around him again.

With limbs strong enough for her but too weak for anything else, Tyrus pulled Dee against his chest. The small room was quiet except for the even breaths that fell in sync with each other. Ecstasy and despondency choked out any words that may have been left to share between them and, instead, gave way to sleep's even breathing.

Only hours later, when Tyrus's overheated blood had cooled and the jut of a table leg against his hip demanded he move did he finally open his eyes. Through the small window, burgeoning beams of light threatened to tint the night sky with reds and burnt oranges. Dawn was approaching.

Tyrus inched away from the desk and sat up, but when he stretched out his wings—carefully, this time, so as not to whack Dee in the chin again—he needn't have worried.

She was already gone.

CHAPTER 3

Present Day

If Drea Arnold squinted hard enough, she could almost pretend the coffee stain on her lab coat blended into the stitched lettering. Almost. She slowly cocked her head to the left. Maybe, if one didn't look too closely, the swirly dried drip on the bottom of the embroidered letters could be mistaken for an added flourish to the E at the end. Not the E in her first name, sadly, but the final looping E punctuating her poor life choices, albeit in pretty royal-blue stitching.

Trainee.

To get her full name decked out on a pristine white lab coat, instead of the seen-better-days handout she currently wore, would mean she'd have to stay at one job long enough for her company's purchase order to go through. Or for the background check to clear. Or for her to focus on the project she was actually hired to do instead of poking around the myriad of other things she had no business poking around.

Which brought her back to the brown blob engulfing more company-owned real estate on her boob than had any right to be there. Whoever thought embroidered stitching on one's chest was a good idea never had to wrangle their tits into a button-down shirt. Honestly, did the penises in charge ever consider that maybe it wasn't the best idea to enforce company loyalty and name awareness by branding it on a woman's top shelf?

Thunderous stomping tore Drea away from her coffee conundrum.

"Got the stain remover!" Molly Resnick, Drea's best friend/roommate and resident domestic goddess, tore into a plastic packet with her teeth, yanked out a folded towelette, and handed it over. "Blot, don't rub."

"Got it."

"No, you don't. You're rubbing."

"How is this rubbing? Besides, I think the blotting thing is really only for dry napkins on fresh stains, right?"

Before Drea could swipe the towel over the stain again, Molly yoinked the thing out of her fingers and held it high in the manner of all playground bullies and no-nonsense mothers the world over. "If you don't want my help, don't ask for it."

And that right there was the crux of Drea's sad sack circumstances. She couldn't remember a time when she *wasn't* on the wanting-and-needing-help end of the spectrum. The predicament was only made significantly worse by her inability to focus, as her mother loved to point out, though focus had nothing to do with it.

Okay, maybe it had a little to do with it.

"All right, I'll blot."

Molly lifted a dark stenciled eyebrow and leveled Drea with her finest mean-old-school-marm glare. Her best friend had first learned the look from her Jewish mother but had perfected it in restaurant kitchens where every male line cook copped a 'tude when she was inevitably promoted and they weren't. Now, Molly was a sous-chef for one of the most in-demand restaurants in Aurora, New Hampshire, and her death stare was legendary.

And definitely something Drea didn't have time for.

"Oh, c'mon. I don't speak glare, and I need to get to work. My shift starts in"—she yanked her phone from her back pocket—"fifty minutes and it takes me an hour to get there."

Taking pity on her, Molly grabbed Drea's lab coat and went after the stain with vigor Drea truly had no hope of matching. "Sounds like some of your math might be a tad off there, love," Molly remarked.

"They don't pay me for my math skills. They pay me for my big old science brain."

"I'm pretty sure they pay you to be on time, and last I checked, you couldn't operate your big old science brain without a sprinkling of math thrown in."

Drea twisted her damp hair into a braid, doing her best not to *zetz* her best friend in the teeth with her elbow. "I'm in the business of bodily fluids and tissue samples. The automated equipment is far better at the analysis than I am, anyway."

Molly stepped back, assessed her handiwork, sighed, and flicked Drea's braid over her shoulder so it draped over the stain. Point taken. There was no hope as far as looking presentable was concerned.

"You won't be in business much longer if you don't get your ass out that door," Molly urged.

"Right." Drea lifted her work bag off the hook on the back of her bedroom door and bolted to the kitchen, where—bless all things Molly related—a travel mug of burn-your-mouth-off coffee was waiting for her.

Two more weeks. Just two more weeks and she could truly exhale the rancid bubble of stress she'd been choking on for the past three months. After that, her ninety-day probationary period with her new laboratory would be over, and she'd officially be rolling in the glory that was full-time insurance benefits, 401(k) contributions, and paid time off.

Not to mention no longer having to witness the disappointed look on Molly's face when Drea informed her, yet again, that she might be a tad late with her portion of the rent. Even sainthood had its limits apparently, and though Molly was more likely to kick up her feet and listen to Drea bitch about her bad day than kick up a fuss, it wasn't right. None of it was.

All that was about to change.

Drea tossed a protein bar and an apple into her bag and spared a second she didn't have for her first bracing sip of coffee while Molly eyed her with exasperation.

"That's hardly a breakfast of champions, but far be it from me to try and change your habits at this point," she remarked, tidying up the couch cushions and folding the throws Drea never bothered to return to their rightful locations.

Drea winced at the burn but braved another sip. "We've all got habits," she said with a not-so-subtle side-eye toward her friend's busy hands.

Got ya, Miss OCD.

Molly dropped the blanket in a huff, then shifted her feet. A second ticked by before she picked up the blanket again, placed it down once more, then resumed her fidgeting.

Tension stiffened Drea's back. She halted the travel mug halfway to her lips. Uh-oh. The lack of eye contact, the hands playing with the nearby table runner's fringes, the pursed lips.

Shit. Not now.

Molly dropped the fabric and fiddled with her nails. "Just, please don't . . . you know . . ."

"Fuck this up?"

The anguished look on Molly's face was half-gratitude at not having to say the words herself and half-misery because, yeah, they both knew they needed to be said.

Drea had first met Molly in sixth grade, when they were two frizzy-haired eleven-year-olds shoved into a new intermediate school before they could even spell the word intermediate. As terms like *cliques* and *popularity* entered their not-yet-preteen lexicons, they both quickly realized the value of sticking together rather than sticking out. Sprinkle in the fact that they were both adopted—Molly from Latvia and Drea from Russian immigrants with Greek roots—and there had been no separating them.

Even when, two decades later, Drea's tenacity had matured in perhaps a different way than Molly's had. Whereas her best friend had been downright ruthless in pursuing her culinary career from an early age because the lucky brat had gotten her first taste of the food fancies at her Bat Mitzvah and had been determined to up her game ever since, Drea was a victim of shiny object syndrome. To be clear, it was a brutal, obsessive work-your-ass-off-and-discover-all-the-secrets kind of shiny object syndrome, but it was a syndrome nonetheless. When she was fascinated by something, she threw herself into it *hard*, until her impossible-to-stifle curiosity would invariably tug her in a different direction.

That was why she pursued the sciences. Well, the types of sciences one could access with an associate's degree. Things as a lab technician were always changing, always moving, and one wasn't penalized for asking questions or volunteering to bounce around on different research teams. Usually. Maybe. Sometimes.

"Oh, I won't. Honestly, this is the best job I've ever had, despite it being an hour away in Drake County." Drea placed a hand on the door but, in true long-goodbye fashion, didn't open it to leave yet. "I have one supervisor, and he only seems to surface about once or twice a week. I get the diagnostic lab all to myself. And"—she dropped the door handle and punctuated the air with her finger—"I've been given the green light to deck out the staff break room with whatever goodies I want! Do you realize what this means?"

"That you're finally going to get all your single-serve hazelnut mocha coffee pods out of our kitchen and bring them to work?"

"Yes! No nut allergies to worry about!"

Molly snorted an *I can relate*. They'd spent many a night and many a bottle of wine commiserating over the dietary restriction hoops chefs had to jump through. All necessary, of course, but it didn't change the fact that Molly hadn't become a chef so she could play gluten gladiator in defense of sourdough bread.

"I don't know. I still think it's really weird you're there all alone and that you can't talk to me about any of it. Who are you supposed to talk to, then? Does your boss seriously just expect you to leave work at work? Does he even know how women operate?"

"Okay, the nondisclosure agreement was a tad unusual, I'll admit, but I'm not really in a place to judge. The sign-on bonus that's coming my way once I make it to full-time employee will more than cover this month's rent and the repairs on my car."

Molly quirked a sad smile her way. "I hear ya. Now, go. I gave you the prime parking spot on my day off for a reason. And let me know what time Malcolm's joining us for dinner tonight."

Shoot. Was it time for Triple B—boyfriend, best friend, and burgers—already? Hadn't they all just gotten together a week ago? Or was it four? She and Malcolm had only begun dating soon after she started her new job, but still, nearly three months wasn't long enough to forget important details like that, right?

Drea twisted her features into one of regret and thanks. "Yes, I will. I'll text you when I get off work."

After the air kisses were thrown, Drea threw herself down the steps and out the door. If she timed the lights right, she'd make it out of Aurora proper and onto the highway with plenty of time to catch up. Speed traps weren't generally a thing on the route she took to work. Besides, the former landfill on site had a little something to do with people keeping a wide berth. Who the hell wanted to patrol that when the Drake County Mall was a few miles away and afforded more regular and reliable prey for the state troopers?

Tires long ago missing any decent tread peeled out of their parking spot and bumped down the road. Once Drea was clear of the bulk of the congestion, she exhaled a shaky breath.

Molly was right. That NDA was truly a killer. How on earth anyone expected her to keep her lips shut about some of the samples she'd been testing, she'd never know. On paper, all identifying patient information was, of course, omitted. However, she hadn't worked at seven laboratories, three hospitals, two medical research facilities, and more doctor's offices than she'd ever admit without knowing a red flag when she saw one.

Drea gripped the wheel tighter and got on the entry ramp to the highway. Excitement, coupled with her sedan's woefully inadequate shocks, nearly had her bouncing out of her seat, because at the top of her to-do list this morning, and all she could think about over the weekend, was to reanalyze the blood samples she'd taken on Friday.

And figure out why the hell, after spinning one blood vial for more than ten minutes in the centrifuge, which was definitely *not* recommended by the manufacturer, the blood's serum still refused to separate from the cells.

Or why, after triple-checking that she used the right tubes and everything was balanced, her centrifuge still overheated and set the rotor on fire. One thing was for sure: Drea would eat her hubcaps before she'd let a mishap like this threaten her job security or deter her from figuring out just what the hell was in that blood.

CHAPTER 4

As far as Chrome's seating preferences went, a boulder caked in bird shit hadn't been on his bingo card for the day, yet there he sat. The acres of parched earth before him didn't look like they were having any better luck either when it came to their own proclivities. The July heat had settled its ass over the area good and hard, and after four consecutive days of temperatures above ninety degrees, Drake County and the rest of its miserable neighbors were solidly in heat wave territory.

And yet, despite the sweat dripping into parts he really didn't want to think about, he'd returned to this perch for the third time this week.

To watch her.

Chrome lifted one numb ass cheek off the rock and peeled out a pack of chewing gum from his back pocket. Popping a square into his mouth, he breathed in the peppermint while his eyes volleyed from the sun's position to the steel-gray door at the mouth of a sewer pump station that was anything but.

To anyone passing through, the chain-link fence bordering the ho-hum dirt road and surrounding property was nothing more than a do-not-disturb sign on a capped landfill. Before the giant waste pimple, the sprawling acreage had been home to Chlor-Chem Labs. The facility was a chemical plant that produced a whole lot of shit that made the metal that was part of him revolt and, turned out, not agree much with the mortals either.

Decades later, after the mortals turned a blind eye to their direct involvement in the area's chemical pollution problem, the site had sat abandoned, until the sentinels caught wind of Cyro using it as his little underground dark magic meth lab and refurbished HQ. However, since Chrome and his brothers didn't exactly have accurate schematics of the holdings other than a largely unfavorable demon-to-angel ratio, the sentinels had been forced to lay low.

That all changed three months ago when they stumbled upon caravans of demon charmers carting around new and dangerous weapons through residential areas like a damn ice cream truck in peak summer. The discovery had nearly cost his brother Steel his life and the life of his brother's soul bond, Bridget.

Chrome checked his watch. The moment the minute hand turned over, the door to the pump station swung open. If it wasn't for the gum in his mouth cushioning his bite, he'd be the new owner of a cracked molar or two. At five minutes after five on the dot every day, she stepped through that door. A door that, by all intents and purposes, shouldn't have opened to anything more than the small masonry structure full of tanks and pipes. Certainly not a door for a mortal to walk in and out of every day like they were clocking into work.

Like the badge and lanyard hanging from the woman's neck would suggest.

The door slammed closed, and the woman worked the latch on the small fence surrounding the pump station. Once she turned her back to the tree line where Chrome was hiding, he stood, risked taking a few steps forward, and, not for the first time, silently thanked the celestial mages for his heightened senses.

Blonde hair dappled with honey highlights was twisted into a loose, if slightly messy, braid down the woman's back. It was a common hairstyle for her, though in the times when he'd observe her in the mornings, the braid started off much tighter and was often damp. Sometimes she wore it loosely braided, and sometimes she'd arrive with it more intricately done like he'd seen equestrians wear. Her head was only a few inches shorter than the six-foot fence she was currently locking up, and for some reason, that fact pleased him, being a large man himself.

And as long as he was sticking to the honesty portion of his peep show, there wasn't much about her that *didn't* please him. Her elegant features and occasionally frantic mannerisms had been stirring up a familiar memory, one he only ever took out to examine when he was at his lowest, which, oddly enough, had been more often as of late.

The white lab coat she wore brushed just above her knees. He didn't need his heightened eyesight to pick up on the garment's profuse wrinkle situation or the small stains grazing the hemline on the back of her coat where she most likely couldn't see. Every time he came here, he could have sworn there was another mark marring what should have been starched white cotton. From the looks of it, however, the coat hadn't seen the underside of a hot iron since it was first woven and pressed at the manufacturer. The thought might have bothered him if it wasn't for the fact that, if his suspicions were correct, her employer was about as OSHA-conscious as a shark was vegan.

Chrome waited for her to walk to her car, and wasn't that a generous moniker for the so-called vehicle? Only two out of the four door handles were the same silver as the rest of the paint job. The rear driver's-side tire was the same doughnut from the week before, which only added to the mismatched—ambiance? flare?—of the poor creature. He didn't know whether the damn thing should be sent to the crusher or put on display as a testament to the tenacity of duct tape and dreams.

One thing was for damn certain: he in no way liked her driving that thing.

The car door peeled open with a rusty groan of all things too old and tired to give a shit, but instead of angling into the vehicle, she paused for a moment, then turned to *him*. Well, not him exactly, but the tree line where he hid. She always did this, and the hell if he knew why, the second she maneuvered his way, he'd alter into his metal skin. With the angle of the late-day sun and the lengthening shadows crawling through the bramble, he would be just another shape among the trees to her. For him, however, his transformation to chrome armor was a visceral reaction to unleashing a memory—a memory that always flooded back whenever he came here.

And after three months, he was going to find out why.

Her chin lifted toward the sun, and a relaxed calm bathed her features. A deep breath or two followed, almost as if she was exhaling the workday from her lungs as well as her mind. What the hell kind of workday did she have that required such a rote wind-down routine each evening? His jaw ticked. Nope, he couldn't dwell on that. The only thing that kept him coming back each week was to make sure that female walked out of there at five after five. The why of it he had time to figure out. How *much* time was the unknown intel he really fucking needed.

The female's long lashes fluttered closed for a heartbeat, then another, before opening again. Slim shoulders sagged in relief, then quickly shucked off the lab coat. She tossed the thing into her passenger seat and flapped her hands under her arms in a futile attempt to cool herself down. If that beater of a car had any sort of air conditioning system, it hadn't worked since the odometer's first lap around the hundred-thousand-mile mark.

Inexplicably, his fingers itched to tear into the thing. The metal he commanded all but barked to get under the hood good and deep. Even from this distance, he could sense the sparsely filled chrome-plated aluminum radiator. The thing needed coolant, which had most likely been leaking all over Drake County's highways for the better part of a month. As soon as the thought entered his head, he debated his stealth Good Samaritan approach. If she had to drive that rust bucket into the charmers' den, the least he could do was fix it up while she was sleeping so her AC would magically work one day. Perhaps it'd help shake up this obsession and take his mind from memories that insisted on being dredged up, even if this female's odd familiarity did more to keep things front of mind than was healthy.

Dee.

The messenger mage, another female with similar honey-blonde hair from limitless lifetimes before, was long gone. Not gone, he hoped, but safe in the Empyrean behind gates he and his brothers had sealed themselves out of to protect heaven from Cyro's invasion.

She had to be safe, he told himself, more to preserve his sanity than anything else.

Or to preserve his peace.

Chrome shook away the morose thoughts and turned to go, but before he angled his back completely, a dark shadow at the base of her wrist caught his attention. With each flap of her desperate hands, the shadow remained stationary. Odd. How had he not noticed the smudge before? If he could pick up on her penchant for fuchsia hair ties and aquamarine nail polish, it certainly wasn't beyond him to catalog minute details like birthmarks. He narrowed his eyes further at the curious shadow, then stilled.

Not a shadow but a tattoo. Small and ivy-like. It was a pattern he'd seen before only once and only on one person. One female.

"No," he breathed out.

Blood pounded in Chrome's ears. Breath turned to ice in his lungs. He stumbled back and shimmered out of his metal skin. His ass returned to bird-shit boulder ground zero. Once his bulk was firmly settled on the rock, he dropped his head between his knees and let his central nervous system have the freak-out it needed.

It wasn't possible. There was no way any mortal could have that mark. Not the mark he'd once pressed his lips to and whispered prayers against before dawn had come and ripped him away from its owner and everything else. From the single moment of peace he'd managed to find in a barrage of death.

No. *No!*

Chrome lifted his head in time with the woman's tires retreating over gravel. As soon as she was out of view, he unfurled his metallic wings and shot to the sky.

Tonight, he would have his answers, and she would give them to him. He was done hiding.

CHAPTER 5

If Drea could trust in anything, it was her neighbors' ruthlessness when it came to scenting out a vacant parking spot. Freaking bloodhounds. On some level, it should have been a comfort, because if she couldn't trust human survival instincts, what could she trust? And securing a parking spot was most definitely a form of survival in her book. Even though all the units came with a designated and *numbered* space, once the workday ended, the complex's lot turned into a free-for-all with no empty spots left behind. There was safety in proximity, and given that she and Molly didn't exactly live in the ritziest part of town, the closer one parked to their unit, the better.

Drea navigated a K-turn in the lot below her second-story garden apartment and sighed mournfully at the Honda Civic taking up residence in the space Molly had given up for Drea. *Ah, well. Next time.* The stop at the gas station had cost her. Oh, sure, she probably could have made it another day without fueling up, but her nervous mind simply couldn't tolerate staring at a gas gauge dipping below a quarter of a tank. Some things were just too big of an ask.

"C'mon, c'mon, I know I saw one," she muttered, leaning over the steering wheel. As she maneuvered down a slight hill, her shriek preceded her fist bump. On a side street, a lone parking spot appeared, bookended by a pickup truck and, of all things, a pink van boasting *The Zoomer Groomer* and a picture of a cartoon dog in a bubble bath on its side door. It was the closest thing to a visitor's spot she'd find at that hour. "Sold!"

With the E-brake fully engaged—well, as engaged as it was going to get—she killed the engine and hustled out. The sidewalk was a modest mix of cracks and character, sprinkled in with the occasional newish slab of cement. She walked as briskly as she dared up the small incline, but when she reached the crest, a tall figure appeared in front of her. A man and not one she recognized.

"Excuse me." Drea dipped her head, though she kept her handbag strap high on her shoulder, and ducked around him. Boots the size of kayaks maneuvered in front of her, blocking her way.

Unease pricked along her spine. She took a step back and lifted her eyes . . . to the most brutally handsome man she'd ever seen. Closely cropped dark hair stood out in stark relief against angled, stern features. A sharp jaw sporting more than a day's worth of dark stubble framed a scowl that could curdle milk or cower criminals. Shoulders wider than her car outlined a rugged physique common among mountain men and the military. Fluttering heartbeats ticked a quick measure in her chest, but it was his gunmetal gaze that worried her the most.

So, yeah, handsome, if one was into the carjacker/kidnapper look, which she most definitely wasn't.

He didn't move, nor did he say anything. He simply stared at her with those lingering slate-gray eyes that raked over her without qualm or consequence. Drea quickly scanned her murder mystery show memories of what to do in such a situation. Pepper spray seemed like it should be high on the list, though she'd taken it out of her purse months ago to make room for her solar cell phone charger. Running or screaming seemed apropos, or maybe she should make the first move and take him by surprise? Did New Hampshire have stand-your-ground laws? Shit. Perhaps if she moved fast, she could jab her thumbs in his—

"Eyes."

The rumbled word caught her off guard. "I'm sorry. What?"

"Your eyes. They're violet."

"Um, yup. Sure are. Well, I've got to—"

He took a slow step forward but didn't crowd her off the sidewalk like she expected, nor were there any vehicles nearby with ominous open doors he could easily toss her into.

The man shook his head but simply proceeded with a new line of questioning. "How did you get here?"

How did she . . . Was this guy serious? "I drove?"

"Before that."

"I drove . . . fast?"

His searching gaze returned to her face, and dammit if she didn't feel every beam of his intense inspection. Those roaming eyes bored into hers, and it was almost as if he sought out answers her words were not providing. Despite the warm weather, the man wore khaki cargo pants and boots that in no way should be out and about in ninety-degree anything. Definitely military.

The only acquiescence to the heat was the white T-shirt wrapped snugly over muscles she suspected might have been earned in a way that didn't include monthly gym memberships and protein powder. Honestly, he looked, well, she wasn't quite sure what to make of him, but the longer they stood there, the less her fear froze her. If she had to pin down the man's behavior, he almost seemed . . . lost.

Drea shifted her weight, placing her right foot on the curb, or so she intended to, but half her sole met air by mistake. Her ankle rolled over the edge, and she stumbled into the street. A car horn blared in her ear. She didn't even have time to gasp before her feet were swept off the ground. Strong arms banded around her waist and lifted her back onto the sidewalk.

"Holy shit! Oh my God, that was—"

"Are you all right?"

"Terrifying!" she gasped out, then slowed her breathing altogether.

Up close, the stranger's features had morphed into something far less menacing and far more, well, she wouldn't call it concerning, per se, but definitely tense. That squared-off jaw she couldn't help but admire a moment ago had hardened into stern angles, revealing faint scars along his neck and beard line. His wide brow had furrowed impossibly tighter, causing a vein to bulge in his left temple. And that nose had a sharp ridge in it, hinting at more than one remodel most likely performed by a fist.

Drea had only been half right. Nothing about this man was handsome in the conventional sense, but everything about him was brutal.

Alarm bells went off in her mind.

"Thanks for the assist, and yes, I'm fine. I'm not usually that scatterbrained, I promise." Drea righted herself and stepped back—really fucking carefully this time—as his arms fell away. Well, arm. One of his hands had slid from her waist to her wrist.

"Yes, you are," he quirked.

"Huh?" She couldn't truly focus on his odd and eerily confident reply, however, because her hand was still trapped in his. Gently, he turned her wrist and examined her tattoo. The small black vine danced in a circle just over her tendons. He brushed a thumb across the design before releasing her. Ah. He was curious about her ink.

Drea shrugged a shoulder. There was little harm in sharing

the story with him, especially after he demonstrated his intent not to kill her by saving her.

"It's seaweed." When he didn't say anything, only kept his eyes on her wrist, she continued. "I got it to remind myself that there's strength in being different. I know it's weird, but if you know anything about me—"

"It's not weird."

That certainly took her off guard. No one understood her tattoo. Even Molly asked for the explanation a good three times before she'd acquiesced to Drea's enthusiasm for the design. She cleared her throat. "Well, did you know that most of the planet's oxygen comes from seaweed and that there's more seaweed in the ocean than plants on land? This stuff is the true unsung hero, and most people don't think anything more of it than how tightly it's holding their sushi together."

He was silent for a long moment, so long that Drea remembered her original destination, but before she could make her awkward goodbyes to a complete saint of a bulldog-like stranger, he lifted wide eyes to her and spoke, or, rather, interrogated. Loudly.

"How did the celestial mages get you out of the Empyrean? The other sentinel angels and I sealed the gates, for fuck's sake! No one can get back in, and we've sure as shit been trying. Unless . . . unless you found a way. Are there others here? Were you hurt when you fell?" He gripped her shoulders hard, nearly shaking her in unrelenting desperation.

What the hell kind of *Dungeons & Dragons* verbal diarrhea was this? Mages? Sentinels?

Time to bounce.

"All right, that's enough, buddy. I've got to go." She backed out of his hold and offered the big guy a thank-you pat on his arm. "Thanks for the leg up again."

"No, I'm not letting you go, not after I've just found you, D—"

"Drea!"

A handsome dark-haired man with a close-cropped goatee jogged down the path leading to Drea and Molly's apartment. One side of his mouth was lifted in an easy smile, and his long legs made quick work of the distance between them. "There you are, Drea. Molly's just about ready to pull the burgers off the grill pan. I'm on condiment duty, and she's threatening to drink the wine I brought by herself if I don't have my shit together by the time the meat is finished resting."

Malcolm sidled up to Drea and placed a light kiss on the top of her head before taking in the tractor-sized third wheel. "Oh, hi there. I'm Malcolm, Drea's boyfriend. Do you two know each other?" His finger bounced between them.

"Uh, no, not really. He just helped me get out of the road before a car almost rearranged my insides to be on the outside."

"Oh, jeez. Are you okay?" Malcolm held her out before him, scanning her body for evidence to the contrary.

"Yeah, I'm fine. Just a little spooked."

"Thank God." Malcolm turned to the stranger and extended his hand out. "Hey, thanks, man. I don't know what I would have done if something happened to her. I owe you." The stranger had grown quiet, but he still took Malcolm's hand and slowly pumped it once.

"No need," he said, but his voice had lost all the animation from a moment ago.

"Well, if you ever need anything, she's in 3B. I'm there most days, so seriously, just holler. See you around." Malcolm tossed a quick wave and hugged Drea tightly to his side before escorting her up the walkway leading to her apartment. As their heavy steps ate up the pavement, she could have sworn she heard a grumbled promise.

Yes, you fucking will.

CHAPTER 6

"Okay, now I know you're being weird, Drea. That's the fourth fry I've stolen off your plate, and my hand is still attached to my wrist. You keep this up and I'll have to assume it's either my cooking or something's wrong with your olfactory system, because it sure as hell ain't the first one." Molly tossed the pilfered potato segment into her mouth and chewed with relish. "Yup, it's definitely you. Now spill."

Drea's eyes drifted toward the paper plate. Yes, paper. Their kitchen's ancient drain pipes could only handle so much grease. Huh. Turned out, her pile of rosemary and olive oil *pommes frites* had significantly decreased in size and, funnily enough, looked rather lonely next to her barely nibbled burger. When did that happen? Though, now that she looked at the display more closely, the potatoes had become far sparser, as if the damn things could sense her disinterest and purposely positioned themselves toward diners who would appreciate all that golden, brown, and delicious. The rebuke had the air of a cat's upturned tail in the face.

Malcolm took his seat next to her, his wide shoulders and

long legs eating up more than their fair share of the dinette set. "She got spooked on the way up here. Almost got clipped by a car."

Molly's eyes widened. "*What?* You didn't tell me that. And here I am, thinking I'm all clever swiping your food from under you. Here." A few potatoes were plopped back onto Drea's plate, though, judging by how the plate dipped under the new weight, those particular fries had been Molly's soggier rejects. Drea couldn't blame her.

"No, I'm fine. It was just a little scare, and I had a lot on my mind about work. My head wasn't in the game."

If by not in the game she meant up in the analyst booth replaying highlights of the strangest encounter of her life, then, yeah, that one. She bit down on a potato in a show of good measure, letting her other wrist fall into her lap.

It was still warm, her tattoo, as was the rest of her ever since she left the stranger's side. Sure, Molly had no problem pointing out Drea's lack of appetite, but her roomie didn't once mention how Drea was on her third glass of ice water. Every part of her itched with a prickling flush she couldn't shake. Though her feet had quickly taken her away from the stranger on the sidewalk, her mind hadn't fallen in line.

Brawn like that didn't casually walk around her complex, especially not on a man with such quick reflexes. Nor did it usually display prominently on a guy whose features were more aloof than antagonizing. No, aloof wasn't quite right. Adrift maybe? Then there was the firehose of tension that hit her square in the chest, but it wasn't so much the usual apprehension between two strangers as it was the way he spoke to her.

As if he knew her.

It had taken the full walk back to her apartment, the trek up a flight of stairs, a nursed glass of wine, and the theft of several potatoes before she finished rummaging through her memory bank. Unfortunately, the result wasn't all that comforting. Drea could say with absolute certainty that she'd never seen that man before.

Then why, hours later, could she still remember how firmly his hands fit around her waist, even as Malcolm draped his hand across her hip?

"I'm just going to chalk it up to me being off my game today." Drea sank her teeth into the buttered brioche bun and medium-rare meat. The moan caged behind her lips said it all. Yup, good. "Remind me again how we can eat so well but still need to schlep our laundry down a flight of stairs, drag it around to the basement in the back of our building, and hope no one's tossed our wet clothes from earlier on the floor before we get there?"

Molly's lips curled around the rim of her wine glass. "Because we need to eat every day but we only need to wash our work clothes on the weekends?"

Drea lifted up her burger in salute. "I'll take it!"

Malcolm leaned over and dropped a kiss on Drea's shoulder. "Aside from your roadkill rescue, what's eating you?"

She touched her chin to the spot in acknowledgment and gave him a soft smile. "Just some things at work that aren't adding up. I reran some samples today, and the math isn't mathing the way I need it to. I'll figure it out, though. My supervisor isn't expecting my lab report until Friday, so I've got the week to noodle over it. It'll give me the time to set up the new centrifuge anyway."

"Look at you, getting things in order. Initiative is damn sexy, babe." Malcolm took a slow sip of his wine.

"Barf." Molly groaned. "I'm getting something stronger than this weak-ass red if that's what I'm going to have to listen to all night."

"Um, my dear, did you or did you *not* drink a third of the bottle before I even got Drea inside? A bottle *I* brought over, mind you."

"Oh, please. If you expect me to cook without wine, then you shouldn't have brought any."

A teasing sparkle lit his eyes. "I had no such expectation, which is why there's a second bottle hidden behind the coffee pot."

Chair legs screeched against the laminate flooring. Molly was up and in the kitchen before her half-eaten fry had time to hit the plate.

"Aaand she's off," he replied.

Drea should have chuckled along with him. Instead, she discreetly freed herself from his hold to wipe her hands on her napkin. Fidgeting was an old habit whenever her anxiety threatened to rear its ugly head. Belts, blouses, phones, test tubes, anything was fair game for fiddling, and she was beyond grateful Malcolm hadn't picked up on the gesture. Yet.

Though three months was hardly enough time to evaluate long-term couple potential, it wasn't nothing. Right? She wouldn't go so far as to throw around the L-word or anything, but she certainly cared for Malcolm enough to move past the honeymoon insta-crush phase of dating. Even when he'd make the occasional comment that may or may not hint at her poor job retention track record.

Drea swiped one final grease stain off her fingertips as she replayed his words. *Look at you, getting things in order. Initiative is damn sexy, babe.*

And there it was, hidden between the lines. Doubt. She thought she'd glimpsed it a time or two over the past few months, but every statement had always been subtle and sweetly delivered. If there was any doubt on Malcolm's part about her ability to follow through, the concern had been wrapped in so many pretty words of understanding and encouragement that the blow was hardly felt. Lately, however, the jibes have been more overt, bolder, even crueler in their deceptive kindness.

Was he waiting for her to prove herself professionally before he could approve of her romantically?

She itched at her wrist, which still tingled slightly from earlier. Perhaps her worry was manifesting psychosomatically? Well, if there was ever something to worry about, it would be over things she *could* control, starting with the results of those blood samples. Results she kept turning over even though they made about as much sense as the logistics of a husky-chihuahua mating. Then she remembered where those results currently sat and where they definitely shouldn't be.

Crap.

Drea stood from the table. "I left some work stuff in my car. I'm just going to grab it real quick."

Malcolm stood with her, never setting down his wine glass. "I'll come with you."

"It's okay. I'll be fast. I can't really share too much about it. You know that."

He rolled his eyes. "Ah, yes, your little NDA."

She pressed her lips together, worrying over the disbelief in his voice. "Back in a flash."

Drea kissed his cheek and hurried out the door, wondering just how much security clearance she'd need to prove she was worth it.

DREA SHUFFLED through her apartment complex's abysmally lit parking area, silently cursing her property management's good-in-theory solar streetlight installation. If illumination was the goal, they could have fooled her. With the abundance of sugar maple and elm trees decorating the property, sunlight hardly made it to the blacktop long enough to heat the stuff. How they thought there was enough solar output to power a necessary streetlight let alone a light-up sneaker was beyond her. As it was, only one light worked for every three that didn't.

She scurried down the hilly road as fast as she dared, well aware the light was enough to be seen in but not enough to actually see. By the time her steps leveled out on the straightened sidewalk, her car came into view. The poor thing sat parked under another paltry luminance distribution pattern, but hey, at least she managed to find it.

The locks clicked over, and Drea grabbed her forest-green notebook from the front passenger seat. Loose-leaf papers stuck out around the edges, while a faded rubber band wrapped around the middle did its level best to hold the mess together. Okay, it wasn't exactly a high-security clearance presentation, but it got the job done. Besides, these notes were more superfluous than secret. Everything she needed to report was already cataloged in her lab's software. These were just . . . well, things she didn't want to lose track of.

Still gripping the notebook, she slammed the car door shut, but not before the door's corner hooked under the rubber band, snapping the thing. Papers and notes spilled out of their binding.

"Shit! No no no, come back."

Drea dropped to her knees and quickly plucked as many scraps as she could back into her notebook. How many unbound pages were there? Oh, hell, at least a dozen, if not more. She secured what she could, working as fast as the shitty lighting would allow. She may not exactly be up to date on her current rent with Molly, but the property management didn't need to know that. As far as she was concerned, being a tad behind on the payment—while having the literal best friend on the planet—didn't preclude her from being able to see at night on the property. Did it?

A relieved breath left her once she spied the last paper. The damn thing had tucked itself up against her rear driver's-side tire, of all places. Drea stretched out her hand—

A large muscled arm fell over her vision and snatched the piece of paper before she could reach it. Drea quickly stood, still scanning the ground just in case she missed something, and wiped her hands on her thighs.

"Thanks for the help." When there was no answer, she lifted her gaze. Beneath the laughable illumination, a familiar crisp white T-shirt stood out against the dark verdant surroundings. Her heart fell into her stomach. "Oh, it's you."

The stranger from earlier didn't address the comment, at least not in the way she was expecting. What was she expecting, exactly? Certainly never to see him again, but now that she had, she wasn't entirely sure she was ready to dismiss him. His heavily muscled chest bobbed on a low grunt while shadowed eyes never lifted from the paper he held. The gruff sound was his only acknowledgment of her standing there. Well, talk about dismissals.

Then he pulled the paper closer under his inspection. Crap.

"Um, I'll take that back now. Thanks for grabbing it." She extended her hand, which she made sure was visible even under the pathetic lighting. He should have had no problem handing it over. Yup, at any minute, he could have tossed the chicken-scratch scribbles her way and gone about whatever it was men like him did in suburban apartment complexes. It dawned on her that she probably didn't want to know what men like him did, especially not at night when she was alone with one such man.

He continued ignoring her.

"Look, I really need that back. It's for work. I signed an NDA. And not for nothing but what are you still even doing here? It's almost nine o'clock."

Even shadowed, his piercing gaze was a beacon all its own. "Visiting a friend."

"Well, don't let me keep you." Again, she held out her hand, hoping her brisk tone was enough to highlight her urgency. She was about to snatch the paper free when his words stopped her.

"These platelet counts are bonkers. Is this all from the same sample?"

Drea's hand fell away before the tip of her finger even caressed the paper's edge. "What?"

The stranger stepped closer toward her, pointing a thick finger at the data scrawled on the top of the page. "Proteins are off, too. I don't see a plasma reading here, though."

"I couldn't get a plasma readout. My centrifuge rotor over-heated before I was able to get things fully separated. The data's incomplete." Drea's hand flew to her mouth, but really, like she could call the words back? Her fingers stilled, then relaxed slightly. Even if she *could* call the words back, did she want to? They were the first things she'd ever said to someone about her lab work that didn't include the letters NDA, but he'd under-stood them.

What the hell was she thinking? She wasn't, clearly, but it wasn't like random people would know about proteins and plasma. Her verbal outburst had been an accident. A simple, misguided, perhaps slightly eager accident. She cautiously studied the man in front of her, who still pored over her research notes with rapt attention.

That wide stern brow dipped low in concentration, gath-ering wrinkles at its center. His jawline tensed, while full lips pursed to one side. She got the impression he did this often, or at least, his features seemed to have a neutral stance they assumed when he was analyzing something. Did he analyze things often as well?

"Those rotors don't usually overheat," he said.

Her fingers fell away from her mouth. "Tell me about it. I just installed a new unit at my lab today. I was going to rerun the samples, but—"

"You thinking parasite? Infection?"

Drea faltered for a second, not because the question caught her off guard, but because she'd been wondering the exact same thing earlier that morning. How did he . . . ?

"That's honestly above my pay grade. I'm a lab tech. I just run the samples and analyze the data." Shit. Why was she saying all this? If her employer found out, she could kiss her full-time employee promotion goodbye, along with her portion of the overdue rent.

He handed the paper back to her, nodding at her notes. "Kind of hard to analyze data when the data doesn't want to get got. What do the other techs say?"

Drea tucked the paper into her notebook. "There aren't any. I work alone."

The man's brows winged up to his hairline, and he crossed his arms over his chest. "Who do you run your questions by? Your supervisor? What did they say about the broken rotor?"

"They don't know about it. It's a small operation. I order what's needed, and as long as I produce my reports on time, I'm pretty much given complete autonomy over the lab. Or at least I will be for the next two weeks."

"What's in two weeks?"

"My probationary period ends, and if all goes well, I'll be hired full time." She cringed as soon as she heard what she said. Holy crap, what was with her mouth? Who the hell was this guy, and why was she spilling VIP beans to a shadow?

Because he speaks your language. He understood your notes and was bothered by the same things you've been scratching your head about all weekend.

And there it was. The prospect of a peer in an isolated environment. She couldn't speak to Molly or Malcolm about any of the things eating away at her in her job. Technically, she couldn't speak to anyone, but this man? He was a stranger, yes, but one who was familiar with her world in some way. An idea scratched just under the surface and quickly made its way to her mouth. Again, the horse left the barn before she could grab the reins.

"You know about clinical lab analysis?"

He nodded. Strangely, he didn't seem surprised by the question. "A bit."

"Are you good at keeping things confidential?" *Whoever's up there, if you're listening, please ignore the irony in that question.*

The corner of his lips lifted, flashing a hint of teeth. "Something tells me you may be a tad off base in that regard."

Drea swept her hand away. "Fine, yeah, maybe a little, but I'm kind of stuck." She released a worried breath and finally relented to let her big mouth do the talking. Hell, it was doing a bang-up job of that anyway. "I need this gig, okay? I'm two weeks away from a permanent position, but if I can't produce the complete data my supervisor is asking for by Friday, I can kiss my chances of that goodbye. Now, technically, I did sign an NDA, but—"

"You'd rather sign off on an accurate report more. Put your name to something solid that'll impress the top brass and get you to your goal."

The truth belted her in the face, and she had to fight not to recoil from the sting. "Yes," she whispered. "How would you like to help me out with some analysis? Just be someone to run things by, look over some data? I can pay you," she rushed out.

No, I can't.

"I don't need money."

Oh, thank God.

Drea released a shaky breath. "Desperate isn't my favorite look, but I've been told I wear it well." Drea infused all the uncomfortable humor she could into her plea.

"Ty."

"What?"

"Call me Ty."

She lifted a brow. "Do you promise not to be a psycho creeper who murders women or adopts puppies from shelters, only to surrender the dogs in a few years when either the dog or the training routine gets too old?"

Stormy eyes pinned her with a look. "If I wanted you dead, I would have just let gravity do its thing earlier." Then he shrugged. "And I'm more of a cat person."

Embarrassment and no small amount of relief warmed her cheeks as she hugged her notebook to her. "Then call me Drea."

The man—Ty—worked his jaw to the side, as if savoring the flavor of her name. "Drea it is."

"Great," she breathed out, then grabbed the pen from inside her notebook's spiral binding. "What's your number?"

They exchanged information, along with a plan to meet up the following evening. Before she turned to walk back, however, his words stopped her.

"Anyone ever call you Dee?" Ty asked.

Her chin touched her shoulder as she looked back. "No, never."

All she could make out beneath the low lamplight was the firm dip of his chin. "Good."

CHAPTER 7

One didn't get to be as old as Chrome without perfecting the art of lying. It wasn't even so much of an art form anymore. When mortals mistook his and his brothers' fall from the Empyrean as some dinosaur-destroying asteroid, Chrome had learned the specific causal relationship between certainty and correctness. In short, being *sure* you were right had fuck all to do with actually *being* right. It was all in the delivery. As long as some twitchy tweed-clad academic could make a claim while forcing eye contact and accepting all major credit cards, it didn't matter whether or not he was lying. Certainty sells.

That was how he found himself at the local community college's library, staring down the columns of a metal detector with a paid-by-the-hour security guard about to wave him through. As if the man's portly belly currently dining on his belt buckle wasn't enough of an allegory on poor life choices. Chrome was about to get his own lesson on the outcomes of speaking before thinking. Could he spin a tale so intricately that he'd have mortals forming a political action committee, conducting a general election, and greenlighting said tale into legislation? Absolutely. Was getting out of Dodge also the key to avoiding the aftermath of his tall tales? Yup.

Then why, for all the blessed mages in the Empyrean, was he about to voluntarily walk through a metal detector and have a sit-down chat with his bad decisions?

If all this is true, she's a mortal who doesn't remember you. Whatever kept her alive all these years did so without your involvement. Leave her alone.

"You're next, sir. Please empty your pockets into the bins and walk through." The corpulent rent-a-cop hadn't gone so far as to make eye contact with Chrome. *Don't blame you there, buddy.* Instead, his blue nitrile-gloved fingers did their shaky best to spread out two gray bins for Chrome to unload his belongings into. Like the poor fellow knew Chrome was holstering a lot more than a pack of gum.

Chrome did a brief mental tally: three 9mm lugers (full size, compact, and subcompact, because you just never knew), two KA-BARs, a switchblade, and four—no, five—extra ammo clips.

And that was just what he had strapped to his legs.

He hesitated for a moment, then gave the metal detector the stink eye it deserved. There was *an abundance of caution* and then there was *overkill.* This academic library had blown so far past the latter, he wondered why anyone even bothered coming here. Then he remembered the sentinels' nighttime activities over the past few months that had regrettably spilled over to campus life: demon charmers disguised as students, weapons found in classrooms, faculty gone missing. The advanced security measures had moved up the college's priority ladder and were installed in time for the summer session.

The grim reality would have soured his mood, if said mood hadn't already been festering.

Chrome let his hand drift to the plastic bins on the conveyor belt. Well, not the plastic so much as the metal runner on the side of the belt. The chromium-plated metal runner.

With his other hand, he fidgeted around in his pockets. "Sure thing."

One touch was all it took. The second his finger caressed the edge of that metal, Chrome threw his power into the connection. The metallic ripple along the conveyor belt's border was so slight, the security guard didn't even detect a problem until the alloy connections at the back of the monitoring system had already pinched closed. The telltale *ping* of dying electronics reverberated through the small entryway, right as the lights dappling the metal detector blinked out.

"Shoot. What the heck?" The security guard waddled over to a hopelessly black monitor and, in true retiree fashion, hunted and pecked his way through a sequence of commands that Chrome ensured wouldn't command shit.

"Everything all right there?" Chrome asked.

"System just went on the fritz."

On the fritz? Jeez. Another second or two and the poor guy would be spouting a few *hold your horses,* along with a side of *dagnabbits.* Enough of this.

"I'm meeting with some of the faculty in five minutes. If you'd like, I can leave my ID with you and pick it up on my way out."

Relief smoothed out some of the panicked wrinkles on the security guard's excessively bunched brow. The man was clearly grateful for an out that didn't completely steamroll his night shift's entire purpose. He gruffly cleared his throat and threw his shoulders back, as if the Hail Mary had been his idea. "Sure, that'd be fine. Library closes at eleven o'clock. If you're not back by then, I'll turn the ID over to the authorities and you can collect it from them in the morning."

Judging by the crumpled fast food wrappers in the waste bin, the only thing this guy had any authority over was his bathroom schedule and even that was dubious, but Chrome kept that comment to himself.

"You got it." Chrome plopped his newest fake driver's license down and prowled into the study space. As far as community colleges went, this one was financed better than most. While it still held all the budget-friendly hallmarks of a county institution (potted fake ferns included), the main floor pleasantly surprised him. Linoleum tile gave way to blue-gray carpet beneath organized clusters of computer workstations and armchairs of questionable comfort. To his right, situated in a square lineup that would make Dr. Rubik proud, were a dozen or so laptop docking stations, with the reference room located just beyond that.

He pulled out his phone and reread the text that would either drag him down a journey toward long-desired answers or mire him in more questions he was too chickenshit to ask.

County College of Aurora. 8 p.m. Reference room in the library. Thanks! -D

Chrome headed toward the meetup spot and was about to yank down the door handle when the top of a golden head poked over the laptop nearest him.

"Ty! Over here," Drea whisper-screamed, then followed that up with an in-no-way-covert wave.

A breath rushed out of him. He tried to steady his hand on the handle, but his fingers just brushed the metal before they fell heavy at his side.

He'd seen that gesture before. That exact fingertip flare and devil-may-care exuberance had once snagged his soul-crushing thoughts away from duty and despair. Long-ago words, spoken in that same smoky rich voice, floated through his mind. *If there's only tonight, I've got to make it count.*

Chrome relaxed his frame, stared unblinkingly at the

woman seated in front of her laptop, and cursed himself blind for not seeing, and believing, things sooner. Blonde hair with a shock of honeyed highlights lay braided down the middle of her back. The weave was loose, yet efficient. It took no effort to remember its heavy length splayed against her blue messenger mage uniform. Or across his bare chest.

Wide violet eyes he'd thought of so often he could paint their exact hue urged him closer. He was a sentinel angel, the prime sentinel's intelligence master, a guard of the celestial mages, and a defender of the Empyrean. One did not *beckon* him, and yet his ass had somehow found the seat next to her.

Drea. Dee. She's really here.

"I certainly am, though I could do without the nickname. It reminds me of a Southern career diner waitress whose life revolves around fire-engine red lipstick and apple pie a la mode."

It was the adorable nose crinkle that did him in. That and the deep husky voice that had Chrome settling his too-big-for-most-things frame into a seat, which he likely maxed out the weight limit on seventy-five pounds ago. That voice. Mages, he could listen to her speak even if she didn't have anything to say. And he had, on some level. It was her voice, above all else, he'd called upon over the millions of years he'd been cast out in the mortal realm, fighting, always fighting to protect souls.

Just like she had, or would have if the woman before him had any memory of who she was.

"Noted. You remind me of someone, that's all," Chrome replied.

"I hope it was a good someone."

He clenched his fists in his lap. "Yes."

She flashed a brief smile, then grabbed the top edge of her laptop as if to close it. "I got here a tad early. We can still go into the reference room if you'd like. The tables are larger, and it'd be easier to spread out."

"Here's fine."

She froze her screen halfway to the keyboard. "Oh, okay. Sure, that works, too." Drea unpacked her notes and laid them out between the two workstations. "You said you've worked in clinical labs before. What do you do?"

"Scientific intelligence. Medical affairs. Mostly whatever is needed."

Her violet eyes widened, bordering on owlish. "Ooh, that sounds secretive."

"Can be. It's pretty boring, though."

"I hear ya on the boring front. Although, I will say what I'm working on now is far from it, probably because it's so frickin' confusing."

Chrome leaned over her notes, tucking his knees under the desk as best he could, and tried to ignore the fresh, lightly sweet scent that somehow touched everything she did. "Tell me what you've got. I'm here to help."

"That's just it. What I've got is a whole lot of question marks and dead ends. I'm supposed to be doing clinical analysis on a patient, but every test I run either comes back with whacky markers or my equipment goes haywire."

Now, *that* caught his fucking attention. A patient? In Cyro's grotto?

"The first few months on the job, my supervisor had me analyzing various elemental samples. Lots of metals for some reason, along with corrosion levels, acidic behavior in general, even testing tensile strength on new composite materials. Last week, however, I was given live patient samples, and it's been downhill ever since." Drea reached into her bag and stole a sip from her water bottle.

His eyes snapped to her lips wrapped around the straw. Tightness enveloped his lungs—and other places. He had to take a breath to rally from the impact that had on him, of the memories they conjured.

"I was doing so well up until then, and my supervisor had seemed pretty pleased. Now?" She tossed her hands in the air. "I'm in panic mode." Right as she took another breath to continue, she seemed to think better of it and stopped. Uncertainty wrinkled her brow. "I can't talk to Malcolm about this either, legally or otherwise."

The way she said *otherwise*, like it was a dirty secret, made Chrome's trigger finger itch. He sneered as he eased back into the chair and lifted the notebook with him in hopes of covering his reaction. "Otherwise?" There, one word wasn't so bad. He could say words without growling. Or cursing. Sometimes.

"It doesn't really matter, but even if I *could* discuss my findings with him, he's not always the most . . . attentive."

"He doesn't attend to your needs?" Well, shit, that definitely came out more as a bark, but like he could help it. That wry sound in her voice when she'd mentioned the guy told Chrome everything he needed to know about a man he had zero qualms burying six feet under. Really, like, none.

Shock colored her words. "No, not *that* kind of attentive. I mean that his interest in my chosen profession kind of comes with an expiration date. He'll listen, but only for so long and then he gets bored. He's a real estate agent, always driving around, jumping in and out of houses. He just doesn't have the head for the things I choose to focus on."

"Lose him," Chrome ordered.

"What?" Drea's confused gaze lifted from her fidgeting fingers.

He held her stare with immeasurable certainty *and* correctness. "Any man with eyes in his head and half a bean knocking around his noggin who's so easily distracted by anything else when talking to you isn't worth the oxygen he's choking down."

The charged declaration filled the space between them, even as he willed some recognition to dawn on her face. *Do you remember me? Do you remember anything?* When only shock remained, Chrome tore his gaze away from her and perused her notes once more.

At some point, they settled into a routine of sorts. She'd point out the tests she'd run and at which intervals, and he'd remark similarly on discoveries she'd already made. It turned comfortable, casual, and oddly soothing. He'd gleaned enough intel to make sense of her previous lab report findings and absolutely nothing regarding the patient samples. The simple fact that there even *was* a patient unnerved him. No human produced labs like that. Ever.

Hours passed, until ten thirty rolled around, and the place had pretty much cleared out. Drea hefted her bag on her shoulder, snagging a few golden strands beneath the strap. It would have been adorable if it didn't look so painful. Without thinking, Chrome reached across and freed the trapped locks.

Drea stood still, curious, until he was finished. "Thanks. Long hair's a hazard, that's for sure."

"Nothing's a hazard if you know how to handle it right."

Drea laughed lightly. "If you say so."

Once Chrome collected his license from the security guard, who silently warned Chrome not to do anything that would screw up the final quiet thirty minutes of the dude's shift, he escorted Drea out into the parking lot.

"I'm over here," she said, gesturing toward the four-wheeled heap that was one of three cars still parked in front of the library. "I know, she could use some work, but she's my baby." She patted the top of the car like one would pat a thirteen-year-old golden retriever, praising it for living beyond its expected years.

Chrome made up his mind. As soon as he saw her home, he was going to spend the night going to town on that rust bucket, at least to the point of meeting conventional safety standards.

That thing had clearly been passed over for a tune-up half a dozen times. Unacceptable. Did that Malcolm prick even give a shit whether she made it home each night? Just the thought of the two of them together, whether night or day, made his eye twitch. In the ten seconds it took for Chrome to open her car door, see her inside and buckled, he'd already planned out her vehicle's entire service and repair schedule, along with the parts he'd need. Some he'd buy, some he'd make.

"Thanks again for looking at my notes. And for your discretion."

He stepped back from hovering over her open window, but that was as far as he could make himself move. Even the car carried her same freshwater scent, like water lilies and lemon. "No problem. Any time."

"You mean it? Any time?"

"Of course. You run into any problems, you know how to reach me." *In case you get a flat tire. Suddenly remember how you survived falling from the Empyrean. You know, anything.*

A sly smile curled her lips, and damn if that didn't tell him everything about how fucked he was. He stood there, staring at her retreating taillights, wondering what the hell he was going to do. He'd never told his brothers about Dee. What he'd shared with her was a private night of desperate passion. She'd been a closely guarded memory he only allowed himself to visit because he *thought* he'd left her safe behind heaven's gates. Gates he had sealed himself. And yet here she was, living, breathing, and apparently working for the enemy.

Confused anguish wasn't a good look on anyone, least of all him. Despite coming up in the business of knowing his enemy's secrets, keeping his own was not his way. It was long past time. Tonight, he'd finally tell the others. He had to, because he needed them. Needed to learn what Cyro was cooking up. Was there really a living being down in the charmers' grotto being used as a test subject?

Chrome strode under a well-shaded tree and prepared to release his wings. Before he called them forth, however, headlights flared from one of the two parked vehicles. One car had to belong to the security guard, but the other . . .

A black SUV exited the lot and headed in the same direction Drea had just gone.

CHAPTER 8

If Drea could figure out a way to bottle up her current excitement, take it to work, and inhale a good whiff of it whenever she wound up scratching her head over lab results, she'd throw her life savings at the endeavor. Was she closer to actually figuring out what the hell was going on with the patient's labs? Not exactly. Oh man, though, did it feel good to have a confidant. Maybe a little too good, if she was being honest.

Once the longest red light in the world finally turned over to green, she kissed the gas pedal with her foot—because one did not do anything quickly in her car—and veered onto the on-ramp. The ride home was blessedly short, only about ten minutes, but given Aurora's rural layout that surrounded the downtown, almost everything required highway access of some form. Thankfully, she only needed to wrangle her car up to top speeds for one exit before she could coax the old girl back down to the car's much-preferred twenty-five miles per hour.

Though ten minutes wasn't much of a trek, it was more than enough for her to completely unravel at just what the hell she was doing, and who she was doing it with.

Ty. The name was about as exhilarating as the color beige and in no way did justice to the brawny brilliance she'd just spent the past two and a half hours marveling over. She'd never shown anyone, breathing or otherwise, her notebook. Ever. Molly would even rib her about spending dinnertime jotting down scribbles instead of eating. Somewhere over the past few months, the ratty thing had turned into her constant companion. Her constant *solitary* companion with whom she shared all her questions and secrets. So, why the hell did she offer up the thing to a stranger as casually as she would a side order of soggy fries she wasn't planning on eating?

Dotted white lines whipped past her periphery. She was vaguely aware of her speed, as her car rarely made it up past sixty miles per hour, but to say she was intently focused on the road would have been a tad too liberal. Replays of her evening with Ty swirled through her memory.

Maybe *that* was the reason for her out-of-character behavior? He echoed every one of her doubts and insecurities she'd only ever revealed to ink on paper. Where she failed to see a connection, he failed as well. Even when he brought up alternate labs to run or different brands of equipment to try in hopes of getting more consistent results, they both settled back to square one: a big fat question mark.

But it was *their* big fat question mark. She wasn't alone anymore.

Drea winced as some part of her interpreted the thought as a betrayal. Of course she wasn't alone. She had Malcolm, who she adored. And Molly, who would sooner poison every patron in her restaurant than see Drea lose another job. She had the perfect trifecta of support. A fierce friendship, an affectionate boyfriend, and the first professional prospect that was less than two weeks away from being a permanent fixture.

With Ty, though, things had been easy. There was no need to apologize for existing. Her questions flowed and were met only with inquisitive insight and agreeable assessments. Even when she tried to smother her laugh at how the library was *so* not made for large men like him, he simply winked at her and made a show of adjusting himself in the chair.

Maybe he hadn't been so bad to look at either, once the library's fluorescent lighting had chased away the nighttime shadows, which had seemed to cling to him like ivy on an ancient keep. His looks weren't classically handsome, but they sure didn't hurt, and they certainly didn't give her a reason to check the clock. There was no law against appreciating uncharacteristically beautiful things, right? Being in a relationship didn't mean you were dead.

Drea passed the quarter-mile marker for her exit and threw her blinker on. As she maneuvered into the right lane, she glanced down at her notebook on the passenger seat and how Ty had neatly placed all her loose papers back within the binding. It took her a second to realize it was even hers, but she had to admit, the idea of him carefully folding and filing her secrets wasn't entirely terrible—

Metal pounded at her side and crunched inward. Glass fractured. Her neck and shoulders were yanked to the left, while her head whipped in the opposite direction. Drea flailed her hands as the car spun out on the highway, taking her world with it. One working headlight illuminated nothing but whirling shadows. The barren road was a brief swipe of darkness before her car completed its arc and settled, nose first, above an embankment. Nearly bald tires churned up grass and tree roots with frightening speed, careening over the steep hill. Drea screamed. Terror tightened her limbs. Her eyes peeled wide at the enormous tree trunk she hurtled toward. She opened her mouth to scream again, but nothing surfaced. Breath *whooshed* out of her as the seat belt sliced across her torso, cementing her to the seat.

The whole car halted. Hair fell free of her braid and

cascaded forward. Through the blonde curtain, a giant black gum tree stood no more than ten feet from the hood of her car. She wasn't moving, or rather, the car wasn't. How? Groaning, she lifted her head and tried to look behind her, but the steep incline, coupled with the throbbing stiffness in her neck, made it impossible. Instead, she squinted into the rearview mirror.

In the partial moonlight, a man stood, heels braced against the embankment's slope and hands secured under the rim of her car's body. Straining muscles flexed against the load. His strong jaw clenched. Powerful determination twisted his features, sharpening everything. Shoulders and legs bunched as he pulled against the two-ton vehicle. The car jostled once, then again, and Drea blinked her vision clear. When her eyes refocused, crippling confusion robbed her senses.

Ty?

The man holding—no, *pulling*—her car up the embankment was Ty, and he was covered in gleaming sheets of metallic armor. Not just his clothes, but his skin and hair were covered with it, as if he had been dipped in a bath of molten metal and left to harden.

"Wha . . . ?" Drea tried and failed to get a sentence out. Her throat was hoarse from screaming. That was probably a blessing, as no words would make what was jutting out of his back even remotely logical. Behind him flared two gigantic metal wings. Feathered, like a falcon's, but looming and large, like some great mythical bird.

Impossible.

Her limbs jerked forward, but the rest of her was still held in place by the seat belt. Her hair shielded her view again, but she didn't have the strength to bat it away. Pinpricks hissed along her bare arms where tiny shards of glass had found her. Another tug had her head lolling forward, while the rest of her, along with the car, was somehow being pulled back up the embankment. How was he doing that? Did he have a wench or something? But what was it connected to? And what the hell hit her?

"Drea! Hold still. The car's almost up."

The tugging resumed, this time with more fervor the closer the car climbed toward the road. Metal groaned in time with Ty's punctuated roars. She didn't have the strength to look back. She could barely keep her head upright when the car finally crested the lip of the slope and leveled out. The engine's steam hadn't even stopped leaking from the hood when her door was yanked open. Cool air flooded in.

Ty crouched next to her, his massive shoulders heaving as they pressed against the doorframe. A ruddy complexion and dark hair filled her blurry vision. All traces of silver had vanished, except his eyes. Roiling pools of quicksilver bored into her, raking over her body with fierce, wild precision.

"Where are you hurt?" he barked.

"Neck," she wheezed out.

Instantly, his fingers were at her throat, pushing and palpating until he slowly lifted her neck so her chin pointed forward and the back of her head was flush against the headrest.

"Keep your head here, if you can. I don't feel any fractures or dislocations, but the EMTs need to get you in a C-collar and on a backboard just in case. Most likely whiplash. Your chest hurting you, too, where the belt nabbed you? Don't nod, just talk if you can."

"Chest is sore."

He frowned and spread his hands over her ribs, pressing and gliding along each bone. His tender ministrations flanked out to her hips, thighs, and feet, where he rolled each ankle and checked for distal pulses. Drea's quivering neck strained to hold her head steady. Adrenaline fueled her shaking limbs, but shaking was good. Shaking meant she was alive and her nerves were present and accounted for.

"What . . . happened?"

Molten eyes flicked to hers. Despite Ty's down-to-business first responder tactics, panic still flared at the corners of his gaze. Full lips thinned over clenched teeth, and nostrils flared the way she imagined a wolf who was about to attack might look. If her heart hadn't already been going a mile a minute, fear would have surely taken it the rest of the way.

Not fear of him, but fear for whomever his target was.

"You were hit on your rear driver's side."

"Hit by what? Another car?" That wasn't right. Surely, she would have heard another vehicle on the road, especially at that time of night. *Would you have, though, or were you too absorbed in your little nightly recap?*

Without answering her, Ty stood and walked around to the back of her car. All her focus remained on keeping her head still, but pain pummeled her body in crashing waves. Muscles throbbed and joints screamed. Her trembling lips released a puffed whimper. Just when she was about to beg and crumple forward, he returned and gently urged her shoulders back against the seat. Her shaking fingers fumbled around for her seat belt, but he stilled her movements. Charcoal gray eyes, not silver, stared back at her.

"Ambulance is on its way. I need you to stay here, Dee, okay? Strapped in, just as you are. It's the safest place for you."

"No." She groaned. "And don't call me that."

The corner of Ty's mouth lifted in a ghost of a smirk, but his lips never lost their grim determination. "If you stay still, I'll consider it."

Exhaustion and blurriness weighed her down, and they both knew her fight was born out of habit rather than any hope she'd actually win. She murmured some protestation right as her head lolled forward. Ty's hands gently caught her under the chin and repositioned her, but he didn't remove his hold. Heavy eyelids fluttered closed, despite her best efforts. Before the murky haze of oblivion fully set in, his deeply whispered words floated through the car.

"You won't see me for a bit, but I'll be with you the entire time."

CHAPTER 9

Faint murmuring invaded the shroud of darkness. Shadows cushioned Drea's body in some veiled inky mist, while tendrils snaked around her arms in a gentle cocoon. She sighed at her weightlessness, as she always did when she visited this place. In that unknown haven, there was no pain or expectations, just a mindless existence. A tad too cold perhaps, but she didn't mind it that much, especially since her time there was always so short.

Her body bobbed among the shadows, cresting over a slight wave, when flashes of silver shot across her vision, gleaming so brightly she was always surprised that they never melted the shadows away. Instead, the darkness lifted her and stretched out her arms toward the shocks of light as if in an offering. Her tattoo burned and writhed on her skin, flaring brightly with each blaze of illumination that punctured the dark. It was so beautiful, and every time, she wished she could touch that shimmering patch of light just once. Whispered pleas burst through her lips whenever the light appeared, only to die just as fast.

More jumbled voices knocked around her dark oasis. A man's voice, high but edgy. He was speaking with a woman.

Older, if Drea had to guess based on the slight warble and lower register of her words.

"Pulse is picking up," the woman said.

"Is that good? Should you get the doctor?" the man hastily replied.

A deep sigh breathed through the darkness. "Sir, I *am* the doctor. Step aside, please."

How strange. There were no doctors here. Only soothing shadows and piercing light. Sometimes the light was just a flash. Other times it'd take the shape of wings. Sometimes silver, always just out of reach.

Something jostled her left arm, then turned her wrist over. Firm pressure flattened her veins. Were those . . . fingers?

"It's no longer thready. A good sign."

A good sign. Signs . . . like those on a road? An insistent memory prickled her mind into awareness. Mile marker signs. Highways. Exits.

The accident!

Drea's lids winged open. She immediately regretted the enthusiasm and snapped them shut again.

"Oh, you're awake. I know, the overhead lights aren't ideal. Let me kill the one above your bed." Again, that woman's soothing voice.

Drea's heart ticked up a bit at the word *kill*, until she recalled that someone in her vicinity claimed to be a doctor. She opened her eyes again slowly and peeled her tongue away from the roof of her mouth.

"Drea! Oh, thank God you're okay."

The sharp outline of dark hair registered first, and her heart beat an anxious rhythm. The hairstyle was neat and familiar, but a tad too long around the ears. No, that couldn't be right. Ty's hair had been cropped close at the sides. Then the groggy blur faded a touch more, revealing a well-trimmed goatee and the panicked blue eyes of her boyfriend.

Malcolm.

Inexplicable disappointment gripped her chest.

Drea barely had time to register the rest of Malcolm's face before he rushed to her side and gripped her bandaged fingers in a too-tight squeeze. She groaned against the pressure, but he misinterpreted her noise of displeasure for need and immediately reached for a cup of ice chips. "Here, suck on these."

Before Drea could respond, an ice clump pushed against the seam of her dry lips like a spoon of peas being shoved into a defiant toddler. Just as she was about to relent and open her mouth, an insistent throat cleared, and the other voice in the room spoke.

"Let's hold off on that for a bit."

Relief flooded through Drea, and the ice fell away.

A woman clad in light blue scrubs and a white hospital coat stood at her side. Judging by the death grip she had on each end of the stethoscope hanging around her neck, her patience had left the room long ago. Dark brown skin muted what, on Drea, would have been a face full of tomato-red rage. The tight lips, firm stance, and take-no-shit stare down said it all. This woman was clearly in charge, and she was *not* in the mood for Malcolm, the well-meaning but clueless bystander.

Ah. She's the doctor. Drea briefly wondered whether it would have been wiser to fall back to sleep or bear witness to a crime.

Wait, doctor?

"Where am I?" Drea croaked out.

"Ms. Arnold, I'm Dr. Lawrence, one of the physicians here in the emergency department at Aurora Medical Center," she greeted, easily jockeying her tone from annoyed to soothing. "You were involved in a motor vehicle accident and sustained quite a few injuries, but thankfully, all of them are minor. Whiplash, soft tissue injuries on your joints and muscles, a mild concussion, and a fair number of superficial cuts on your arms and hands. You definitely gave me a run for my money fishing all that glass out, I'll tell ya."

Her warm smile and attempt at levity were entirely lost on Malcolm, who still wore a deep scowl, but softened Drea immensely. She returned the woman's kindness in what she hoped was a grateful smile, but even the muscles in her cheeks felt swollen.

Dr. Lawrence adjusted the IV bag. "How are you feeling?"

How was she feeling? Up until she'd been yanked from her pleasant dark stasis, she'd been just fine. Now, however, an insistent pulsing beat against the backs of her eyes, and despite Dr. Lawrence's efforts, the lights were in no way dim enough. What she wouldn't do for a good set of blackout curtains and a sleeping mask.

"Head hurts."

"Migraine-like symptoms?"

"Bingo." Drea closed her eyes and practiced blinking them open in small increments. Better, but not great.

"That will go away with time. I know everyone always hates that answer, but I haven't found a better one yet. Until then, NSAIDs are your best friend. We can evaluate to see whether you need something stronger, but those usually do the trick for minor head wounds."

Drea grunted her acknowledgment, and Dr. Lawrence gave the knowing look of all physicians not used to being the most loved person in the room.

"Do you remember anything about the accident, Ms. Arnold?"

Drea considered the question carefully. "I was driving home from the community college's library. It was close to closing, I think, so maybe ten thirty? Quarter to eleven? I was about to get off the highway when something hit my car and I spun out." For some reason, she wasn't entirely ready to mention Ty's involvement in front of Malcolm. It wasn't like she was doing anything wrong. She was a grown woman who could make friends with whomever she wanted, but as she ran through the series of events, her memory snagged on things she wasn't quite sure even she knew how to explain. "Wait, what time is it?"

"Three thirty in the morning."

"Oh, wow, that's late. Or early, I guess."

"Funny thing about hospitals," Dr. Lawrence quipped as she typed some notes into the computer next to the IV stand, "we're kind of a twenty-four-hour operation."

Drea's shoulders bobbed on a chuckle, then she winced when her body protested the movement. As she breathed through the pain, a thought occurred to her. "Do you know what hit my car?"

"Caller said it was a moose."

Drea snorted, then cringed at what the reaction had inadvertently dislodged that she had no choice but to swallow. She cleared her throat and asked, "A moose?"

Dr. Lawrence's tapping never let up. "Yeah, I know. Not super common at night, but not entirely unheard of either. Caller said he witnessed the animal dashing across the highway and clip the back of your car. The animal must have thought it could make it and misjudged its timing. My brother's a hunter, and he's told me moose aren't that well adapted to seeing in the dark. Their senses of smell and hearing are much stronger."

Malcolm finally put the cup of ice chips on the table and wiped the condensation on his pants. "Did the police ever identify the anonymous caller?"

Anonymous caller?

The doctor's bored brown eyes peeled away from the computer long enough to pin the man with the force of his idiocy. "Anonymous callers are anonymous. You should be grateful someone was around to witness the crash and call it in at all."

"No one's really anonymous." He scoffed. "Who the hell was driving by at that hour anyway? And they didn't stop?"

"Visiting hours are over, Mr. Brand. I made an exception for you to be here when she woke up, but now I must insist that you leave. It's very late."

Drea got the sense Dr. Lawrence wasn't used to *insisting* on anything. The tension in the room fueled the tension in her head, and she shut her eyes for a moment to take in a bracing breath. Drea could count on one hand the number of times she'd seen Malcolm back down from an argument, with fingers to spare. Usually, she loved his tenacity. Once, he had even used it in her defense when a waiter got her order wrong after they waited weeks for the reservation. Now, however, the whole thing sent her pounding cranium into a tailspin.

"Malcolm, I'm really tired. I don't think I can honestly do more than fall back to sleep anyway, and you've got to be exhausted. Don't you have a showing scheduled for tomorrow? Or, today, I guess?"

"Sleep is the best thing for you at this point, Ms. Arnold. We'll see how you do later in the morning, but if you're not experiencing any signs of nausea, dizziness, or decreased coordination, we could discharge you by lunchtime."

Lunchtime. Crap. She'd have to e-mail her boss and explain her absence. The moment her logistical wheels started spinning, however, a bone-numbing exhaustion took the reins, telling her just how she'd be spending the next few hours.

Malcolm swiped a hand down a similarly tired face. "It's in the morning. I can be done and back to pick you up by noon." He squeezed her shoulder, then lifted her hand and brushed a kiss across her bandaged knuckles. When his eyes lifted back to hers, the telltale sparkle that always managed to win her over fluttered dimly beneath a veil of his exhaustion. How long had he been waiting with her? All night? Her chest tightened with emotion.

"I'm just going to go back to sleep. I won't be the best company, I assure you. All these beeping monitors will just annoy the crap out of you anyway."

"They're not annoying if they're keeping you alive," he fired back.

"Ms. Arnold is only wearing a pulse oximeter and a blood pressure cuff. She's hardly critical."

"See?" Drea said, waving her machine-clamped finger for emphasis. "Totally fine."

Malcolm scanned the monitor next to her bed, squinting at the neon green numbers as if they were hiding something.

Dr. Lawrence rolled her eyes and walked toward the door. "I'll give you a few minutes before lights out again. You need anything urgently, Ms. Arnold, just hit the button hanging over the side of your bed."

As soon as they were alone, Drea gathered Malcom's hands and gave them a gentle squeeze. "I'll be fine. Seriously."

"I know. Still don't like it, though."

"I've slept in worse places."

His eyes snapped to hers. Indignation curled his lip into a sneer. "You've slept in better places, too. By my side, to start."

The kiss that came next melted any words from her thoughts, not that there was much she could say. The comfort of his mouth drowned out the confusion in her head, so she sank into him with as much tenderness as her battered body would allow. He broke the kiss only to bestow one more gently on her forehead. "I'll be back at lunchtime tomorrow."

After Malcolm finally left her room, Drea sank into the pillows and waited for sleep to claim her. When it eventually did, however, there was no return to that sublime dark oasis as she had hoped. Instead, silver wings visited her dreams, along with the prickling sensation of being watched.

CHAPTER 10

"You're sure he's coming, Ms. Arnold?" The harried, though obviously practiced, words of the tiny-but-mighty nurse wheeling Drea down the emergency department exit ramp matched the woman's quick steps.

Drea suspected the concern was twofold: anxiety over whether Drea's caregiver would show up and, more significantly, detached frustration because Drea's bed had already been filled by another patient. To state it plainly, there was no more room at the inn, but until Drea's discharged butt was out the doorway and offloaded to someone else, the hospital was still responsible for her. She'd worked in enough medical settings to know the power of legal liability. Completely understandable, though severely unfortunate for all parties involved, as there was no sign of Malcolm, despite the bevy of "yes, I'll be there, just finishing up" texts he'd sent over the past hour.

"He'll be here." Drea threw as much self-assured emphasis into the words as possible, though the effect didn't land the way she'd hoped.

The nurse simply pursed her lips and craned her torso over the back of the wheelchair, eyeing the entrance to the parking garage around the corner. "What kind of car does he drive? Do you see him pulling up at all? Maybe he went into the garage, instead of pulling around to the front?"

The questions were more hopeful than helpful. If the nurse leaned forward any farther, the woman was liable to roll Drea down the exit ramp herself. Going by the on-your-mark jitters coursing through her attendant and vibrating down the metal frame of the wheelchair, the nurse was one starting gunshot away from hauling ass back into the hospital and leaving Drea to fend for her recently-concussed-though-still-able-bodied self. From the chatter Drea heard on her way out, a summer camp school bus full of preteens had gotten into an accident, and Aurora Med was the nearest hospital. The staff was about to get slammed with a slew of very injured and very nonconsenting minors.

Drea ducked her chin and checked her phone again. Nothing. Where the hell was he? After passing all her tests, she'd been given her follow-up instructions and discharge papers. That was at noon. Solidly lunchtime, which she had pointed out to Malcolm in her most recent text. The staff was beyond gracious and took no small amount of pity on her situation. They let her wait it out in the room for another thirty minutes, until the emergency department erupted and every quick-thinking nurse gave their most polite version of the same speech to any lingering patient. Can you breathe? Can you walk? Good, do it outside.

And so Drea sat, with a wheelchair half under her butt and half being inched back inside the emergency department. Embarrassment warmed her cheeks, and sweat that had nothing to do with the heat misted her brow. She was about to scan the cars lined up for the garage again when her phone pinged.

All wrapped up, but the clients want to see another house that JUST came on the market fifteen minutes ago. I'll make the showing as quick as possible. Hang tight.

All the breath was punched out of her.

"Is that him? Did he just park?"

Drea gripped the phone and slammed it facedown in her lap. "Yup. He just parked." She shot the words out in tight spurts. Disappointment clogged her throat, and she didn't trust Nurse Eager Beaver not to poke at the wound that had most definitely been ripped open. Once she'd gotten her quivering vocal cords under control, she gestured toward the bench next to the exit. "He had to park far, though. I can sit here and wait for him. He's coming."

The nurse eyed the bench, then twisted her lips into the conflicted expression of someone being given an out when they knew they shouldn't take it. "I really can't do that. Dr. Lawrence's discharge instructions state you need to be sent home with a care provider, given the head injuries. Technically, I'm supposed to make sure you're picked up."

So was Malcolm. The betrayal stung worse than any of the myriad of injuries dotting her arms and pulsing down her neck. Their conversation from last night, which had been tender and comforting in the moment, sliced her through with morbid humiliation.

I'll be fine. Seriously.

I know. Still don't like it, though.

I've slept in worse places.

You've slept in better places, too. By my side, to start. I'll be back at lunchtime tomorrow.

Big engines turned over, and ambulances began lining up in front of the ambulance entrance. EMTs emptied out of rigs and rolled preteens on stretchers single file through the automatic doors.

Drea frowned. She shouldn't be here, nor should she continue taking up this nurse's time and skills when others needed the woman more.

"He just had to park at the top level of the garage. He'll be down any minute." She nodded with fake resolve.

"Oh, good." The nurse had already pulled the wheelchair alongside the bench and bent over to apply the brakes. Once finished, she held out her hands for support. "Up you go."

Drea's butt was kissing the synthetic wood before her feet had a chance to settle. Holy crap, that nurse meant business. Drea briefly wondered what damage the woman could inflict on a stumbling drunk. Probably slap the sober right into him.

The nurse visored her hand over her eyes and scanned the people exiting the garage. "Where's your guy? You see him yet?"

"Here."

The gruff word yanked both women's attention from the throng of visitors. Ty stood on the sidewalk to Drea's left, his powerful stance nearly taking up the entire width of the concrete slab. Muscled arms hung heavily at his sides, and an icy expression twisted his full lips into a warning. For what, exactly, Drea couldn't fathom, but the pedestrians skirting around him on the walkway clearly understood the threat.

Nurse Time's Up dropped a fist to her hip and did something Drea had never seen the woman do before: stood still. The slow smile came a heartbeat later, followed by an appreciative appraisal that made Drea want to run the woman over with the wheelchair. Or an ambulance. Confused, she tucked that thought away as Ty stepped forward, but the nurse's mouth was faster.

"For future reference, care providers are instructed to drive around and pick up here at the door. Save the garage for when you want to do the obligatory visit for your cousin's newborn. Normally, I'd say you can head inside to get your parking ticket validated, but it's a shit show in there. It's your eight dollars, though, so I'll let you square away your priorities."

"We're good."

We're good? Did he expect Drea to leave with him? She

fumbled for her phone again and checked her texts. Radio silence from Malcolm.

"Great." The nurse grabbed the wheelchair and hauled ass back toward the automatic doors. Before they closed all the way, she hollered over her shoulder, "And just call the number on the discharge papers if you have any questions."

"Wait! He's not my—" The doors clanged shut, leaving her alone with her outrage and the man who had more than a hand in causing it. Drea whirled on Ty. "What are you doing here? Why did you tell her you were my boyfriend?"

"I didn't. She asked where your guy was, and as I was standing there sporting a Y chromosome and a vehicle capable of taking you home, I figured I fit the description rather nicely." There wasn't a hint of smugness in his matter-of-fact retort. If her mind had any more capacity for fury, he'd have just topped it off.

"You . . ." Then the rest of his words poked through the sarcasm. "You have a car? To take me home?"

"No, I have a vehicle—a truck, technically—which is more than I can say for whatever your boyfriend's supposed to be sporting. Where the hell is he, anyway?" While Drea's anger was a slow simmer under tender skin, Ty's seemed like an inferno barely held together by birthday balloon rubber. One sharp poke and she imagined he was liable to erupt, shattering that perfectly clenched jaw of his. Maybe it was her overwrought fragility of the moment, but she didn't truly mind someone exploding in rage on her behalf just then since her body sure wasn't up for the excitement.

"He got held up at a house showing." Even as she said it, the excuse stung her lips.

Ty scoffed. "Dude had one fucking job, and that was to get you home safe."

Drea's throat tightened, and she lifted a shoulder. "Something came up."

"Yeah, me." Ty's nostrils flared, and he pinned her with those harsh eyes. In a blink, they melted from a burnished gray into swirling liquid silver. She gasped, but when she inched her head forward for a closer inspection, the pewter flames extinguished back to the sea-storm sky she was used to. Then he carefully lifted her by her elbow.

The rest of her couldn't help but follow.

"Where are you taking me?"

"Home."

CHROME EASED his black dually pickup truck into Drea's parking spot at her apartment complex and wished like hell her fuckwad boyfriend's head had been the Heineken bottle his front tire just crunched over. As long as he'd live, and he'd lived a long damn time, he'd never get over the sight of Drea sitting helpless and expectant in a wheelchair outside the emergency department, waiting for a man who didn't know what it was to be one. What kind of alleged testicle-toting tool would ever leave a woman like that on the side of the road waiting, let alone after she'd nearly choked down a tree and spent the night in a hospital?

Not one who'd be walking around much longer, if Chrome had his say.

He yanked the gear shaft into park and nearly strangled the steering wheel. Below Chrome's skin, his angel fire burned high in a torrent of rage and the particular need to incinerate a certain goatee and the skin it was attached to. He slammed his eyes shut and prayed to the mages Drea hadn't noticed the fire dancing in his irises. The last semblance of his celestial power wouldn't do either of them a lick of good if he blew his wad over a corpse Chrome hadn't yet corpsed.

That man had *kissed* her. Touched her. Held her hand like

she was spun gold and then *abandoned her?* If Chrome hadn't forced himself to stay in the hallway outside her hospital room last night, he'd have popped in for a quick hi-how-are-ya and emptied his gun into the lackey's shit for brains.

Fuck, he needed to hit someone. But first, he needed to make sure Drea was all right.

"You want me to carry you upstairs?"

The statement snapped Drea out of her silent stewing, but only in the way a large dog acknowledges a bee sting. "What?"

"The stairs."

They both regarded the bright red door of her unit, behind which held a single staircase that led to the apartment she shared with her friend, Molly.

"Oh, I'll be fine. Thanks for the ride." Her hand drifted over to the car door latch, but when she went to pull it, her lax grip never really got the thing all the way to Openville. It was like watching a ghost trying to flick on a light switch. The next time Drea reached for the latch, the door swung open wide before her fingers could curl around the lever. Chrome was already on the other side of the door, offering her a hand to get down. Her expression teetered between stunned and confused, neither of which he very much cared for.

"I'm good, really," Drea insisted, though she still accepted his hand. The moment he got her upright, a clenching grumble cut off her words. Her hands shot to her stomach, and deep crimson crept up her cheeks. "Oh my God, you didn't hear that."

A wry smile touched his lips. "Sure did. Sounded like marching orders for my next assignment. Judging by the bandages on your hands, I'm guessing juggling kitchen knives is not on your list of recommended activities."

"I wasn't going to juggle them," she mocked indignantly. "Opening jars on the other hand . . ."

"Won't be your problem." Chrome held his palms up to her and wiggled his fingers. "These meat hooks can more than manage a jelly jar or mayo lid." He tossed extra levity into his voice, hoping to coax a smile out of her, but Drea's brushed velvet words snapped him right back to the shitstorm swirling around them.

"Can they also lift a car off an embankment?"

Fuck.

Hesitant violet eyes found his and left him little room to hide the truth. She'd seen him in his metallic form, no doubt wings and all. The big reveal should have been a relief. His heart should have finally eased enough to fling the questions that had balanced on the tip of his tongue the past few days. He wanted to plow her memories so he could map every path she had traveled these long years. How had she survived? What the hell was she doing on the wrong side of the gates? What had she lost and learned? Did she think of that night?

Did she think of him?

He and his brothers had a strict track record when it came to interactions with mortals, however, and as much as it killed him to admit, the woman before him definitely was one now, inexplicably so. The less mortals knew about celestial beings, the longer those mortals tended to live. Only recently had a few mortal women been welcomed into their fold when some of his brothers found their soul-bonded mates, restoring those sentinels' full celestial powers in the process. The bonds had been discovered by skin-to-skin touch. Well, he and Drea had sure checked that box once upon an eternity, and his power was still locked up tight on a rechargeable time limit. The thought itched under his skin and screamed for more examination than he was willing to give.

They weren't soul bonds. Just two souls who had shared a bond, sort of. At a time when his soul had been so tainted with despair he couldn't recognize his own skin until it had been wrapped in hers.

And she had no fucking clue who he was.

Illogical resentment gave way to stoic resolve. No, he couldn't tell her. Not until he got some more intel on the situation and not until he could get to the bottom of her involvement with the charmers. Strands of an idea began to tighten in his mind. Perhaps he could stoke her interest while still securing his.

Heat simmered beneath his eyes while he weighed the risks. "I'll make a deal with you. I'll talk if you eat. Ask me any question you'd like, as long as it's between bites."

That curious gaze of hers tracked his, then brightened at her apparent win. "All right."

"Under one condition."

"What's that?" she called back over her shoulder as they made their way toward the door.

"You tell me everything you know about that lab you work for."

Drea's climb faltered mid-step, and Chrome steadied her with a hand on her waist.

"I've already told you about my research. Why does the lab matter?"

Ice hardened his vocal cords, and he quickly dropped his hand. *Guide her, but don't tell her.* "Because it wasn't a moose that ran you off the road."

CHAPTER 11

Peanut butter and jelly wasn't the best choice of nourishment when one had a thousand questions dancing on the tip of their tongue. Questions that were barricaded behind a sticky wall of obedient chewing while Drea's new research-partner-turned-rideshare-runner stood in her kitchen cutting up apples for her like she was a child in need of an after-school snack. Her good fortune, while regrettably late to the party, had definitely shown up now, however. And its shoulders were currently widening her small galley kitchen while putting ninja-grade knife skills to use.

"So," Drea mumbled around a mouth full of bread, "should I make a list and start from the top? Do we just go back and forth with our questions?"

The honed back muscles facing her shifted on a chuckle. "Most women I know would be crying into their Frosted Flakes after what you've just been through."

"Most women I know wouldn't eat Frosted Flakes. Too much sugar."

Ty turned back to her, touching his chin to his shoulder. "Oh yeah? How's that purple grape-flavored high fructose corn syrup taste? Or does it need to be paired with the tan peanut-scented high fructose corn syrup to really make those flavors pop?"

Drea's eyes narrowed, and she tossed her final PB&J bite into her mouth, chewing with as much relish as the sweetened shoe paste would allow. "Duh-lish-ush."

"Sorry, what was that?" Ty cupped his ear. "Were those words?"

The balled-up napkin hit him on his rounded shoulder, and Drea got the distinct impression he didn't catch it on purpose.

He passed the apples through the little window separating the kitchen from the dining room and joined her at the table. Drea tossed a prayer up to a being she'd never believed in that the *vintage* in Molly's antique dining set meant it was made from an actual tree capable of supporting the mountain that was Ty's body. Only when he'd successfully settled next to her without any groans, snaps, or buckles from the furniture that would otherwise point him toward eating the carpet could she relax a bit.

Then the silence reminded her nerves they had a job to do: freak the heck out over a man who was quite possibly strong enough to lift a car.

"You need to start first, because I'm thinking all sorts of nonsensical things over here."

Ty's jaw widened with a teasing smile. "Let me guess. You want to know whether I'm stronger than a locomotive. Able to reach tall buildings in a single bound?"

"I'll admit, I can't exactly imagine you in a red-and-blue leotard, but I'm woman enough to admit my brain's not totally firing on all cylinders at the moment."

An unreadable expression colored his features, and his chest lifted on a deep inhale. The slightly stubbled skin beneath his chin rippled with a firm swallow, and Drea's lower lip, now free of its peanut butter prison, fell open slightly. His eyes snagged her gaze, and she quickly looked away.

"I was heading home, and I saw another vehicle from the library's lot follow yours out. I thought it was odd, given the hour, and by the time I caught up to you, I saw your rear driver's side get nailed by a black SUV and your car go over. Before it did, I grabbed it."

Drea blinked at him. "You . . . *grabbed* it. A car."

"Ever read those stories where a mother lifts a car off her kid who's trapped underneath? It's not unheard of." The explanation was delivered with such frankness, he may as well have been talking about picking up a penny from the street or plucking a lint ball off his shoulder.

Blindly, Drea patted around for her phone while Ty leaned to the side and grabbed a piece of gum from the pack in his back pocket. The phone screen's blue light was *not* post-concussion friendly, and she reflexively dimmed the display while she typed out anything she could to verify a theory she'd always assumed was just that. Her stomach recoiled when the search results populated.

Hysterical strength is a physical and spontaneous phenomenon when a person experiences extreme distress or peril . . .

Adrenaline floods the lungs and heart, increasing oxygen to muscles . . .

Endorphins are released, lessening the body's perception of pain . . .

For people with high fitness levels and peak physical condition, the phenomenon, while still very rare, can be more likely . . .

Drea's gaze floated to the enormous man before her, whose strength couldn't help but be on display. His cotton T-shirt was practically painted onto sculpted shoulders and biceps, leaving little room for anything else to fill in the gaps, be they hormones or otherwise.

Ty shifted his jaw back and forth on the peppermint square for a moment, though she wasn't sure whether it was to work on the gum or work out a response to what she'd say next. It seemed like the man had an answer for everything.

"Okay, so Superman moments aren't entirely made up," she relented, swallowing back the quiver in her voice. Something else niggled at her, though. A memory she couldn't fathom coming up with on her own. She cleared her throat tentatively. "I also recall seeing . . ." God, was she really going to say it? Could she even look him in the eye? Would he think she was just as crazy as she felt? The strange thought sent a shudder through her and clouded her mind with uncertainty. Why should his opinion of her carry any more weight than that of a stranger's? Which was exactly what he was, right?

"Recall what?" he prodded.

Do it. You don't have a meek bone in your body. Rip that sucker off and deal with the chips wherever they fall.

"Wings," she rushed out. "Silver wings on your back."

A single dark brow climbed higher. "You saw wings?"

"Through the side mirror. Huge, twice as wide as you were tall. They were silver and reflected some of the moonlight, I think." *I think?* Crap, if there was a way to put any more disbelief into her statement, that just about did it. Judging by Ty's small smile and pitying gentled gaze, her argument had all the weight of a little girl stomping her foot at her parents while pointing toward the empty chimney where she *swore* she'd just seen a red-and-white-clad ass shimmy topside.

"You were in pretty rough shape when I pulled you out of the vehicle," he said pointedly. "Took me more than a few swipes just to clear all your hair away from your face so I could make sure you were breathing. Can't see how you'd be able to see much of anything clearly."

Drea's heart sank, and she threw another apple into her mouth to cover her embarrassment. He was right, of course, though she supposed it was a testament to his irritatingly extreme good manners that he didn't flat-out call her a crazy lady.

"I'll tell you what confuses me, though," he said, scooching his seat forward a tad. "When you told me you were running lab samples on a live patient but all the reports came back batty, do you remember what your initial thoughts were?"

The change of subject was a subtle relief, perhaps on both their parts, for it was clear her accident was bringing up more questions than either of them had the heads to accurately sort through. It took Drea a moment to switch gears before she answered. "I thought I had run the tests incorrectly at first."

"So you reran them."

"That's right."

"And when you got the same numbers again, where did your mind go?"

Drea had to think carefully for a moment, as even the day before seemed like a lifetime ago. "That the equipment was damaged. Mechanical errors or faulty tubes. Maybe I didn't store the samples correctly."

Ty nodded in encouragement. "Has any of that ever happened before? Is that a mistake you usually make?"

"Hell, no," she barked. Her employment history may leave something to be desired, but she sure as shit knew how to do her job. It was sticking with it that had proved difficult, in her managers' eyes, at least.

"Didn't think so." He leaned back in his seat a touch but let his relaxed legs fall open in a casual show of comfortable conversation. "So, if you didn't run the tests incorrectly and all the equipment was functioning according to factory settings, what's the next logical conclusion?"

"That the sample results are correct, but that would be impossible."

"You sure?" A dark brow lifted in question as he crossed his arms. "What if there are other things, something else in your lab that's alive and kicking, that biologically wouldn't behave the way a human would?"

Drea's brows dropped low, and she shook her head as she considered his words. "Not possible."

"No? Tell me, you ever see anyone else at your lab on a regular basis? Your supervisor, other employees?"

A disconcerting pall weighed down her senses, even as her heart tumbled around her ribs. "I see my supervisor about once or twice a week. It's never for very long, though, quick pop-ins here and there. We mostly interact through e-mail, as I'm the only one who works there during the day. That was one of the things that drew me to the position, actually. It's private, quiet, and if I make it through my probationary period, I get full autonomy of the lab. It was a freaking miracle gig, especially for someone with my track record. But no, I don't see any other employees regularly. Or anyone, for that matter."

What had struck her as a fortuitous employment opportunity before was quickly being stripped of its glittery package. She'd worked in enough medical settings to know that nothing, not even the janitorial services, operated in a vacuum. So, how had her company managed to do so?

"You signed an NDA."

"Yes, but that's not unusual."

When he didn't answer, she looked up, only to find stern and stormy eyes calling her out on what she had never bothered to examine too closely before. "Well, it might be, now that I think about it. Typically, if a lab is operating within a medical setting, HIPAA privacy rules apply automatically, so it's a given that no employee's going to sign any additional liability agreements. Their employment is consent enough and conditional on upholding those rules."

Shit. With each new layer peeled back, more and more of Drea's nerves were exposed.

Ty picked up the thread and continued unraveling it. "The

way I see it, people typically don't go to such extreme lengths unless they want to keep things—"

"Hidden," she finished for him.

Ty let the word settle between them for a moment before continuing. "If your employer has a secret patient whose human labs are coming up screwy . . ."

"Then the samples might not be human in origin." The reality was one she'd never considered. Her lunch formed an uneasy lump in her stomach. Had she been working on animal samples all this time?

"And I'll toss one more fiery turd on the pile," Ty added. "You want to talk about extreme lengths to keep things hidden, well, a hit-and-run seems like it would fall in line nicely with that particular *modus operandi*."

Drea's head bolted upright. "What? No." Then his words from earlier sank in. "The doctor at the hospital said an anonymous caller identified a moose hitting my car." But her tone conveyed the question her words didn't. And when he shook his head, her mouth dried up.

"I called it in." His voice had taken on an edge that wasn't there a moment ago. "That car tailing you from the library was intentional. I'm willing to bet your boyfriend's next commission that someone knows you're sniffing deeper into something you shouldn't. And whoever it is, they don't like it."

"But I . . . I'm just doing due diligence. Anyone in my position would ask the same questions when things don't add up." She shook her head vehemently.

"Hey, listen to me." Ty reached forward and settled his warm hand over her bandaged one. His touch was surprisingly gentle despite his size, cradling her hand in a light blanket of comfort. One look at that large hand told her he did very few things gently. And yet she'd predominantly seen that side of him, with her notebook, texts, computers. Even when her racing mind called forward the memory of his firm grip that had yanked her out of the street the first time they met, it wasn't without its softness.

His thumb smoothed against hers, drawing her attention back to him. "How many people in your industry are more motivated to punch a clock at the end of the day than spend an extra hour or so poring over why one of their lab results was a fraction of a percentage off from what it should be?"

Well, shit, he had her there. "A fair amount," she admitted.

"Exactly. But your employer didn't get that with you. Instead, they got someone who's motivated, inquisitive, and gives enough of a shit to figure out the problem so it doesn't become someone else's."

Drea shook her head. It almost sounded like he was complimenting her, like he was *praising* her nosiness instead of condemning it for the disruption it usually caused. No, that couldn't be right. All he had to do was look at her employment history and he'd see just how detrimental her constant questioning could be. Her curiosity didn't just have teeth, but claws and heels as well. Malcolm had highlighted that very point to her when she shared with him how exit interview after exit interview kept coming away with the same language: insubordination, failure to follow directions, insufficient ability to adhere to management's guidelines.

I know you have questions, he'd say in that cajoling manner of his, *but it's not always your job to find the answers. Let the higher-ups do what they're paid to do.*

"I'm the problem," she whispered.

Ty nodded gravely. "And until we can figure out what they're hiding, you've also become the target."

CHAPTER 12

In Drea's experience, there were few things a woman's firm chin and sardonically lifted eyebrow couldn't deter. To her aggrieved frustration, one of those things included Ty with an agenda. His heavy gait around her small apartment threatened to knock over every book perched precariously on her particleboard bookshelf. Once he'd finished whatever he had been inspecting in her room, he'd stomped across the hall to Molly's. A fresh wave of fear curled her gut. Oh Lord, if one of her best friend's stuffy old cookbooks hit the floor because of the not-insubstantial tremors Ty's boots were leaving in their wake, she'd never hear the end of it . . . or be fed a decent meal ever again.

"That's enough," she called from the kitchen as Ty left Molly's room, only to double back on Drea's for the third time. Oh, for fuck's sake. She had known working-line German shepherds with less tenacity. Gritting her teeth, she set her proverbial foot down. "I'm in a top-floor garden apartment in a complex even men with criminal records couldn't be bothered with. Half the windows in this place have broken sash cords with zero balancing weights to speak of and haven't been opened since the Nixon Administration. Why do you think we have Gertrude the Growler cooling the place down?"

Ty stalled out in the hallway and leveled a sneer at the commercial-grade in-wall air conditioner pumping out enough BTUs to freeze a meat locker. So what if the old girl, who Drea and Molly wholeheartedly believed was really just misunderstood and would perform better if given a proper name, had seen more summers than management-required yearly tune-ups? She got shit cold, and that was enough.

Then Ty's unimpressed stare zeroed in on the dinosaur of a control panel sporting one or two noticeable vacancies. "There's no temperature knob. How do you turn that thing off?"

"We don't. She kicks off when the heat kicks on."

The furious expression on Ty's face was enough to scare the stripes off a tiger. Oddly enough, his features had been stuck that way ever since the two of them realized the past twenty-four hours had most likely been an orchestrated event. She'd be a fool to say the circumstances didn't affect her. Of course they did. Fear wasn't unique to certain people, a fact she was grimly reminded of every time the pounding behind her right eye flared up.

Which was why she had every intention of going to work the following morning. And also why Ty had taken it upon himself to glower around her apartment and lock it down like Fort Knox.

The brooding brute in question pointed an accusatory finger at Gertrude. "*That* is something I can't even begin to tear into right now."

"Good. Every woman's entitled to her secrets, be they mechanical or otherwise," Drea retorted, but when her joke didn't smooth out the tense lines at the corners of his eyes like she'd hoped, she tried a different tactic. "Look, I'll be perfectly safe here. As soon as you leave, I'm calling Molly. We usually catch up when she's having her staff meal at the restaurant anyway." Drea paused another moment, then added, "And Malcolm will be by later."

A derisive snort filled the room, then landed with the force of a toppled oak tree. "Just like he showed up at the hospital?"

She knew it was coming, knew he had every right to throw the jibe, but the expectation of the hit did little to block the stinging blow from Ty's words. Once they arrived home, she'd sent Malcolm a text letting him know she'd gotten a ride. That was when the profuse apologies and virtual groveling began. Sort of.

Sorry, babe. Glad you're home safe.

Want me to grab dinner?

You like that Thai place, right? You want your usual? Pad see ew?

Sorry, again. Finishing up soon. Molly's there, right?

I'm so glad you're OK. You have no idea how worried I was. See you soon.

There had been a time in their relationship when every *ping* of his texts had done the same to her heart. When he spoke and she leaped with joy at the attention. She'd had few boyfriends in her life, and Malcolm's fondness toward her spackled over a loneliness she'd never had time to dwell on. She'd always been too busy saving the world from itself, one test tube at a time, as Molly liked to put it.

Until today, when Ty's hand had been the one to help her into a vehicle instead of Malcolm's. Before that, it was the few hours she'd spent with Ty in a quiet library, their heads ducked low over her scribbled suspicions. This sort of attention was altogether different, more caring than carnal, and she wasn't entirely sure what to make of it. One thing was for certain: she didn't hate it, though what that admission said about her was a separate problem altogether, one she was definitely *not* ready to unpack just yet.

"That's a fair statement," she agreed, "but it doesn't change anything. I plan on fueling up on a buttload of sleep after I check in with Molly and maybe pop a few more ibuprofen somewhere in between. It's the best way I can recover before I head in to work tomorrow."

Ty glowered at her with such vehemence, even the hallway seemed to shrink around him, which only accentuated his swelling shoulders and tension-locked biceps. Ooh, he was pissed. "Dr. Lawrence said two to three days of recovery before you resume normal activities."

"No, she *recommended* two to three days of recovery. And if you think for one minute I'm going to sit around here waiting for an arbitrary number of days on a calendar to pass before I bolt toward whatever poor thing's being tested on at my lab, you've got more than a few screws loose, buddy."

"It's not an arbitrary number of days," he ground out, his aggravation apparent in every breath. "It's a physician's order for a recommended clinical recovery period."

"Again, *recommended*, not required."

"You almost—" Gunmetal eyes flashed to shards of smoky silver, cutting off his words. A sharp gasp squeezed her throat before he tore his gaze from her and gave her his back. Her startled confusion beat back the burgeoning throb behind her right eye that all the excitement had stirred up. Finally clear of the discomfort and with his back to her, she was left examining the strain tensing his shoulders again. A strain that hadn't relaxed since he'd begun battening down her hatches, so to speak. Thick cords of tendons held his neck in a permanent and what looked to be an uncomfortable stretch. When he slowly turned to face her, the small lines she had hoped to smooth away with levity earlier now remained pinched in impossibly tighter creases. Once he finally met her gaze again, it was with far-thrown exhaustion.

Drea wrestled down any remnants of her own concerns and turned her focus to the glaring one before her. God, he didn't just look tired but ragged in the way of emergency responders during a natural disaster or fourteen-hour shift workers juggling two jobs. As traumatic as her life had been the past several hours, she'd not taken a moment to consider how Ty had fared. The man had been too busy seeing to her needs for her to even stop and examine whether the cup he was pouring from had been empty or full. Had he even slept? Where did he live? Was it nearby? How the hell had he known she needed to get home?

Then a more chilling question added itself to her worried overload. Did it matter?

Mortification at her lack of concern for him hardened into determination to reverse course. Drea carefully took his larger hand in hers and guided him to the couch in the living room. Once she got his tightly strung body settled on top of the cream-colored leatherette, she steeled herself for words he needed to hear, but more so, words she needed to say.

"I cannot thank you enough for everything you've done for me and continue to do for me. And don't even think about rolling your eyes over my corny declaration of gratitude. I'm not a words person, but that doesn't make mine any less earnest." She jerked his hand sternly for emphasis, and he had the good sense to bite back whatever retort he had been gearing up for. "Am I scared? Sure. Who wouldn't be a little bit unsettled? But what scares me more is the possibility that I may be playing a part in something that's potentially harmful to another creature. I had no idea my employer was involved in animal testing. None. If I did, I assure you I'd have reported their asses so fast, they wouldn't even have had time to get off their chairs before their facility would have been raided by animal control."

She paused, falling victim to the intense emotion her imagery conjured. Only when an unexpected pulse of encouragement squeezed her fingers did she look up. Ty's gaze danced across her features, touching her everywhere with intense solemnity, as if he were memorizing a map or searching for a lost trail. What she *didn't* see was condemnation. Her breath caught in her throat, and she summoned the courage to keep going.

"If there's any living creature down there that's hurting, I couldn't live with myself if I turned the other cheek. If that means I slash off a few recovery days so I could give those days to some poor animal, then that's exactly what I'm going to do."

Ty broke the contact first, sliding his hand free. Grim determination steeled his mouth and brow, further sharpening the strained lines of exhaustion.

"You didn't sleep last night, did you?" Drea asked.

He paused for a moment, then quickly shook his head. "Busy night."

"Understatement of the century," she quipped before considering her solution, then added carefully, "I think you need to sleep. What if we slept together?"

Every noise in the apartment sputtered into silence. Two sets of lungs simultaneously slammed the breaks on the whole breathing thing. Even Gertrude's signature growl quieted to an idle rhythm as Drea realized the mistake of her words.

"No, not sleep *together*! I didn't mean that. I meant we both should sleep at the same time but in, like, different beds."

Ty's astonished expression began to soften, but the bastard still didn't speak, seemingly content to let her hang herself with her verbal diarrhea. His mouth curled into a tucked smile, and just when she thought he was going to say something gentlemanly to smooth over her obvious embarrassment, that dangerous mouth didn't move. Instead, mischief lingered on those lips.

Drea did *not* fixate on how roguish it made him look or how, once upon a time, rakes and rogues had been her favorite brand of book boyfriend red flag.

Shit. Shit. Shit!

"You sleep in your home, and I'll sleep in mine!" She nearly screamed the words as they tumbled out of her in rapid succession. "We both need a good night's sleep, just, you know, separately." On the far wall of the living room, below the picture window, Gertrude's compressor kicked on and her monotonous growl resumed its auditory onslaught, as if satisfied with Drea's clarification.

Drea exhaled and let her head hit the overstuffed couch cushion behind her. Leave it to her to have an air conditioner with a penchant for chaperone duty.

"I do need to recharge," Ty agreed, if somewhat reluctantly, and Drea thanked whatever pain meds were still coursing through her bloodstream that his chivalry went deep enough not to berate her for her little gaffe. "But I'm going to have a few of my brothers swing by the complex and keep an eye on things."

That got her attention.

"That's not necessary—"

"You won't even see them, though I'll have them introduce themselves before they start their shift."

"Shift?"

Ty stood, and some of that starch from earlier had returned to his shoulders. When he reached the front door, he wiggled the handle and tested the lock one last time. "Yeah, they'll be around all night before I drive you to work tomorrow morning."

Drea bolted from the couch. "Excuse me? I don't need a ride." She began to stomp toward him, but he pinned her with a droll look.

"How do you plan on getting there? Last I saw, your car, if you can even call it that, was having its last rights read before its appointment with the crusher."

Yeah. It was. And screw him for pointing out something

perfectly valid and logical when she was in the mood for none of it. "Malcolm could give me—"

"Tomorrow's Wednesday. You ever see anyone around the lab on Wednesdays? Your supervisor ever pop in midweek?"

"Well, no. If I do see him, it's usually either Monday or Friday, but I can't just let you—"

"Good. Looks like tomorrow's Bring a Friend to Work Day. Lunch is on me. Break room coffee's on you. Pick you up at eight o'clock."

"It's a secure lab!" she huffed out, exasperated by how fast things were unraveling. "I have a keycard for a reason!" She flung the words at him, but they landed on his back as the door slammed behind him.

CHAPTER 13

Chrome's angel fire, a celestial magic so powerful he once used it to raze a football stadium's worth of charmers with little more than good aim and better timing, now barely fended off the den's bad chill. The angels' self-made underground cavern-structure-turned-fortress had been their home since the Sealing blasted them out of the Empyrean and they'd learned that the mortal realm was their new and permanent Motel 6. Too bad Magic Fingers weren't still a thing. The vibrations might have helped distract Chrome's body from its hard-earned and even harder-to-avoid exhaustion.

Drea had been right about him being dead on his feet, but not for the reason she suspected.

As Chrome pushed the granite door to the den closed—with two hands instead of one, and boy, was that fucking embarrassing—a low whistle, followed by a *tsk tsk tsk* echoed through the great room.

"Someone forgot to eat their Wheaties again."

"Can it, Bronze. I'm not in the mood." Chrome stalked around the stone support columns separating the farmhouse dining table and eating space from the living area and all but collapsed onto a sandstone sectional. He used the dregs of his energy to heft his booted feet fully onto the sofa and let the cushions support him the rest of the way.

Damn. He had been aboveground for too long, and it was not a good look on him. Already, though, the metals and minerals in the surrounding stone went to work, bolstering his celestial energy and fire like a lizard baking in the sun. The metal in him sang at the relief of the restored elemental connection, which would only grow stronger throughout the night.

Did he regret his decision? Fuck, no. Staying aboveground for entire evenings wasn't a healthy long-term strategy for him or his brothers, as it deprived them of their much-needed fuel source for their celestial power, but it could be done on occasion. A slowly simmering irritation threatened to bubble up at the thought of how Drea's outcome would have changed had he not been there, but he dismissed it just as quickly and sank that sucker back down to the realm of Never Would Have Fucking Happened.

And speaking of past, present, and future items on his to-do list . . .

Chrome lolled his head to the side and took in the impressive array of Bronze's bladed weaponry decorating the walnut coffee table. His brother's shoulder-length red hair flopped to the side, and copper brows pinched in concentration as he organized his knife vest and assorted holsters.

Chrome eyed the leather suspiciously. "You know you swap that shit out like women swap out handbags?" Then he instantly recognized Bronze's vest as . . . one he didn't recognize. "Jeez, is that one new, too?"

"Yup," Bronze said, giving the P the pop it deserved. "And I'll have you know, brother, that little diddy didn't land the way you wanted it to." The auburn angel flashed his perfected shit-eating grin. "Handbags are usually swapped out seasonally.

These I swap out at least once a month." He hoisted the empty vest for inspection (read: appreciation). The brick-colored piece of leather apparel still had the price tag dangling from it —a price tag, Chrome noted, that was handwritten and denoted a nice round number with plenty of zeros hanging off its tail.

"More custom work from Falcon Leatherworks?" Chrome shook his head with equal parts indulgence and approval. "Ritchie's too good to you."

Bronze fired back a knowing smile. "Yeah, he is. Doesn't ask questions, always comes through on the specific modifications I throw at him, and makes a hell of a lot more from our business than the renaissance fair circuit and cosplay crowds."

Chrome grunted his acknowledgment. "Definitely pays to have an armorer on call, and speaking of on call . . ."

No sooner had he said the words than four sets of measured steps reverberated through the cavernous hall. One by one, his brothers joined him and Bronze, melting into the surrounding furniture as if they were all getting ready for family game night. A sharp smack on Chrome's ankles knocked his feet off the couch, and Titan, the sentinels' second-in-command, took up the newly vacated place. The angel's dark finely barbered beard did nothing to hide his annoyance at the dirt smudge Chrome's boots had left behind.

Across from the couch, behind Bronze's perch, stood Tungsten, their prime sentinel, with his arms folded across his barrel chest like a commander waiting for an intelligence report. Next to him, with trim hips casually leaning against the edge of a pool table—well, as casually as any flannel-clad angel with the shortest fucking trip wire one could manage—was Iron. To his left stood Brass, whose closely cropped auburn hair glinted under the lantern light, as if in a subtle nod to how calculating the bastard could be. The angel had assumed his usual no-nonsense stance of hands firmly clasped behind his back, while his notoriously calm demeanor gave away nothing of what he was thinking.

Chrome sat up straight, then remarked, "Where's Steel?"

"Driving Bridget back from Boston," Titan answered. "It was her week to be on site at her design firm."

"Ah."

Bridget was the latest mortal woman to enter their fold, when her soul bond with Steel had revealed itself after the angel nearly wound up dead on her back deck. Talk about your hard transitions. But they'd been sickeningly inseparable ever since, even making accommodations for when her remote job called her into the Boston office once a month for a week.

Chrome's jaw twitched, and he exhaled the rust from his lungs. Fuck, this was going to be hard. It wasn't like he was a stranger to hard things, but this? He took another rasping breath, allowing the cavern's cool air to smooth over his nerves. "You guys ever think about that night?"

As predicted, an uncomfortable silence thickened throats throughout the room. Boots shifted uncomfortably over the stone floor. There was no need to clarify which night Chrome was referring to. There never would be. Kind of hard to forget the last moment of one's existence before everything they knew was ripped from them. That they survived at all was a testament to whatever celestial magic had the good sense to hang on while their angelic forms were being shredded apart and transformed into mortal bodies with benefits.

Titan cleared his throat and, as usual, was the first to speak. "Yeah. All the time." His silver gaze brightened with the iridescent heat of his metal, then glazed over to land far away. "I still see their faces. The legions I trained, the way their eyes held mine while I rattled off whatever empowering words I could. I never learned . . ." His voice thinned, snagging on emotion they'd all spent eons avoiding.

Chrome clasped his brother's shoulder. "None of us ever

learned what happened to anyone in the Empyrean after we fell. But I may have."

Startled heads whipped to attention so fast, Chrome was waiting for a neck to snap. Or three. Barked confusion echoed off the chamber walls.

"What?" Bronze screamed.

"How?" Brass looked to Chrome, then to Tung for clarification, but the stunned expression on their prime sentinel's face mirrored the others.

"That's not possible. It's just not possible. Is it?" Titan bolted to his feet, nearly toppling the coffee table at his knee. Luckily, Bronze had already affixed his blades to the vest or they'd have one heck of a knife-throwing show on their hands.

"Steady." Tung's booming command settled around the room. His mane of golden hair shifted across his shoulders as he leveled a calm but assertive look at Chrome. "Please, brother, explain."

Chrome stood and walked over to the bar that separated the living space in the great hall from the rows of practice targets and cases of arrows and ammo. After pouring himself three knuckles worth of bourbon, he took a bracing sip and let the words fly.

"I spent that night with a mage. A messenger mage," he clarified. "She was—" Fuck, why was he choking on the memory as if he hadn't just spent the last day with her? As if she wasn't still alive and well and gifting smiles to a man-child who couldn't be bothered to cherish them for what they were?

What Chrome had once coaxed out of her while her strong thighs gripped his neck and her moans chased his hell away.

"Who?" Iron asked.

Chrome summoned her name, which he had tucked away in some sacred space inside him, and forced it through his tightened chest. "Dee. She said her name was Dee. I got the impression she wasn't high up in the order." The memory tickled his senses, and he shook his head with a smile. "Probably had something to do with the fact that she'd still been shuttling souls in after we gave the lockdown mandate. She had a rebellious streak, for sure."

Tung relaxed his arms, though his face remained grave. "She had been shuttling souls through the Veil? Impossible. It had been shattered."

Chrome shrugged. "She figured out how to get through the mist and had just returned from one of the water worlds that night. She was so goddamn concerned about logging the soul on the celestial map, about fulfilling a promise to the family. It didn't matter that heaven was literally falling down around her."

The brothers exchanged inquisitive glances, silently seeking out whether the others had known of her, but they all shook their heads. In denial, not judgment. Every angel in that room knew all too well the power of desperation. It was yet another thing that strengthened their eternal bond, for better or worse.

"The woman Steel and I saw leaving the charmers' grotto bore a striking familiarity to her, and it had been bugging the crap out of me for months. Then, on one of my reconnaissance patrols, I saw the tattoo on her wrist," Chrome added.

Titan leaned against the back of the couch. "A tattoo? Like the mark of the soul bond?" Titan's mate, Rose—along with Rose's twin sister, Tammy, mate to Tungsten—and Bridget each bore a quarter-sized symbol tattooed on the inside of their wrist. The writing revealed the name of their angelic mate in the celestial language and appeared once the soul bond had been completed.

"No, this was different. It was black and more of an image than a symbol. Very distinctive and *very* specific."

Tung stepped forward slowly. "What are you saying, Chrome?"

"I'm saying that Dee is mortal, and she's here in *this* realm, though she goes by Drea now." He nearly spat the words, then took another sip of liquid composure before adding, "And she doesn't remember anything. Not her name, not the Empyrean, not who the fuck she's apparently working for or why."

And not me.

A deeply seated emotion clawed at his insides, threatening to get out, screaming at his subconscious to reveal the true depths of his connection to Dee during that night. How he had been one desperate footstep away from dragging himself onto that battlefield and begging Cyro to do his worst in exchange for the safety of those who shouldn't have had to bear it.

How her glowing warmth and beautifully foolish soul chased away the dark for the briefest and brightest moment of his existence.

How, eons later, he'd never stopped thinking about that night or stopped fighting for a way back to the Empyrean.

The others had always assumed his desire to return home was like theirs, one born of longing for what was lost: a home, a community, friends and comrades, duty and service. While all that was true, Chrome had never shared his deeper, darker motivations, and what might happen to him if he returned to an Empyrean where she no longer existed?

"Hold on," Bronze said, putting his palm out and squeezing his eyes shut. "How the hell is any of that possible?"

"Fuck if I know," Chrome answered, slamming down his glass, "but until I can figure that out, I've got more pressing action steps. The research lab Drea thinks she works for has been churning out some less-than-kosher samples."

Iron's predatory tone reverberated off the stone walls. "What sort of samples?"

"Live patient samples. She's only worked there for just shy of three months, but from what she's told me, they just started asking her to analyze soft tissue, blood, and urine last week. Before that, her samples had been inanimate and largely mined for metal analysis." Chrome's anger flashed, echoing his brothers' unrestrained and equally volatile rage. "Acids, corrosive behavior, and the like. Same shit, different day."

While the charmers were adept at dark magic, the sentinels' angel fire was far stronger and the only true recourse they had at eliminating the demons. It was why every weapon the angels used—whether it be bullets, blades, or bolts—was infused with their celestial fire. In recent years, however, the strongest among the charmers had devised ways to slow, though thankfully never fully thwart, the fire's lethality. Since angel fire was still fatal to Cyro's dark demons, even despite its slower reactions, the charmers had been hard at work with efforts to level the playing field, weaponizing metals by manipulating them with magic. To hear that humans were now involved, whether knowingly or otherwise, was a sickening turn of events.

Chrome shook the macabre thoughts from his mind and met his brothers' gazes, all of which sparked with fiery intent. "I think the charmers have caught wind of Drea sniffing around. Someone in a black SUV tried to run her off the road last night. I got to her in time, but I wasn't able to follow them. As best as I can figure, the charmers need her as a skilled lackey to facilitate their research, especially when a portion of the work requires daytime analysis or interacting with the mortal world to get the supplies they need. Drea's no mindless lemming, though. If she sees something off, she'll go after it with a ruthlessness that rivals any of you assholes."

"And the charmers now view her as a threat," Titan surmised.

Echoing grunts of acknowledgment flitted around the room, cramming out any pity and instead fueling the air with grim determination.

Chrome shot to his feet and rolled out the ache in his shoulders. "Tonight, I need three of you to watch her apartment. Tomorrow, she's reporting for work as usual . . . and I'm going with her. A quiet in and out, no large raids. She doesn't remember me or know about us or who she's really working for, and at least for the time being, I'd like to keep it that way. Her keycard gives her access to the grotto, and I plan on taking things just a bit further." Blue fire sprang from his fingertips, curling around his clenched fists. "Whatever's down there, it's coming topside. I'll need you all ready when we hit the surface because nothing will survive the place when I'm through with it."

CHAPTER 14

The sun's early morning rays stretched lazy lines along Molly's deep mahogany dining room table, keeping their own—and far more accurate—time than the cooking-themed clock above the stove. No matter how many times Drea changed the batteries in that sucker, its soup spoon hour hand loved to hitch a ride on its dinner fork minute hand, while the butter knife second hand gave zero fucks to either and spun happily around the clock's face at its leisure.

Suffice it to say, Drea wasn't entirely to blame for her chronic tardiness. This morning, however, was a whole other ball of wax as she white-knuckled the gauzy curtain liners and stared out at the parking lot. Behind her, Molly gently tugged Drea's wet hair into her customary braid, a habit her friend had started on days when Drea's nerves weren't conducive to dealing with flyaways. Once the elastic was snapped into place and a second one added for good measure, Molly joined her bestie at the window.

"Wow, they're still there, aren't they?" Molly murmured.

"Sure are."

"And they're brothers, you said? Because, Good Lawdy, they certainly make them differently wherever they're from."

Drea had to agree. As promised, Ty's brothers (in muscles and bone definition, as well as blood, apparently) had patrolled the apartment grounds the entire night and into the morning. An hour or so after Ty left, three men who would have had to squish to fit in a warehouse aisle if they stood shoulder to shoulder showed up at her door. The first one sported a kind smile through a neatly trimmed dark beard and introduced himself as Titan, before casually bobbing a head toward the other two redheaded, though otherwise very different men. The more stoic of the two, introduced as Brass, had politely shaken her hand, though his reserved demeanor cut off any *nice to meet you* she was about to throw out. The other man, however—Bronze, she'd learned—was all smiles and charm as he offered his fist to her for the commensurate bump. Drea had stalled out for a moment at their unusual names before her brain quickly corrected course. After all, one didn't go through the blander-than-bland New Hampshire public school system with a name like Drea without having to justify her existence.

Yes, that's my real name. It's Greek. No, I've never been to Greece, but my birth parents were from there. Yes, I'm adopted. No, I don't know how to say, "So is your mom," in Greek.

So, yeah, she wasn't throwing a dollop of shade on their name game.

Behind her, Molly had poked her dark head around Drea's shoulder. Even from Drea's periphery, it was hard to miss her roomie's dilated pupils as they struggled to take in all that testosterone clogging up the doorway. With the patience of patron saints Drea had only heard about from Internet memes, each man dipped their head in acknowledgment and went through the roll call again for Molly's benefit. The amber gaze of the one in the middle, however—Brass, if she remembered correctly—followed Molly around the living room while she nervously arranged pillows that didn't need arranging. Once she caught on to the anxious show she had been performing and who kept watching her, she muttered a quick "excuse me" and bolted for her bedroom.

That was the last either of them had seen of the three men, until this morning.

Drea fiddled with the curtain liner's fraying fringe and exhaled as much of her nervous energy as her tense lungs would allow. In the parking lot below, Ty had joined his family, and the four brothers now stood with matching scowls and meaty fists on lean hips. She didn't need any advanced degrees to figure out they were talking about her.

Molly pressed her nose to the glass. "I can't say I fully understand the need for all those homespun security bros, but I find myself hard-pressed to complain."

Her shrewd, yet curious eyes followed Ty's hulking form as he separated from the pack and headed toward the walkway that led up to their apartment. Once Ty had disappeared from view, Molly pulled in a soft gasp. The other three remained in deep conversation, including Brass, whose tense arms had settled into what Drea had come to think of as his comfort crossover: forearms braced over each other, hands clasping the opposite biceps. But even as he nodded at whatever Titan was saying, his amber eyes wandered up to their window and snagged on Molly.

Her friend dropped her side of the curtain, jumped away from the glass as if the stuff was a petri dish housing salmonella, and shook out her hands. "OK, gotta go. Love you. Good luck with Mr. Muscles. Bye!"

Molly air-kissed Drea's cheek and dashed down the hall in a blur of dark hair and pink slippers. The bedroom door slammed shut before Drea had an opportunity to even turn her head, but not before Ty entered the apartment.

He clapped his hands, and the startling sound nearly had her heels clicking to attention. "Truck's loaded. All that's missing are butts in seats." His lips tilted in a half-smile, which surprisingly summoned one of her own.

"I can't imagine what you've loaded up in that thing. I'm just going to work."

A long finger pointed out the window where she and her voyeur best friend had just been staring. "That *thing* is going to be your new ride for a while, and I'll kindly refer you back to our earlier conversation entitling women to their hard-won secrets. My baby is no better." Then that charming smile melted a touch. "Unless your boyfriend helped you work out transportation logistics already."

The words took the warmth right out of her. Malcolm.

While she'd spoken to him on the phone several times since she got home yesterday and exchanged numerous text conversations whereby she received four words from him for every twenty of hers, he still hadn't stopped by. At first, the disappointment hadn't been that acute. After all, she had a lion's share of trauma to process and an even greater deal of questions to sort through. But after the headaches receded and the plans with Ty formed, she'd kept clutching her phone and willing it to ring to life with Malcolm's name emblazoned across the screen. It never did. Ever a woman of action, however, she relegated that particular problem to her *to be dealt with later* pile—a pile that was getting bigger by the hour.

"He's busy," she murmured, already hating the excuse or why she felt the need to toss it out there in the first place. Electing to give the issue no more room in the spotlight, Drea steeled her spine and hiked her handbag strap higher up her shoulder. "Unless you have any more questions, we better leave now. I don't want to be late for work."

Ty studied her for a moment, and she prayed to whoever happened to be in charge of this stuff that he wouldn't pry further. *Please* don't pry further.

His eyes assessed her for a heartbeat longer before he shook his head in one swift, almost imperceptible motion. "Wouldn't dream of it."

"And you *promise* to keep yourself scarce? I'm usually the only one there, so this is a huge breach of trust. I could get fired for this."

"You almost got killed for this," he bit back.

"We don't know that, not for sure."

"Which is why I'm coming with you. I'll keep to myself while you do your thing. Once we find out where the living samples originate from, I'll be out of your hair."

A pang of unease thumped in her chest, though its source was as well-known as the nuclear launch codes. Did the notion of him being *out of her hair*, as he put it, bother her? Or was it the foreign weight of walking into her place of business with an uncertainty of what she'd find that gave her proverbial hives? Would the snacks in her desk drawer still be there? Her samples? Was there something else in the facility that needed help? That needed . . . her? She didn't trust herself to speak, so she simply nodded a big fat *yes* to all of it.

Taking her head bob for the agreement it was, Ty extended an outswept hand toward the door. "Your chariot awaits."

***

FOR A RACE OF DARKNESS-BOUND DEMONS, the charmers sure had their basic institutionalized lighting patterns down pat. It saved Chrome the trouble of burning through his angel fire, which coursed under his skin at the ready, when he'd much rather light his quick-to-catch fuse on something that would actually char up nicely. Like, you know, demon bodies.

Chrome leered at the overhead fluorescent bulbs casting their *hey, look at me* glow through a corridor that could have been plucked right out of any research lab on the planet.

Considering how charmers couldn't survive in solar or celestial light and tended to prefer darkness in general, perhaps Chrome should have given the fuckers more credit for the effort. Off-white paint covered bare walls that were only interrupted by an occasional matching outlet or fire alarm pull station. He didn't need his celestial senses to figure out that those supposed building necessities were all for show and carried exactly zero volts of electricity. As any good counterfeiter could attest to, the devil was in the details.

In this case, that particular expression hit differently.

"Here's my lab." Drea ambled up to the only door in the hallway and swiped her keycard, which, to his annoyance, didn't provide any other details aside from her picture, name, and position. But c'mon, like they were going to post their tax ID number on the thing?

The door swung open, and Drea scurried over to her desk in rote movements. Carefully, he closed the door behind them. Once he heard the snick of the door sealing them in, he finally loosened his taut hold on his power, replaced it with his connection to the metric ton of firearms he was packing, and got a good look at what he had to work with.

Drea perched herself at her desk and had already gotten busy logging into mages only knew what sort of server system the charmers had cooked up. To her right and extending along the rest of the wall was a whole lot of white counter space displaying a microscope, an autoclave, an incubator, a shaker, a freezer, and an empty space where he suspected the new centrifuge was going to live.

On the wall to her left, shelves of endless beakers, test tubes, pipettes, and burners were lined up like good little soldiers waiting to be called into service. Freezers and industrial ovens were stacked toward the back of the lab, while tables in the center supported her mass spectrometers, blood bank analyzers, and cryostats. Except for the lone coffee station and standard break room refrigerator/freezer, the rest of the perimeter was taken up with shelves of disinfectants, culture products, nitrile gloves, safety gear, and anything and everything one would need to store, label, and catalog test samples.

Chrome let out a low whistle. "Color me impressed." He didn't want to think how long Cyro had been cooking this up while the sentinels had been dallying around on the surface putting out fires and otherwise *not* cutting off the head of the snake.

Insistent taps drew his attention around to Drea, whose slender fingers just finished punching in whatever sequence was required to pull up the data they needed. As she leaned forward in her chair, her adorable nose inches from the screen, his knees seized up and locked him in place. He flung his hand out and had to grip the edge of the metal exam table to keep the linoleum out of his teeth. Memories of another time assaulted him, one where Drea's long graceful neck had been angled just so as she frantically input data of a different sort. Celestial data.

The stolen moment grabbed hold of him, and that fucker had teeth. Black dress slacks gave way to the flowing bolts of a lavender messenger mage gown, secured tightly with a royal-blue sash around a delicate waste. Elegant fingers flew furiously across a console while wisps of braided honeyed hair hung over a slender shoulder.

A shoulder he'd once bared by dragging that gown down with his teeth and branding every inch of potent skin with his tongue before unwrapping her further.

Chrome's chest tightened as Drea's petal-pink tongue darted out of the corner of her full lips to aid her concentration. The curious, teasing appendage casually roamed over the juncture of her mouth, conjuring recollections of a flavor he had never forgotten. Slightly sweet, though citrusy, with an eternal freshness that had his balls drawing up tight when he thought about tasting that tongue again. Of where it had been. Of how many lifetimes had passed since he'd claimed it and nearly broken down from its slick torturous caresses.

Of the last time he'd fucking felt anything that wasn't rage masked with comedy or despair shielded with misguided hope.

Metal softened beneath his grip. The table's edge sank against the weight of his inadvertently fire-fueled hold. He jerked his hand away and threw his body in front of the deformed table corner. *Shit.*

"Any luck?" he called out and hurried over to Drea's side, careful to keep his back to the damage.

"Not really." She sighed, her lower lip in full pout. "I don't have any new notes from my supervisor. Usually, when I come in, new samples are waiting for me, along with an e-mail from him detailing the needs. Today, there's nothing." Slim shoulders deflated beneath her white lab coat. "I was really hoping there'd be something here, something that would give me an idea of what sort of animal they're testing."

Chrome peered down at the screen, trying to make sense of the jumble of e-mails in her inbox, all originating from one name. "This Dr. Blake Sorrento guy your supervisor?"

"The very one."

"Can you pull up his signature for a second? I just want to see—"

Steady, rhythmic steps grew louder in their approach. Chrome and Drea whirled toward the door. The beep of a keycard swipe echoed through the small lab, followed by the distinct click of a disengaged lock.

CHAPTER 15

Breath caught in Drea's lungs. In a movement born of sheer terror more than rational thought, she jumped around Ty and scrambled for the door. With a yank made easier by an equal force pushing from the other side, Drea prevented the door from swinging wide and instead positioned herself in the six-inch crack.

"Dr. Sorrento! Good morning. I was just about to send you an e-mail, but since you're here, we can just chat instead." Her usual alto voice had kicked into solid mezzo-soprano territory, and every bone in her body locked up tight while she hoped her supervisor wouldn't call her out on it. Maybe she could play it off as women's troubles? Most men were oblivious to the less obvious mechanics of the female gender anyway, so the that-time-of-the-month excuse wasn't out of the realm of possibility.

One uneasy look at the single pointed blond eyebrow inching toward Dr. Sorrento's hairline told her all she needed to know: fat fucking chance. If incredulity were a religion, the good doctor would welcome the masses and preach weekly sermons on the subject. It was a quality that had propelled his career in the research field, he'd once told her, even if it did little for him in the endearment department.

"Good morning, Drea. I—" The side of one high-polished loafer pressed against the door in obvious entreaty, but Drea hefted her weight against the intrusion.

"Oh, actually, mind if we talk in the hall? It's kind of fumy in here. I realized I forgot to do a thorough wipe down on some of the equipment last time I left and went a little heavy with the disinfectant this morning to compensate."

Given the tight bit of space Drea was desperately trying to defend, she had no choice but to look up to meet the man's gaze. What she usually thought of as a solid zero on the hardship scale, since the man couldn't have been older than thirty-five and had that Clark Kent glasses thing going, quickly escalated to a Richter-level crisis. Dr. Sorrento's fastidiously barbered blond hair and tortoise-brown horned-rim glasses provided the perfect backdrop for the discerning planes of his sharply angled face. A face that was now twisted with consternation instead of its normal tight-lipped smile.

"Has something happened? Was there a spill again?" He made to push past her, but before he could place his palm flat on the door, she shut it behind her and joined him in the hall.

"No, no spill. Just taking some extra sterilization precautions. You never can be too careful."

A wary gaze bounced from her to the door. "Yes, well, your attention in that regard is appreciated. You know how highly I value safety."

"Mm-hmm." She pressed her lips together and rocked back on her heels, hoping to provide enough of a distraction so he wouldn't want to investigate further. Despite having only worked there just shy of three months, she knew every inch of that lab. If Dr. Sorrento insisted on going in, there was no place for a six-and-a-half-foot-plus man to hide.

"While we're on the subject, how are you faring? I nearly fell over in my seat when you e-mailed me about your accident."

"Much better. Thankfully, most of my wounds were superficial, outside of the mild concussion. But with some highly effective pain meds and a boatload of sleep, I'm doing all right. All cleared to return to work." Sort of.

A small smile played at the corner of his mouth. "I'm glad you're feeling better. I don't know what I would have done without you."

Her throat tensed at the many ways she could interpret that statement. Instead, she simply waved a dismissive hand. "Like I said, all better now."

"Good," he replied, then shoved his hands into the pockets of his lab coat. "Since you're back, I wanted to go over a few things about what you'll be working on over the next several days. It's a bit different from the usual crop of tests you've been running."

"Oh, sure."

Dr. Sorrento adjusted his glasses higher on the bridge of his nose, then returned his hands to their hiding spots. Something about the gesture struck her as odd, though not being a glasses-wearing person herself, she couldn't attest to the cohort's potential nature for futzing with the rims, even if she'd never seen him squirm or make an unsure movement as long as she'd known him. The man usually dripped so much confidence, she was inclined to mop it off the floor in hopes of wringing some free for herself. Lord knew she could use it.

"I'll be having some new equipment delivered, mainly focusing on more cell analysis. We've just taken on a client involved heavily in the bone and skin grafting sector. Our company has been brought on to examine tissue efficacy for skin connected to spinal nerves."

Drea's stomach twisted in on itself. "That's quite the contract, sir, but I've never worked on anything like that before."

He swiped his hand casually. "No worries at all. I have absolute confidence in you. There's nothing coming down the pike that you can't handle." Punctuating the statement's finality, his thick-soled loafers turned on a dime and carried his lean frame away from the bomb he'd just dropped on her. "The cryopreservant agents should be arriving in a day or two," he called over his shoulder. "Further details will be sent to you by the end of the day."

Drea stammered slightly. "Oh, um, yes, Dr. Sorrento! Sounds good." *Not really.*

When the clips of his heels mellowed into bare echoes, she swiped her keycard on the pad and pushed the door open with her shoulder blades. "Hey, what the—"

Her rubber soles scraped against the floor as Ty shoved her behind his back and muscled the door open before it could close. "That the good doctor?" he asked with the unimpressed air of a lawyer getting paid to ask questions he already knew the answers to.

"Yes," she said through clenched teeth, slapping him between his shoulder blades that didn't even have the common decency to rebound from the hit. "Get your ass back in the lab or he'll see you."

"No, he won't."

"How the hell can you be so sure about anything? This is *my* lab, *my* freaking job on the line here." Drea pushed out an angry breath through pursed lips and tried to calm her heart rate before asserting her point. Fighting never helped anyone. Persuasion was a far more useful tool, even if it wasn't one she'd mastered quite yet. "Let's go back inside and take another look at the data. Dr. Sorrento said I'll be working on bone and skin graft analysis in the next few days. Maybe we can figure out why some of the cultures—"

"Or we can follow him and find out ourselves."

Words she'd never considered swirled between them. "What? No. That's not part of my purview."

"Why not?" He leveled a sharp glare at her. "You ever do bone analysis before?"

"Well, no, but Dr. Sorrento's always been really good at making sure I have the resources to learn about new testing methods—"

"Tell me, Dee," Ty said, each word dripping with desperate impatience, "where are those bone fragments coming from, you think? Hmm?"

"I-I don't know."

Liar. A sharp pain pinged against her breastbone, as it always did when her heart and head got into sparring matches. This time, however, the usual agony wasn't born of indecision so much as bone-deep certainty.

Certainty that the company she'd hoped to finally put down roots at wasn't operating on the up and up.

Ty leaned closer to her. The faint tingle of peppermint teased her nose and forced her bottom lip to open slightly. Cool, stinging relief invaded her dry mouth, bringing her back to their time in the library together. Heads bent over hasty notes, brains working in tandem to make heads or tails of a scene she couldn't map out, that stinging scent of peppermint kissing her papers each time he turned one over.

"You do know."

Her head bobbed slightly before she could even get the words out. "An animal is being tested for something, brutally so if spinal nerves are now part of the conversation." Drea lifted the end of her long braid and absently toyed with the fringe while her thoughts clung to images of her supervisor's atypical fiddling.

"Something about Dr. Sorrento was off. I've never seen him so squirmy."

Ty shut the door behind them, enclosing them in the hallway. "Seems like we've got a lot of answers to uncover. Let's start with figuring out where your supervisor prefers to spend his time when he's not ignoring his sole lab employee."

IT TOOK everything Chrome had not to palm his .40s and tear into the place like it was a mall on Black Friday. The only thing keeping him even close to well-behaved—as well-behaved as his short fuse and twitchy finger would allow—was the woman beside him. By a mutually unspoken agreement, they'd stayed silent as they crept through the labyrinth of hallways, chasing the barest rasp of Dr. Sorrento's heels.

Doctor. Fucking please.

Chrome's molars met with an audible clack. He had nearly melted down the door he hid behind while Drea chatted it up with the man. Correction: demon. Charmers were notorious for adopting the look and skin of whomever they liked. It was one of the ways they'd been able to acclimate so well into the mortal world. Kind of hard to rob a human of their soul when your eyes glowed piss yellow and your face looked like Darth Maul with a glow-up.

And Drea had been working for them, *with them*, for fucking months.

A sharp tug on his elbow drew his attention toward Drea, who was craning on her toes to whisper in his ear. The fragrance of lilies and lemon brought his olfactory system to its knees, pulling him down closer. He *definitely* didn't focus on how her warm breath pulled every nerve in his body into a pleading awareness. Nope.

"What happened to the overhead lights? What are all these green glowing lamps? I can hardly see two feet in front of me."

"Just stay close."

"Do you think there are photosensitive animals down here?"

"Anything's possible." He drew out the words, hoping that the less-is-more tactic wouldn't cause him to accidentally reveal more than he should. It already drove him up a wall knowing the dark magic scantily lighting their way was even within spitting distance of Drea.

Up ahead, the doctor's footsteps grew slightly louder, as if the two of them were catching up to their quarry. The more they closed the gap, the darker the halls became, and the more dark magic lanterns stood sentinel over the passageways. Passageways Chrome knew full well the charmers didn't need any light to see in.

Which meant the illuminating magic was for another creature's benefit, one that very much *did* need light to see.

What the fuck were they keeping down here?

Chrome urged Drea behind him and led the way around a corner, homing in on the footsteps' echo like a sonar ping in the sea. He shifted his shoulders slightly and angled his head, ensuring his eyes were shielded from Drea as he released a ribbon of power into his vision.

"Okay, looks like we've got a few options. There's a closet and HVAC room on the left coming up, and about thirty paces ahead of that, there's a door on the right that's built like the door to your lab. I'm guessing we start there," he whispered. "Or we can keep following your boss's trail and see where that leads us."

"How the hell can you see anything? I feel like I'm in a freaking touch tunnel at a kid's science museum."

"What can I say? I like my carrots."

Drea blew out a frustrated breath but stayed close despite it. "You know, that makes a lot of sense, actually," she anger-whispered. "I've been around a thoroughbred or two when one of Molly's friends used to do equestrian racing. I can see the hot-blooded big-mouthed resemblance. Those horses loved their carrots, too."

Swagger replaced stealth, and he couldn't help but let some of his deviant confidence drip into his smile. Too bad she couldn't see it. "Oh, Dee, you're leaving me wide open there. How can you set me up like that and *not* expect me to make any hung-like-a-stallion jokes?"

"That's it, I'm done talk—"

"Wait!" Chrome grabbed Drea's shoulders and pinned her against the wall, placing himself in front of her and caging her with his arms stretched behind him.

"What are you doing? Get off—"

"Shhh," he demanded.

Drea stopped moving long enough for both of them to pick up the distinct thud of boots—a thud made by thickly treaded rubber, not the light leather of a loafer, and it was coming from behind them.

Chrome ushered Drea to the nearest door—the closet—and pulsed his power into the metal to quickly maneuver the metal pins within the lock. The click of the final pin's retreat only just reached his ears before he fisted the doorknob and shoved them both inside.

CHAPTER 16

Drea was plunged into further darkness as Chrome put a door between them and what sounded like a set of size fourteen doesn't-fuck-around footwear. She only managed to retreat a few steps before her calves, hips, and shoulders collided with ceiling-high shelving. The air was soggy with a familiar astringent scent, and when she bumped her heel along the bottom shelf, heavy gallon jugs of what she assumed were bleach bumped back. She turned around and ran searching fingers over the other items but only came away with rows of cardboard and the occasional pile of plastic-wrapped something or other. After a few heartbeats, the gloom morphed from dark to disorienting, and she fumbled with her hands out to find Ty.

Heated palms plucked her nervous fingers from the shadows like they were night-blooming jasmine. Before she could speak, he brought their combined hands to her mouth and tapped a single finger to her lips. The gesture was insistent and unmistakable: *I've got you. Don't make a sound.*

Outside, each heavy footfall thumped against the floor with a measured approach. The weight of the prowling movements reverberated through the walls around them until Drea was certain it would only take another step or two before items flung themselves from the shelves above. Even though it made no difference, she squeezed her eyes shut and tried to calm her breathing. Could whoever was outside hear even that?

The irrational thought floated loosely in her mind before she wrangled it back. No, of course not. Whoever it was probably just worked with Dr. Sorrento and had as much of a right to be here as she did. Okay, maybe not *exactly* where she was skulking around and most definitely not with an unverified visitor, but it was close enough, right?

Then why the hell did her skin crawl with tense prickles of warning? When it came to self-preservation, her logic train may have missed a few stops over the years, but the part of her brain that controlled the flight, fight, or freeze mechanism had always worked just fine. So, why was it sounding the alarm like she had just been caught breaking into the Pentagon?

Her fingers curled in on themselves and threatened to freeze into panicked fists. Everything went tighter than tight, until even the backs of her legs were so rigid, they threatened to topple her against the shelves.

She'd lost jobs before, plenty of times, but this fear was different. Getting canned had never caused her spine to tingle or her mouth to go ashen. A deeply rooted instinct knocked at her subconscious, screaming at her to run. Drea swayed backward on an exhale, angling toward the shelving—

Ty's strong hand met the small of her back and pulled her forward. Caught off-balance, she bobbed slightly, then frantically pushed away when her breasts brushed against the cotton of his T-shirt stretched across masculine muscles.

His grip didn't lessen, though. He didn't rear back or adjust his stance in the slightest, while she flailed about like a stray animal swept out to sea. He kept his grip loose but firm, giving her what minimal space he could to resettle herself without injuring both of them.

The steps outside grew louder, mimicking her heart with each thud. Drea didn't dare speak. She could hardly take in a breath. Another few feet and whoever was outside would pass right by them. Heat scorched her back where Ty's hand lay, and the skin beneath her tattoo burned in response. Out of options or relief, she dipped her head forward and leaned her misted brow against Ty's chest. Her lungs pulled him in with each ragged breath, extracting the scent of peppermint from his shirt. Frayed nerves sprang to awareness, and the hand at her back molded more solidly against her. With nothing left holding her together, her body fell flush against his—

An insistent, angry buzzing rattled through the closet's quiet. Drea arched back and scrambled for the vibrating phone in her rear pocket. When she pulled it free, the screen's atomic brightness beat back the shadows. Even though she cupped the phone in her hands and tossed the thing back and forth like a vibrating hot potato, she couldn't coordinate her fingers enough to silence the call.

Malcolm. He was calling her. Not a text or a thumbs-up reply, but real voice-to-voice communication that she'd been craving ever since she'd gotten home from the hospital. Her brain short-circuited and she froze, torn between silencing or answering it. Ultimately, neither option was truly viable, as she couldn't make a single part of her body do what needed doing.

Including her mouth.

Drea clutched the unanswered phone and bared her teeth at the vibrating screen. "*Now* you call? *Now* is when—"

One of Ty's hands slammed over her mouth, while the other snatched the phone from her, silenced it, and pocketed the thing. Plunged into darkness once again, she had to blink away the dancing remnants of light swirling in front of her. She squeezed her eyes closed, and the letters of Malcolm's name flashed against the backs of her eyelids. Then Ty's hand returned to her back, and the biting tension of his hold on her mouth lessened.

Blood pounded in her ears as her body was bombarded with thoughts and senses she couldn't make heads or tails of. An insistent thudding grew closer, louder. Her chest, her wrist, her head, the footsteps, Malcolm's name across her screen—everything blared with a confusion that threatened to melt her bones and singe her skin. She opened her mouth—to what, scream?—and her trembling lips brushed against the inside of Ty's palm. She reared back slightly, but he just followed her, never breaking contact. Never saying a damn word.

The subtle peppermint that usually followed him around was replaced by something headier, like leather and earth. Something inexplicably male and entirely too alluring. In the darkness, her mouth became her eyes. Under the protection of his cupped hand, no one could see how close her lips were to his skin or why, held securely as she was, her only instinct was to explore this man further. In that cramped closet, where shadows told no tales, she wouldn't have to explain the attraction away, even as dangerous curiosity lifted her chin higher.

In the darkness, trapped, frozen, she wouldn't have to face Malcolm.

Malcolm, with whom she had shared every secret dream and motivation these past few months over burgers and red wine.

Malcolm, who made excuses instead of making time to pick her up at the hospital and ghosted her with tiny texts instead of heartfelt conversation she desperately needed.

But Ty had been there, and locked away as they were in that closet, no one would witness how damn relieved that made her or how ardently that relief had somehow begun chasing the guilt away.

The moment that realization dawned on her, all the oppressively crowding worries evaporated from the small dark space.

Here, she was protected. Here, her body sang with what made sense on an inexplicable level and there was no one to judge her for it.

Just as Drea opened her mouth again behind the shield of his palm to say so, his heated hand fell away.

"He's gone," Ty whispered. "Whoever was following us passed by. We'll wait it out another minute or two, but we should be good to go."

His warm breaths mingled with her previously trapped ones. The sound of his voice danced around them, and her face angled toward it, chasing it like a beacon. The soft inhale to her left alerted her to his mouth's exact position. Drea corrected her course, and her instincts took her lips the rest of the way until they found his.

CHROME HAD SPENT his entire existence fighting off the darkness, but once Drea's soft lips punched their way through the haze and crashed against his, he'd never welcomed it more. Their mouths came together with equal zeal and, for him, a measure of desperation that again made him grateful for the dark.

Irony, the horny mistress that she was, apparently had a sense of humor.

Power warred with passion as each blind sip of her lips hardened every inch of him. Fire and need unmanned him, and he pulled her graceful body tighter against his. Starved instincts drove his actions, booting all rational thought to the curb. He moaned into the haven of her mouth, swallowing up a few delightful mewls of her own. Chrome's lungs swelled to capacity, gifting him the fervent fuel he needed to seek out the one flavor he never thought he'd taste again.

Slender arms crept around his torso and farther behind, until they hooked over the backs of his shoulders. Once wrapped around, Drea's trimmed fingernails dug into his flesh and pulled. He grunted in surprised approval and leaned his hips forward against hers, letting her know the full extent of his reaction.

"Drea." He breathed the warning into her mouth before deciding that wasting any energy on speaking was ill-advised. The final rational thought in his mind left the station, along with the frayed remnants of his self-control. Good, because whatever magic was present in the darkness was surely ephemeral. Her freshwater fragrance permeated everything, from memories to muscles. Soft breasts crushed against his chest. Even through the clothing, his skin remembered their pillowy smoothness, the two ripe nipples dangling above his mouth, the way her lower back would arch when he captured one between tongue and teeth. There was no telling for how long her sensuous skin would be under his, and he was a greedy enough bastard to grab hold of the opportunity.

With claws.

By the mages, how she had liked to pull, peck, and overall plunder just as good as he gave. Each time her nails bit into his shoulder, his lower abdominals twitched from a core-deep memory.

Dee. Writhing beneath him, bucking above him, capturing his moans, and guarding his sanity. Her smooth skin and sleek curves had been his haven from the worst parts of himself. Parts he locked away from his most trusted seraphim scouts, his sentinel brothers, even his own reflection at times. Every scorching kiss he stole and she returned forged another brick on the wall in his mind that blocked out the helpless terrors of his existence, of who he'd failed.

And she was here, branding her flavor on his soul as if she'd never left. Like their separation spanning tens of millions of years had just been one long layover before he reached his final destination. Her.

His hands settled into the curve of her waist and hoisted her high on his body, urging her legs to settle around him. Strong thighs met his own strength while their mouths kept mapping out familiar pathways. Heads angled, tongues lapped, teeth bit and pecked at lips rubbed nearly raw with frantic need.

Perhaps it was the lightening of his soul or the burgeoning of his angel fire stirring within his core. Perhaps it was the desperate claiming that called two pseudo-strangers to crash like Titans, but he was there for it. The burning, the breathing, the fierce beat of his heart, all of it.

That inferno fueled his hand to cup the graceful line of her neck and trace it down the front of her chest. Fingers that had more business oiling a gun than caressing a woman played at her collarbone through her shirt before dipping lower. The soft weight of her breast met his palm and molded to him like perfection. Utter fucking perfection.

She gasped softly into his mouth, then arched her back so her chest moved toward him, filling his hand. His desire had grown teeth, and his other arm wrapped more tightly around her waist until her ass filled his palm.

Too much. It was all too much.

He broke the kiss and tracked a trail down her throat, dragging her scent into him as he went. "So fucking beautiful. You have no idea how long—"

Her phone in the back of his pocket vibrated against his ass, freezing him against the door, a prodding reminder of who was calling her.

And what the douchebag was to Drea.

Fire barreled through Chrome's nerves, threatening to punch through his fists. Anger, either at himself or the jerkoff currently lighting up Chrome's hind quarters, tightened every muscle. Then his forgotten circumstances flared to life, chasing away any remaining protective shadow.

To her, he was simply Ty, a big man with a big brain and handy timing. She didn't remember the Empyrean or the souls she risked saving before Cyro's armies came for them all. She didn't remember any of it, but he would never forget the blonde furrow between her brows and the wide confused panic in her violet eyes when he'd found her again and tried to shake answers out of her on how she survived the Fall. Whether other mages survived.

Whether she had been able to get back.

After so much time living among mortals, Chrome knew a thing or two about crazy, and in that moment, Drea had sized him up as the fearless leader of the batshit crazy battalion.

Malcolm—and fuck if Chrome could even say the fool's name without needing to throw something heavy—was safe and real. Someone she trusted. Someone who didn't spend his nights dismembering demons before sequestering himself beneath the ground.

Chrome's tense fingers relaxed from feverish grips to supportive handholds as that damn phone continued to make itself known. Drea's endless legs slowly unwrapped from around his hips, and he guided her to the floor. Even in the dark, his celestial senses could make out her kiss-swollen lips and how he had no right to make them so.

"Here," Chrome said, handing Drea her phone. "You're a popular woman."

The screen's glow briefly illuminated her pinched features and disheveled braid before she clicked the thing off and let the call go to voice mail. "Not that popular, really."

"For the right person, yeah, you are."

Chrome quickly cracked open the door, hoping to let out the giant elephant in the room before Drea could respond. No such luck.

"Ty, what we did, I—"

"You don't have to say a word," he said over his shoulder as he scanned the hallway. Satisfied they were alone, he grabbed her hand and led her out of the closet and toward the room down the hall with the door that resembled the one from Drea's lab. The glowing green orbs hardly gave off appropriate wattage, but they were a good sight better than the closet's darkness. Plus, dim lighting sure made shame and regret much harder to read on one's features.

"No, I need to say something. I think—"

Chrome halted, and once he was sure she was able to fall in line with his steps, he dropped her hand and looked down at her. "Message received. I overstepped and took advantage. I won't touch you again. Once I help you figure out what's going on here as I promised I would, I'll be good as gone."

CHAPTER 17

Drea walked with stilted steps behind Ty, painfully aware of the traitorous tension that had spilled out of the closet along with them. The appeasing side of her itched to fire off an *all good, talk later* text to Malcolm so her shame could relax for a hot minute. A different side of her, however, the one with curious senses and unanswered questions that had been prowling beneath the surface of her skin, was absolutely loving its day in the sun. Well, shadows, technically.

She'd kissed Ty. Not just kissed him but practically climbed him like a rock wall, intent on finding the best places to put every part of her. There was certainly no shortage of agreeable crags and handholds, that was for sure. Even as he led them down the blessedly empty hallway, electric green light danced over shifting back muscles her fingers itched to cling to again. Occasionally, when he would turn back to make sure she was still following close, some of the lantern light would catch the edge of his stony jaw, revealing the dusting of crisp hairs that peppered his chin. Hairs that had scored her mouth so thoroughly, so deliciously, that her lips still tingled from the memory.

Drea dipped her head and used the excuse of insecure footing to make damn sure no more of her uncertainties reared up from the shadows. With each step, she wanted to take her phone out of her back pocket and hurl it against the stone wall. Maybe even stomp on it a time or two for emphasis. Who or what she was truly angry at, however, she still couldn't voice.

What a murky, humiliating mess, made even murkier by Ty's last words to her before he about-faced them both out of the closet.

I won't touch you again . . . I'll be good as gone.

Drea palmed the keycard dangling around her neck, and her itchy index finger immediately went to work picking at the laminated edges of the plastic. It wasn't until she'd gotten a good corner separated that she was able to identify the crux of her nerves.

Under zero circumstances did she want Ty to go . . . and under equally minuscule circumstances did she want him to never touch her again.

Despite the dark they'd found themselves in, her body had been lit up like fireworks. Not some backyard barbecue sparkler nonsense, but something expansive and heart-pounding. The kind of show people from all over flock to that was backed by a big budget and lots of fanfare. It was a once-in-a-lifetime concert over the regular bar band making the Thursday night circuit. Kissing Ty was something one didn't miss and certainly something one never forgot. The angle of his mouth as he'd attacked hers was equal parts skilled and sensuous. Each time he turned her exactly where he wanted, a thrilling jolt would punch through her core. It was as if every part of him was connected to a corresponding part of her. Every swipe of his tongue against hers drew her thigh higher up his hip. When his hands pulled her closer, her breasts arched in an answering, needy response.

If her body had been an abandoned string instrument before, it had been transformed into a concert-worthy Stradivarius under Ty's masterful touch.

A touch she had no claim to. Her giant brick of a phone weighing down her back pocket was more than enough of a reminder of that.

Specifically, what her infidelity would cost her, who it would crush. Not just Malcolm, but Molly as well, as he had become just as much a part of her best friend's life as Drea's. In the three short months they'd known each other, the three of them had formed traditions and shared inside jokes. She loved their Three Musketeers camaraderie and cared deeply for Malcolm. Every time he'd close on a house, Drea would be his fiercest cheerleader, and likewise, he'd been hers the closer she got to securing her full-time position at the lab.

He was happy and adored her. She was ecstatic and content. And Molly was the glue that held them all together.

So, why did Drea's stomach feel like it was going to turn in on itself if she didn't stay close to Ty?

Drea caught herself a second before she nearly slammed into the object of her thoughts. He threw her an unreadable glance, then hunched over the door lever while she mumbled her apologies. The entrance was a mirror image of the aluminum-frame door to her laboratory, complete with an uninspired gray matte paint job and a silver handle. Unlike hers, however, this one sported no room placard or other identifying information.

Before she could ask the myriad of questions she had primed at the ready, Ty's whispered baritone echoed off the stone walls, stalling her thoughts. "It's locked, and there's no keycard pad here, but I can get us in. Turn around and stand lookout for me, would ya?"

"You can't be serious right now," she hissed. These were the first words he'd said to her since he refused to let her explain her side of what happened between them and he wanted her to play *lookout*? "As if you wouldn't hear someone coming at the exact same time I would. And what would you like me to tell them, anyway? I could explain myself out of trouble with Dr. Sorrento at *my* lab, sure, but not here. Whatever's behind that door is above my pay grade and access, clearly." The words had no effect and merely pelted his broad back while he resumed his work over the lock, so she scooted around to his left and tried for better aim. "If you think—"

"There, I'm in."

The softest click pinged between them, and it was just enough to rob the remaining words from her tirade. Before she could gather her senses and proceed with her verbal onslaught, though this time one of a very different anti-B-and-E nature, he lifted that damn shushing finger to his lips and gestured for her to get behind him.

Self-preservation was the only thing that got her in line as she stood shielded behind Ty's back, though she made sure to leave her displeasure seated firmly on her features. She tossed him her best *we'll discuss this later* glare, which he acknowledged by giving her the back of his head.

Ass.

Intent on his task, Ty slowly peeled the door open and revealed more of the same eerie green light that dotted the hallways. It wasn't until he swung the door wide and they both entered the room, however, that the similarities ended.

Drea cupped her nose in the crook of her elbow at the force of the smell. The room was too dim to see clearly, but urine was urine no matter what kind of light shone down on it. Then the other biological scents permeated her surroundings, and she had to choke down a gag.

"How many animals do they have in here?" Drea whispered through a tight throat, then fumbled around in her lab coat pocket for the tube of mentholated lip balm she always had. Once the cylinder kissed her palm, she went to work applying a generous coat to her lips and the skin directly under her nose. "Here, want some? It'll help with the smell." She held out her tube to Ty, but when her offer dangled in the air unanswered, she turned to him. "Ty?"

The dingy green lantern light was enough to make out the fury etched into the grooves of his cheeks. The man stood so stock still, with fists tight enough to crush diamonds, she almost blanched. A faint trick of the meager light illuminated the silver in his eyes, which seemed to churn with the force of a typhoon. Drea swallowed a gulp of fetid air and followed his gaze across the room, then gasped.

Floor-to-ceiling metal bars extended across the back of the room. Not cages, but a single cell. Growing out of the cell's floor, as if the facility had been built around it, was an erected stone altar supporting a seven-foot slab of rock. The distinct form of a man's bare arm hung over the rock's edge.

Drea's eyes widened as the disgusting realization took root. She'd been so wrong. The lab wasn't keeping animals in captivity for testing purposes.

They were keeping a human.

RAGE COATED CHROME'S vision in bloodshed red. The *only fucking* thing that kept him from incinerating every meltable object in the room and shooting through the rest was the barely there tattoo on the inside of the man's forearm. Power surged through Chrome's body, strengthening his vision, until he couldn't shake away what he was seeing.

The celestial eye fixed atop the flaming scepter, etched in silver translucent ink only visible by the sentinels and celestial mages.

Chrome had branded the symbol and tattooed it with his own angel fire when he'd appointed his most trusted seraph and friend as the new leader in Chrome's intelligence unit.

The tattoo was the talisman of Chrome's seraphim commander. The one he'd sent into Cyro's territory the day before the invasion and had never returned. The one whose loss had sent Chrome spiraling headlong into oblivion, only to fall into the arms of a messenger mage who unburdened the weight of the pain, if only for one brief, blissful moment.

Axtar.

Ax . . .

Chrome barreled through the room, tossing furniture as if they were throw pillows. The room was set up much in the same way Drea's lab was, with stainless steel tables filling out the center floor plan while the perimeter housed the equipment and workstations. Workstations, he grimly noted, that bore evidence of very fucking recent use.

It was all scrap metal on stone as Chrome reached the cell. No sense in staying quiet now, not when he was one good swift kick away from imploding the place around them in a supernova of power.

Drea's short footsteps finally caught up to him. "Oh my God! Is he . . . is he still alive?"

The devastation on the other side of the cell silenced them both.

On top of the stone bed lay his friend's once-powerful frame. Cords of muscle and sinew had been drained away, leaving an emaciated shell of pale flesh clinging to protruding bone. He was nude, except for the two-inch-thick metal manacles encircling his bony wrists and ankles. What Chrome remembered as long thick blond hair laced with warrior braids at the temples was now a bleached matted mess, lying in sweat-damp strings beneath mottled skin.

By the mages, his skin! Bruises of every color, along with

blown veins, painted the insides of his arms and legs, signs of repetitive IV injections, and they didn't stop there. Angry purple shaded the delicate skin beneath his eyes, echoing the shadows in his sunken cheeks, still visible despite his scraggly overgrown beard.

Chrome followed the chains up, until they ended where the stone ceiling began, punching through the rock as though they were extensions of the earth. In the corner sat a single bucket—and the source of the smell. A quick distance calculation revealed that those chains were long enough to allow movement to the bucket from the stone slab and nowhere else. Agony for his chosen brother blocked out all reason.

All this time he had been here, imprisoned. Worse.

Chrome gripped the bars and covertly surged his power into the cell, extinguishing the invisible dark magic that guarded its perimeter. The instant the ward fell, Axtar's chest rose with a full shaky breath. Too-prominent ribs expanded, stretching the taut skin of his torso even farther and highlighting the concavity of his belly.

Alive.

"Yes," Chrome breathed out. "He's alive but barely." A vicious rasp tinged his voice with the warning threat of a predator. "We're getting him out of here. Now."

Drea flung into action and hobbled to the far closet, where she pulled out lab coats and towels and anything she no doubt thought could be used to cover him. When she returned, arms laden with supplies, she dipped her chin in a firm nod. "Let's do this."

Chrome kept his back to her, blocking her view of his hands as he used his fire to burn through the metal lock on the cell door. With a grating snap, the metal separated and the door hinged open.

Just as every glowing orb around them extinguished into darkness.

CHAPTER 18

Those gnarled lifeless fingers held the whole of Drea's focus. The next moment, they blinked out of sight, along with everything else around them. Darkness blanketed the room, and she and Ty were left without even an exit light to guide their way.

"What the hell just happened?" she snapped, long past the point of whispering.

"We've got to move." Ty's voice moved past her, until his words echoed off the cell bars from the inside. Four sharp snaps preceded the tinkling of metal puddling to the floor.

Did he just break those shackles?

Drea tentatively stepped forward, one arm out in front of her, the other clutching her stack of linens running-back style. Once her toes hit the base of the stone altar, she plunked down the towels and blindly spread them across the man as best she could before Ty hoisted him onto his shoulder.

"We went through seven hallways before we left the one where your lab is located. I memorized the turns. Grab onto the back of my belt and do not let go unless I tell you to, got it?"

"This is insane. This is totally insane," she murmured as her shaking fingers latched onto the worn leather still warm from the heat of his skin. Any further protests died on her lips at the first tug against her hand. Ty moved with sure steps through the chokingly thick darkness. The only indication he gave that he was carrying an extra burden was the occasional way he'd jostle his shoulder to redistribute the man's weight. Otherwise, he was a panther on the prowl, both searching for and steering them toward their next conquest.

They navigated the first turn, and Drea only managed to lose her footing once without careening into stone. By the second turn, she'd learned how many of her steps equaled one of Ty's, and she didn't have to pull quite so desperately on his belt to keep up. As she ran, the slack man's greasy hair licked at her wrist in sickly brushstrokes. She tried to secure his head with her other hand, but Ty was moving so fast, the bouncing pace made it nearly impossible.

"Almost there," she whispered on a rushed breath to the back of the man's unconscious head. "We'll get you out soon."

"Not likely, I'm afraid." The conciliatory words were spoken with an all-too-familiar charismatic demeanor, though the accent was slightly different. Slavic, perhaps, though mildly pronounced in the way one from another country might speak to try and hide their origins. She'd recognize the saccharine, crooning voice anywhere, though.

"Dr. Sorrento," she breathed, momentarily forgetting her pace and dropping her grip on Ty's belt. Drea slowly turned around, prepared to conjure up whatever groveling she needed to do but was only greeted with more darkness.

Except for two glowing gold eyes advancing toward her, eating up the shadows like the sun through morning mist. Her limbs locked into place. Indecision paralyzed her breath, her heartbeats. Clammy fingers splayed around her for Ty's belt, but there was nothing to grab hold of. Nothing except stale air thick with her fear.

A sharp implement struck against the stone, and more of that green swirling light appeared before her, originating where she'd last heard Dr. Sorrento's voice and barreling down the tunnel straight for her. The abrupt illumination stung Drea's eyes, forcing her to slam them shut. She couldn't move, couldn't see.

"Ty . . ."

A strong hand clamped down on her shoulder and yanked her backward. Her eyes flung open as she struggled to gain her balance. Before her, a single blue flame streaked across her nose. It trailed by so fast, she'd have sworn it came from a gun, but there was no ear-piercing discharge. Only a muffled *pfft* that ended as soon as she detected it.

Then the screaming started.

"Did you just— Was that a gun? Oh my God. I saw blue fire! Is Dr. Sorrento on fire? That's him screaming, isn't it?" Each question tripped over the one before it, though they never had time to land as Ty dragged her down the hallway. The man on his shoulder bobbed along, still unconscious.

"I swiped some copper chloride from your lab, and I cleaned my knife with rubbing alcohol recently. The two combined give you blue fire. Helped show me where to aim."

"You . . . you expect me to believe you lit your knife on fire so you could throw it at my boss? You're insane. Truly freaking insane. No one throws a knife from that distance and hits the target. No one! And knives don't make sounds like that!"

A predatory growl vibrated through Ty's body, transferring through his palm where he gripped her wrist just tight enough to get his point across. "Two more tunnels. Try and keep up."

Behind them, the smell of fire and charred flesh chased their heels. Only when they turned down the final tunnel did Drea's nose stop twitching from the sulfur. Oh God. Did Ty *kill* Dr. Sorrento?

No, this was wrong. This was so wrong. She shouldn't be

running away from him. He needed an ambulance. She didn't leave people to die. She could at least stop any bleeding until the medics arrived, maybe smother some of the flames with her lab coat.

She was just about to rip her hand free of Ty's hold when another cold realization slowed her haste. Medics. The man in the cell had needed far more than simple paramedics. He was on the brink of death, and might still die, truth be told, if it hadn't been for Ty.

If Dr. Sorrento had a hand in that man's captivity, would you still go back and save him?

Guilt and terror jockeyed for the privilege of igniting her gag reflex. Mist collected along her brow, and her face heated, though less from exertion and more from disgust. Disgust for what she'd witnessed and for what her soured gut was twisting itself in knots to tell her. That had been Dr. Sorrento in the hallway, and though she couldn't see clearly, a part of her knew that green light had been a weapon of some kind.

And he'd hurled it at her.

But Ty had intervened first, once again saving her life.

More footsteps pounded down the tunnels behind them just as they made it to the elevator that went to the ground floor.

"Stairs," Ty bit out, his clipped demand showing the first sign that his strength was faltering.

"Around the corner by the back of the elevator."

Again, Ty grabbed her wrist, though this time, she led the way, keeping one hand along the steel of the elevator and dragging it around the shaft's walls until her toes nudged the first step.

"It's four flights. Can you make it?" she asked.

"Just go!"

With the practiced hustle born of lunch breaks where Drea needed to get her steps in, she flew up each riser like Rocky Balboa attacking the Philadelphia Museum of Art's staircase. When she cleared the last landing, daylight greeted her through the seams of the closed external door. Just as she touched the push bar, Ty barreled behind her, punching their sad trio through the exit. They landed in an exhausted heap on the sewer pump station's concrete pad. Ty immediately dropped his charge, rolling the man limply onto the nearby grass, then donkey-kicked the door closed.

"We need to run. They were right behind us. I heard them!" Drea gasped each word as she crawled on her hands and knees away from the exit, only stopping briefly to grab a fistful of Ty's shirt to ineffectually tug him along with her. She'd have had better luck pulling a semitruck.

"No need. We'll take it from here."

Shadows on the grass, which she hadn't noticed a moment ago, elongated as they drew closer. Six sets of black boots filled her vision. Drea angled her head up while Titan, the owner of the shadow nearest to her and the one who had spoken, crouched down to meet her, offering a hand. She grabbed it instantly, and he swung her to her feet. Beside her, Bronze and Brass were hunched over the unconscious man. They worked in silent tandem, though their bodies blocked her view of what they were doing.

One thing she *didn't* miss, however, was the dire expressions exchanged between the men.

Ty sprang up and immediately ran to his redheaded brothers, then tossed a set of keys to Titan. "Get him in my truck and get Drea home."

"Wait, where are you going? You can't go back in there. We need to call the police." Drea lunged for Ty, but he spared her no notice. Her fingertips only brushed the edge of his cotton shirt sleeve as he stormed past her and back toward the door they'd just fled through. The dismissal hurt, but indifference she could handle. What she *couldn't* deal with was Ty going back down there.

Or, more specifically, what would happen if he never came back out.

Titan wrapped firm but gentle hands around her shoulders and guided her toward Ty's truck. "Drea, we need to see the both of you to safety. Time is not on our side."

Her blurry gaze swung toward the vehicle, where the other two men were carefully loading their unconscious patient into the back seat. Titan's urgency gave speed to her steps, and her legs followed in hurried movements. Her thoughts, however, remained firmly with the man she was leaving behind.

This felt wrong. So wrong. She shouldn't be running away from Ty when he was the only reason she was even alive to run away at all. Her chest tightened, and tears sprang free, spilling messy tracks down her cheeks.

The controlled tenor of Titan's voice barely made it through the screaming in her head. "Has he ever shared with you what he does for . . . work?"

The question was so out of place, she couldn't help but give it attention.

"Um." She wiped her sleeve across her nose while Titan settled her into the passenger seat. "He said he worked in scientific intelligence and medical affairs and that he mainly did whatever was needed, whatever that means."

Titan's stern features met her gaze. "That's exactly what's needed now. He'll be with our other brothers, who are all in the same line of work, and he'll come find you when things are all taken care of." When she leveled him a disbelieving glare, he simply shrugged his shoulder. "Family business."

The corner of his lips tilted slightly, letting some of that charming masculine arrogance shine through.

Just like Ty would have done.

Though she'd never admit it out loud, his ridiculous trick worked, and her fingers found a more neutral place to fidget that didn't include the hem of her worn lab coat. They settled on her braid instead.

"How do you know he'll be okay, though? There are people down there with projectile weapons of some kind, but I've never seen them before. It was so dark. Everything was just so dark."

Titan paused for a moment, studied the ground with an odd intent, then met her gaze again. "I'm not in the habit of asking women to trust me without proving I deserve it first. Learned that lesson the hard way a while back. But I will tell you this: he's a miserable miscreant on a good day, yet ever since he's been spending time with you, he's been a thousand times worse around us."

Drea cringed. "Lovely as that sentiment might have been, I don't think it had the effect you were hoping for."

"Well, it should have, because whatever happiness he's capable of has preferred to hitch a ride with you and no one else. The rest of us just get the scraps."

She sniffled, and her fingers stalled out on a hair tendril mid-curl. "What?"

Titan merely winked, then slammed the truck door on the rest of his words before he walked over to speak with Brass and Bronze. Drea could hardly shut her mouth, let alone involve herself with what they were saying, even though it was highly likely she was one of the main topics of conversation.

All of her senses were trained on the door to the sewer pump station and the fearsome man in the front, flanked by three other men of equal intensity and build. The four of them stepped through the door with the nonchalance one would use to enter a movie theater.

Whatever happiness he's capable of . . .

With you and no one else . . .

Titan's solemn words batted around her brain as the shadows once again swallowed up Ty, and his commanding frame shifted out of her view. Then the morning's exhaustion finally took over. Drea melted into the cushioned car seat, whispering Ty's name on her cracked lips.

"Happiness. Yes . . ."

Her lips spread into a secret smile right before the phone in her back pocket began to vibrate again.

CHAPTER 19

The sun was finally submitting to the night when Chrome dragged his tattered body over the den's threshold. The blood running down his back had dried at some point, stiffening his skin and causing the gashes to bleed anew with each step he took. What remained of his shirt had been scorched onto his flesh in streamers and shreds. One particularly painful scrap had adhered itself rather artfully across his left nipple, its edges seared to his areola. That'd be a bitch to deal with.

He barely made it to the couch before he collapsed. Blood crusted over his left eye, which had already swollen shut, so he couldn't see how Tungsten, Iron, and Steel fared. Judging from the grunting and panting, they weren't much better.

Chrome hinged his upper body off the cushions since his ass was the only thing on him that could deal with the pressure of sitting upright. Slowly, he unclipped every firearm and weapon strapped to him. Thousands of dollars' worth of metal machinery plunked to the floor like discarded clothes. He'd already ditched all his ammo clips hours earlier after emptying them into every demon that swiped across his nose. Repeatedly.

Tung hobbled toward the dining table, favoring his left leg, and dropped onto the bench seat. His bloody brow immediately hit his folded arms still bulging with muscle strain. That golden mane of shoulder-length hair covered a split lip and fractured cheekbone Chrome in no way envied. Steel, who had just returned from visiting Bridget that morning, supported a semi-conscious Iron through the great room. The russet-haired giant's right foot was cranked at an odd angle, and his entire left side was charred with acidic corrosion and pitting. Bits of rust flaked off onto the floor as Steel all but carried their brother to his suite of rooms to heal.

Steel's injuries, at least the ones he let anyone see, had been minor, thank the mages. Chrome closed his eyes and did his best to take in a breath of gratitude through his broken nose for that small mercy. Suffering wasn't discriminatory, but if any of his brothers had earned the right to be spared its misery just this once, it was Steel. That angel had been dealt the shitty short straw more times than Chrome could count. One could only handle so many demons, both personal and realized.

After today, Chrome considered himself a fucking expert on that particular subject.

"It's done. For now, at least." Tungsten's regal, yet slightly muffled words sank to the floor with a finality neither of them truly felt. It was the same after every battle. The killing only got easier due to practiced moves and honed responses.

The mindfuck afterward was the cleanup on aisle four no one wanted any part of.

"Maybe," Chrome whispered, his throat cutting off the word with a cough.

Chrome hadn't even waited for his truck's tires to peel away before his course of action was set. He trusted Titan and the others to take care of what needed taking care of.

Just like they trusted him to do the same.

So he did. Persistently. Ruthlessly. He, Tung, Steel, and Iron exploded through that grotto on a wind of berserker rage. Trapped underground from the sunlight, the charmers were a feast for the angels' starving predators, those dark and dangerous parts of them that only came out without a leash or conscience.

The second Chrome's boots hit the bottom floor, he discharged a tidal wave of angel fire that engulfed every beating demon heartbeat it touched. What followed was a swarm of charmers who met the angels with a clash loud enough to level a building. Portals opened, and bodies flooded in and out. Some retreating, others engaging, all destroyed. Only when the last portal winked closed on the heels of aborting demons did Chrome finally exhale.

And then level the entire grotto to ashes and rubble.

By some stroke of sheer dumb luck, Drea hadn't pressed her curiosity further when he'd fired off his gun at the charmer masquerading as Dr. Sorrento. The silencer did its job, as did his angel-fire-infused bullets. He still couldn't believe he'd been able to explain it away with that copper chloride nonsense.

If he hadn't, though, and that demon had gotten his shot off . . .

That single thought had been the kindling to Chrome's fury. He kept it with him, locked tight in his chest, as he and his brothers laid waste to their plague.

A plague he was certain would come back deadlier than ever.

The thought of illness brought his consciousness back around to the other black mark on his soul. "Where's—"

Brass rushed into the room, his short hair pulled at odd angles. "He's in the sick bay. Vitals are stabilized, and Bronze is monitoring them, but he's still unconscious." Concern wrinkled the furrows between his brows. "We couldn't manage the chamber, not with you still . . . out."

The hyperbaric chamber Chrome had created years ago

served as their main source of healing when faced with life-threatening injuries. Chrome's elemental magic, when mixed with oxygen and infused into the chamber, created a protective layer of chromium oxide. The resulting compound resisted and reversed the corrosive effects of the charmers' weapons. But it only worked with *his* power.

Power that he'd been completely drained of.

"Chrome, I need to ask," Brass hedged, stepping closer, wariness swirling in his amber eyes. "Is that really Ax? Bronze and I saw the tattoo, but neither of us could believe it."

They couldn't believe it because of the implication's reality: that Cyro had imprisoned Axtar all these eons, and none of the sentinels had been the wiser.

Cold dread turned Chrome's depleted muscles into blocks of ice. "Yeah, it's him. Somehow."

He let the final word hang in the air along with everyone's confusion, both about how it happened and where to go next. Somehow, Cyro had gotten his hands on two of the most important people in Chrome's existence.

And somehow, neither of them had survived whole.

MOLLY PLUNKED A STEAMING mug of something chamomile and lavender scented on the coffee table in front of Drea and took a seat next to her on the couch.

"Want another blanket?" she asked as her gaze danced over the expertly tucked corners around Drea's still body. Her elfin features and wide eyes betrayed every single worry she no doubt was trying to hide.

"No thanks. Two's plenty."

Molly nodded stiffly, then shot a worried expression toward the window, which Drea tracked instantly.

"No, Ty's brothers aren't out there. At least, I wasn't told they would be."

"I wouldn't be surprised if they subscribed to the *it's better to ask for forgiveness than permission* mantra."

Drea shrugged, then freed her hands from their blanket fort to pick up her drink. "Wouldn't mind if they were here, honestly."

"Do you want me to stay tonight? I could get Benny to cover for me. It's the middle of the week anyway. The restaurant's never that busy on Wednesdays, especially in the summer, what with the food trucks taking up shop downtown for tourist season."

If there was any scrap of Drea's personality that she could claim to love—and it was a *very* short list—it was her inability to whine, especially about a problem of her own making. "No, I'm fine. I'm just . . ."

"Thinking about how your employer locked a man in a cage and potentially did experiments on him for who knows how long?"

Drea took a casual sip, as if Molly's comment was the most natural conclusion in the world, and set her mug back down. "Yeah, that. And how I'm going to find another job. Again. Though whether that's before or after I speak with the police, I couldn't tell you. I haven't heard from Ty yet."

It wasn't for her lack of checking her messages or, in Malcolm's case, ignoring his. The sun would be setting soon, and the only thing keeping her from driving Molly's car back to the lab was the fact that her amazing best friend offered to go in to work late to stay with her.

If Drea's anxiety wasn't already suffocating her, the guilt would surely finish the job.

And speaking of guilt . . .

"Molly, there was something else that happened."

Her best friend's concerned gaze melted into wariness. "Okay," she said slowly.

"I . . ." God, she couldn't get the words out. Even thinking of voicing them was the equivalent of pulling the sole foundational brick out from under everything she held dear. It was only a matter of time before everything crumbled around her, burying all of those she cared about in a crushing pile of her deception.

But *not* saying it felt like deeper deceit.

"Molly, look, when we were at the lab, Ty and I—"

"Drea! Are you all right?" Malcolm burst through the apartment door with a bouquet of pink carnations in one hand, and, judging by the smell, a bag of Thai food in the other. Sometimes her favorite. Always his.

He dropped the food onto the dining table and ran over to her. Before Drea could fully register what was happening, his knee hit the carpet next to the couch and his hands were cradling her jaw. The fine hairs of his goatee brushed across her lips and chin as he captured a kiss she hadn't been expecting to give. Her shoulders froze, and her jaw locked up. The tang of too-bitter coffee clung to his mouth, assaulting her nerves rather than assuaging them. When his lips pressed against hers once more, her mistaken senses reached for peppermint that wasn't there.

Malcolm pulled away and rested a forearm on his bent knee. He still wore the navy-blue suit and light brown dress shoes he always wore on Wednesdays.

As if today had been a run-of-the-mill hump day that *hadn't* resulted in her losing her job, saving an imprisoned man, almost getting killed, and kissing someone whose flavor she could still taste hours later.

Whose happiness was now linked to hers, if his brother was to be believed.

"Here," he said, holding out the bouquet. "Flowers for my flower."

All thoughts of happiness were thrust from her mind. Instead, Drea turned her attention to the bouquet she'd just accepted and deflated slightly. Green cellophane hugged the bundle of carnations that were more suitable for prom queens and funeral floral arrangements, though years of pounded-in people-pleasing would never allow her to say so. Graciously, she tucked the carnations into the crook of her elbow, pretending, as she always did, that they were her favorite white lilies, and smiled her gratitude.

"Perfect. As always," she recited. *Perfect for someone else, perhaps.*

Down the hall, Molly's door snicked closed, no doubt so she could get ready for work and hurry out now that Malcolm had returned.

With all distractions removed, there was nothing to disturb her and Malcolm except the tantalizing aroma of *pad see ew* and the weight of her shame.

Malcolm rose from the carpet and took over Molly's seat next to Drea. His charming features, made more masculine by his facial hair than any natural angles, softened as he took her in. Lord, she didn't even want to think about what she looked like. Her cuts and scrapes had begun to pinken up a bit, and she didn't need bandages anymore, but her vanity had been thoroughly warned about the bruises' incubation periods. She imagined there were entire art galleries boasting work with fewer splotches than she had.

Strangely, it was something she hadn't given a thought to when she had been with Ty, not even during their hour-long drive out to the lab. Not once had she caught him staring at her hairline, where the bulk of her facial lacerations had been scored. But under Malcolm's roaming gaze, her nervous energy itched for any distraction that would force his eyes elsewhere. When he looked at her mouth once more, she got her wish apparently and regretted it instantly.

Malcolm studied her features a moment longer before his brows dipped and a foreign sort of bleakness stole over his expression. "I'm such a fucking asshole, Drea. I'm so sorry I couldn't get to you sooner. Can you forgive me?"

Drea blinked, not at all certain she'd heard him correctly. "Sorry?"

"Yes, that's exactly it! I'm sorry!" He leaped to his feet and paced an agitated rhythm in front of her. "Two of my sales fell through. They would have been huge commissions, like, year-end-profit-busting commissions. But both buyers just backed out. The first couple decided to look at real estate in Maine so they could be closer to family. The second had their financing fall through right before closing. It all happened so fast, and I was planning to tell you everything, but you never answered your phone." He pinched the bridge of his nose in a gesture Drea didn't recognize, at least on him. Malcolm was a rock when it came to emotions. In his work life, however, he often resembled a border collie who only had two settings: go and go faster. But this was different. This was . . . remorse that tightened his usual charming demeanor.

He took a deep breath and turned to her. "It wasn't until hours later when I found out why . . . when the hospital called me."

Her accident. He'd meant to tell her all this before, but then she'd gotten run off the road and nearly killed, and when she woke, it was to a phone full of missed calls and Malcolm arguing with her doctor. But none of that explained why he hadn't been there for her afterward, like he'd promised.

"I didn't see you when I got home from the hospital, though. You only sent a handful of texts." *And then I went back to work and kissed another man.*

It was then she noticed it. The red veins spidering along the whites of his eyes. The gray shadows darkening the hollows of his cheeks, barely detectable against his goatee. The lack of Malcolm's fastidious dimple in his tie.

Drea's face burned impossibly hotter from a new level of shame. *God, how hard has he been working? How did I not see it?*

Malcolm returned to the couch, and she immediately grabbed his hand. He simply looked at her. The exhaustion and worry were painted clear as day on his face. "I couldn't call you, because I was pulling my hair out trying to course correct. I was in damage-control mode. We all were. About a dozen other real estate agents in my firm all lost major leads within the past few weeks. The market in Aurora just up and went to shit, for some reason. Houses taken off the market, buyers backing out to go direct with property developers, would-be buyers choosing to rent instead."

All zero-to-low commissions. All things that directly affected his bottom line, when he was already dating someone with known job security issues and even more well-known financial scarcity.

"I couldn't let you see me like that. I didn't *want* you to see me like that. But that's all going to change," he said pointedly, some of the animation returning to his voice. "I got off the phone with three families this morning, all choosing to list with me, and all of whom are selling vacation homes that will go for low seven figures, easy." His eyes brightened. "They hit the market on Monday, but I've already lined up five showings a piece. The bidding war on one of the properties alone will make up for what I've lost, and I fully expect all three properties to sell by lunchtime on Monday, if not before. This'll be huge for me! For us."

His face flushed red with the heat of his excitement, and she couldn't help but smile for him. "That's wonderful."

"I tried to tell you," he said, tempering his enthusiasm with something akin to disappointment.

Tried but couldn't, because she kept silencing his calls. While she was with Ty.

Her heart hammered out a traitorous rhythm against her chest. "I know." It was all she could say, all she could offer. "I was—"

"Come away with me for the weekend."

She blinked, uncertain she heard him correctly. "What? Where?"

"Anywhere. I'm busting my ass tomorrow to get everything in place for these listings, and then I'm taking Friday off. Just you and me. We could go camping in the White Mountains, drive out to Vermont, stay at some posh hotel somewhere and never leave the room. Whatever you want, I don't care. I just need you."

Drea's mouth fell open. "I . . . I don't know what to say."

"Say yes." He brought his lips to her forehead, but his mouth did little to kiss away her confusion. "Say yes, Drea. Just you and me," he whispered against her skin.

Her trembling arms found their way around Malcolm's back, though her embrace was an automatic gesture intended for comfort rather than nonverbal agreement. He'd been trying for so long to get a hold of her, to guarantee he'd shored up his prospects before he shared his vulnerabilities with her. And she'd silenced him. Dismissed him.

Hurt him.

Pain of a different sort lanced through her eyes, and she quickly slammed them shut and clutched him tightly before he could see. Words spoken at separate times in separate timbres battered against her heart like waves sparring for the same patch of shore.

I just need you.

Whatever happiness he's capable of . . . With you and no one else . . .

Malcolm's need versus Ty's happiness. Neither was a choice

she wanted to make. Neither was a choice she had any right to make.

So she said the word she always said whenever anyone asked something of her. The one word that defined her spirit but condemned her hope.

"Yes."

CHAPTER 20

Dawn's approach was evident in the cool granite against Chrome's palm. No natural light breached the den, buried so deep at the base of the White Mountains as they were, but that never stopped the stones from rising. Crags stood more stoically, minerals put on their best shine, and the great rock around them groaned with renewed vigor every time that star got it in its head to awaken.

All things beyond a mortal's notice, but was any of it truly worth the price of immortality?

There'd been a time when Chrome thought so. Now, he didn't know what to think.

Chrome's groan echoed off the granite stairwell until the reverberation was so strong, the stone nearly bled from it. For once, he was more than happy to be alone with his aches and pains. Since he needed to take the steps one riser at a time, he had zero interest in Bronze's ball-busting.

The night had been brutal. Healing, whether done by elemental energy or good old-fashioned surgery, was never without pain. Though the ancient stones fed his fire and restored his celestial power, growing skin back and resetting bones was a bitch any day of the week. The cave's energies worked wonders for his angelic powers. His nose, on the other hand, he'd had to shove back into place himself—twice, after he'd done it wrong the first time. And then there were the nightmares . . . one specifically he couldn't bring himself to escape until he'd faced it down.

The base of the stairwell opened out into a hallway lined with lanterns powered by the den's geothermal energy stores. While his torment had begun in a similar hallway illuminated by vile green magic, this hallway was bright and orderly. The walls were made of carved stone, but they fit all the dimensions and included all the standards common among any industrial architecture: light switches, air vents, room signage, etc.

And he was on his way to visit one room in particular.

Chrome depressed the door handle for the newly renovated sick bay and let himself in. Given the hour, he wasn't surprised to be alone. He'd been counting on it.

When the sentinels created this space during the past year, it had been out of a necessity they'd never had to deal with before. It wasn't until Titan discovered his soul bond in Rose that they realized the true power the charmers had over them. The women his brothers had bonded to all carried a spark of the Eternal Flame within their souls, which made them *persona non grata* in Cyro's book. The demon ruler answered in kind by devising weapons far more vile and sophisticated than anything the sentinels had previously fought. Abominations of elements. Magically altered metals. Artillery that was far more deadly for a target list that had grown in number and value. The injuries Chrome and his brothers had sustained had quickly gone beyond what his power and hyperbaric healing could accomplish.

They'd needed a medical suite, and the sick bay was built some months later.

The heart rate monitor's gentle beep and the steady squeeze

and release of the automatic blood pressure cuff offered Chrome a teaspoon's measure of relief. The rest of him twitched in his own skin at the sight of Axtar lying prone on the bed. Someone must have bathed and groomed him while Chrome healed. Brass, most likely. While he wished he could say it improved matters, what they'd uncovered of the seraph commander only enraged him further.

Removing the layers of grime and excrement cast a harsh spotlight on the angel's mottled skin and garish contusions. His complexion was so sheer, he nearly appeared translucent in spots. If Chrome had to, he could map the entirety of Ax's circulatory system by simply tracing the rivers and deltas of his veins with a ballpoint pen. Beneath the thin hospital gown, there was zero muscle definition to speak of. The flimsy fabric settled over Ax's frame like a shroud over the dead. Only the gentle rise and fall of his atrophied pectorals gave any evidence to the contrary.

Desperately needing something productive to do to keep the rage at bay, Chrome rummaged through the chart that had been created. Every hour had a scheduled slot for one of them to check in, including sections for recorded vitals, bathing needs, and any changes to note. As none of them had any idea what they were working with, these seemed like good places to start.

Soon, however, numbers blurred and the papers in his hand fell back where they had been. The seraph had been shaved from chin to head. The matting had made the warrior's once proud mane beyond saving. Chrome was shocked to find that even the angel's scalp wasn't safe from the network of prominent blue veins painting his pate.

A thousand and one questions weaved a network through Chrome's thoughts. They ranged from the gruesome nature of Ax's torture to how he'd survived to Chrome's internal war with what had happened the day he delivered his friend into the hands of the enemy.

Friend. Such a benign and wholly ineffectual word for what he and Ax had shared, what they once were. Though the prime mages only saw fit to birth seven sentinels from the Eternal Flame to guard over the Empyrean upon its creation, had they opened the ranks to another, there would have been none worthier than Axtar. An intelligence master in his own right, just as brutal with a blade, and flawlessly loyal to those who'd proven themselves, he and Chrome had been like-minded on all things. Brothers by choice and in every sense that mattered.

Until he'd gone and fucking forced Chrome's hand after Ax's latest legion of scouts returned from Cyro's camp in pieces. He could still hear his battle brother's insistent words upon the lost's return.

"I'll go."

"No you fucking won't, Ax. Not you. I'll send another."

"Who? Who will you send? Who can you spare?" Ax's scowl gentled. *"Who can you trust, Tyrus?"*

Trust. It had been the sticking point for anyone who worked in intelligence who had also been in embarrassingly short supply of the stuff. Secret seraphim locations had been discovered, plans dismantled before they'd been enacted. Their legions had been crumbling from the inside.

Chrome had been desperate. They all had been.

"Send me, brother. I will not fail you."

Brother. Not Sentinel.

Ax's umber eyes threatened his own course of action: the bastard was going to undertake the mission anyway.

Chrome's hand curled around Ax's lifeless fingers as the memory of their final words sliced across his heart.

"If you go out and get yourself killed, Ax, I'll fucking kill you. You hear me?"

A teasing smirk and a solemn gaze beaming with ardor cooled the intelligence master's anger. "Likewise, brother."

"Then go and let us end this."

Chrome had lived an eternal lifetime mired in regret of one form or another, but never had the damn emotion come at him with such force that it ripped the air from his lungs. The stone floor rose up to meet him, prying further pain from his healing wounds. His legs tangled beneath the table, until the only sight that made any sense was the dimmed overhead light above Ax's bed. The hues cast the room in soft ambers, enough to see but not enough to wake. His eyes twitched, then refocused on the ambient lighting and when he'd seen its likeness last.

The celestial sun dipping below the horizon, right before Dee sprang into the records room, disrupting his melancholy with a light of her own.

The first time he'd reunited with Dee as Drea, when he snatched her up from a four-inch drop off a curb and his arms found their home in the curve of her waist. The sun was setting, bathing her blonde hair in rays of golden honey.

Drea.

Chrome tucked his chin to his chest to peer up at Ax's still form, at the lifetimes of words unsaid and actions he wished he could reverse. It'd nearly eaten him alive, and some days drove him into a melancholy even his true brothers struggled to pull him out of.

How were his actions with Drea any different? She didn't remember him or the world they'd existed in, but what had once sat like solid conviction on his shoulders now threatened to crush him into oblivion. Was he using her memory loss as an excuse to push her away from knowing the truth? By some miracle of the mages, if her memories did return, could he live with what she saw in him? What he'd had to do, what he'd had to become? The thoughts chimed in time with the heart rate monitor before transferring to his body, keeping rapid pace with the pounding in his chest.

And then it all stopped. The spinning wheel in his mind had

spun so violently, all the anxious questions had ripped free of its vortex, until only his intellect remained once more.

Chrome slowed his breathing and let the solution spawn from the silence, as it always did. This was the part of him that had remained all these eons. His cunning, analysis, and strategy. *That* was what he'd show her, because it existed in him across time eternal, regardless of one's recollections.

He was a sentinel. The intelligence master.

Boots scraped against the stone as he scrambled to his feet, energized with a course he'd not considered viable until now. After scribbling a few hasty notes in Ax's chart and whispering a promise of profuse thanks to his friend, he bounded up the stairs, heedless of any lingering pain.

He was done waiting, done wishing for things to be different. If Drea didn't remember him from before, there was no reason she couldn't know him now. Know all of him, family included, and, dear mages, even the mates.

If he couldn't resurrect her memories, then he'd just have to make new ones.

PERHAPS THE FACT that Drea and Molly's building was one of the few structures in New Hampshire with a flat roof was a good thing. Built by a developer at a time when tenement-style garden apartments were popular and building codes were not, the roof offered many benefits. No-frills architecture, an outdoor common space for tenants to gather, and a super convenient ledge to pitch herself over.

That last one wasn't strictly mentioned in the property listing, but that didn't diminish its value, at least in Drea's mind. It certainly seemed like a decent alternative given her options.

First, admit infidelity to her boyfriend, who had almost lost a good chunk of his income and nearly given himself a stroke for fear of failing to provide for her.

Second, confess to authorities her (admittedly unknown) involvement in her previous employer's apparent testing and torture of a kidnapped man.

Third, search for yet *another* job, this time without the benefit of employer references. If that failed, look into the going rate for pictures of her feet and possibly sell them to make August's rent.

Fourth, pretend she didn't remember the taste of Ty's mouth on her skin or wonder what happiness actually looked like.

The black rubber roofing material shared its reserved warmth with her, heating her butt to just shy of toasty, while the soles of her sandals waved out at the parking lot. In a seedier-than-seedy development, it paid to be high up, to have this little patch of ledge where what lurked on the ground couldn't come for you and the only thing that could truly do a number on you was your own demons.

Demons.

Drea grimaced at the headache pulsing behind her eye again whenever that word inexplicably floated through her mind. The pain had only gotten worse ever since Titan had dropped her home and she kept replaying the harrowing events of the day. A part of her had hoped the fresh air would help.

No such luck.

She stood, intent on hunting down more pain relievers, when a shadow in the parking lot moved until it was nearly visible under the single streetlight still up to doing its job. She knew who it was before the man's shoulders had even fully materialized under the mediocre rays.

Ty.

Half shrouded in shadow, his face angled toward her position on the roof. Though he was far away, the tension in his features was crystal clear. Tight jaw. Thinned lips. Brow furrowed in determination.

Nearly silver eyes that clung to hers.

She froze. Even from this distance, she could see his chest hitch on a breath. Then he turned slightly and revealed irises more slate gray than silver. Her bare wrist warmed against her thigh.

Malcolm had never looked at her like that, she'd realized soberly. Never sought her out on a roof in the middle of the night like one searched for a soft place to land after flying through hell.

She didn't know what made her do it, nor did she care to analyze actions she didn't want to explain, but when Drea gestured her chin toward the front door below, Ty followed without hesitation.

And so did she.

CHAPTER 21

The door to the roof swung open before Drea even finished brushing the gravel from her butt. Another time, with another person, she'd have paused to analyze how Ty made it upstairs so quickly or how he even knew where the access door was. Taking in his presence backed by little more than the soft glow from the stairwell, however, she profoundly didn't care.

Drea flew across the roof and lunged at him with open arms, no small feat considering she was nearly six feet tall herself and had long since trained her body to shorten its stride. Training went right out the window the moment he was within arms' distance. He caught her with the grace of a figure skating partner and, with one hand, supported her around her waist while he closed the door behind them with the other. She squeezed him so stupidly tight. There was no room in her adrenaline-fueled frame for gentle caresses or ladylike anything. Not after the last image she had of him was the back of his head walking into a lab filled with potential human traffickers and some sort of unknown chemical weapons.

But he'd come back, and he was here.

And holy crap, did he look like hell.

Drea straightened a bit when he softly winced beneath her grip. Even with both arms wrapped fiercely around her and his head dropped into the crook of her neck, he couldn't hide the way his back muscles reflexively arched away from her touch.

"What happened down there? Oh, Ty . . ." Drea pulled back but left her fingers to hover anxiously over his face, shoulders, and a collarbone that sloped at a slightly different angle than its partner. She was just about to twirl her finger, insisting he spin for her inspection, when his hands caught hers.

"Easy. I'm fine."

"No, fine is being unharmed. You're clearly harmed." She freed her hand from its cage and gestured toward his bruised nose to prove her point.

"Nothing a few days won't fix."

"A few days? You need a hospital and probably a surgeon. Jesus Christ, what the hell—"

"It's gone. The lab is gone."

Drea tensed. "What do you mean, the lab is gone?"

"I mean, it's been . . . dismantled."

Something about that word, dismantled, set off warning bells. "How was it dismantled, exactly? Ty, what did you do?"

The set of his jaw hardened, rivaling the roof's solid structure beneath their feet. Stormy eyes slashed to the ground before they returned to level a look of lethal precision. "Called in some industry alerts and favors. High-up friends of mine in the appropriate medical and scientific regulatory channels, along with other law enforcement agencies. The lab was infiltrated, all parties apprehended, and every operation they were conducting is under investigation. The man we pulled out is under medical care and has a team of providers helping him around the clock. Trust me, by the time the sun's up, that facility will be just another barren hole in the ground the worms wouldn't even bother with."

Drea inched back and marveled at the man before her. In just a few short sentences, he'd summarily explained away one of the most frightening experiences of her life with the casual cruelty one used to step on a spider. Her head swam with the magnitude of all that would be involved, of the names, access, test samples, equipment leases, all of it that this man, with his powerful prowess, managed to poof out of existence like a traveling circus that was here one day and gone the next.

This wasn't real. None of this could possibly be real, and yet . . .

"Who *are* you?" The whispered plea rushed out with such force, her head sagged forward. Ty's firm chest cushioned her forehead, while his hands positioned her until she rested comfortably against his sternum. Rough calluses toyed with her braid, testing the downy hairs at the base of her neck, even massaging the ridges of her cervical column, releasing tension she hadn't realized lived there.

There was so much about this man she didn't know. Cocooned against him as she was, however, and with his hands offering seductive solace, the need to grill him became far less pervasive.

"Let me show you."

Drea's lashes fluttered against his shirt as her eyes flew open. She reared back slightly, her brows arched in inquiry, but he never let go of her neck.

"Come to lunch with me tomorrow." The gruff plea was anything but gentle. Certainly not a question. It was unapologetically direct and hit her with the ferocity of a runaway train.

"I . . . What about Malcolm?"

The question shouldn't have been the first to leave her mouth, but it was, and she instantly regretted it.

Ty's chest hitched, the only indication of him being thrown off guard, and a marked hostility tightened his lips. "He can come too, if you want. Doesn't make a difference to me. Only thing I care about is putting some of that light back in your eyes after your world turned to shit on my account. Figured you could meet my family, their . . . partners . . . eat some kofta. Relax a bit. Then, once your mind has stopped racing, you can hurl any question you want at me. I can take it, so long as I'm fed first."

A placid reserve had smoothed over the stoniness in his expression from a moment ago. Sharpened cheekbones supported the corners of a rare smile instead of a scowl, and wide brows arched over a soft gaze. Drea blinked at the secret radiance of it. She'd never seen him this casual or earnest and briefly wondered what she'd done to elicit such a brilliant shine from this man. How many others had been the benefactors, or dare she say the cause of, his hidden joy?

None! her heart roared, though the thought was tinged with sadness rather than thrill. A tug behind her breastbone urged her to memorize this portrait of him somehow, as if she could tuck the image of his happiness away and protect it.

Nothing would make me happier.

But then one curiosity did come to mind so fiercely it burst from her tongue heedless of where it would land. Not a question, exactly, but certainly something that needed answering.

"You said you wouldn't touch me again," she breathed into the humid night air.

The corners of Ty's eyes crinkled, and his throat worked on a swallow. "Do you want me to stay away, Dee?"

Dee.

It was how she'd come to think of herself lately, as well. Dee was a confident cohort to a like-minded hunk and hulk of a scientist. He didn't condemn Dee for her quirks but respected and encouraged them. Dee was a sexual creature who wasn't afraid to tear into what or who she wanted.

Drea, on the other hand, was an unemployed lab technician who struggled to find her way around a relationship with a man she should be head over heels for. Drea had nothing but a stack of problems with a severe deficit of solutions and was well-practiced in the art of gracefully absorbing pity and rejection.

The two couldn't be more different, and yet they had somehow taken up residence in the same woman. It all begged the question: who was the squatter?

Do you want me to stay away, Dee?

Ty's words floated through her mind as he glanced down expectantly. He'd do whatever she said. There wasn't a doubt in her mind about that. He was too noble, too kindhearted, too disgustingly honorable. Did she want him to stand down, though? What *did* she want?

The questions hammered around the cage of her heart, and Drea almost sank in surprise to find the miserable organ had never really been given the opportunity for freedom. She loved Molly, yes, but it was a sisterly love born from childhood that was as innate and as much a part of her as breathing. It certainly wasn't an all-consuming love that strengthened her heart the more she used it. What else caused the miserable beating thing to blossom beyond its confines? What made her happy to the point of delirious and gloriously unfettered euphoria?

Do you want me to stay away?

She blinked once, twice. By the third blink, the answer was on her lips. It was the first honest phrase she'd ever let her heart voice.

"No."

CHAPTER 22

When Ty invited Drea to lunch to meet his family, she hadn't entirely been sure what to expect. Perhaps a backyard barbecue, a game of corn hole, and small talk about what everyone's summer plans were.

You know, in case anyone else had a penchant for shutting down super sketchy clinical laboratories on random Wednesdays.

But as Ty escorted her into Sultana, the popular Moroccan restaurant in Aurora and the only culinary spot from their sleepy small town to garner multiple esteemed write-ups from national news outlets, all Drea's preconceived notions were tossed out the window.

The door chime tinkled behind them, shutting them into a lush world of soft lantern light, golden platters, artfully arranged hookahs, and rich purple tapestries. Maroon and gold couch cushions took the place of rigid dining chairs and were enticingly positioned around rows and rows of resplendent gold trays.

Drea had walked by this place countless times but never ventured in, half out of fear that they'd check her bank statement to qualify her as a serious patron. The restaurant wasn't merely a place to eat but an immersive experience that, as soon as it ended, was immediately booked again by diners for the next available reservation, which was usually several months out. Once or twice, she'd almost worked up the nerve to suggest the place to Malcolm, but the guilt over the cost quickly tamped down any enthusiasm she may have had over the magical meal.

Drea, as Malcolm's girlfriend, couldn't dream of stepping foot in here, but Dee, as a guest of Ty and his family, was not only welcomed with open arms but, upon entry, was immediately handed a cup of honeyed mint tea by the waitstaff and escorted to the only table with people at it.

"There they are!" Bronze was the first to his feet and nearly toppled over the platter in front of him in the process. He and Ty exchanged animated backslaps, though there was a bit more excitement on Bronze's part, and she wondered whether he naturally moved through life with the same enthusiasm. The dim golden light cast the brother's red hair in subtle shades of burnt orange, accentuating the saffron and paprika hues woven into the mahogany and purple tapestries adorned throughout the room. Drea did her best to keep her eyes on who she was about to meet, but everywhere she turned, another vibrant color stole her attention, until one startling realization made itself obvious.

"We're the only ones here," Drea murmured, searching the dining room for some Moroccan timepiece to confirm that, yes, it was definitely prime mealtime and the place should have been swarming with patrons. "It's one o'clock, right? Where's the rest of the lunch crowd?"

Ty gripped the back of his neck. "We rented out the place. Titan knows the owner, Amira. He and Rose are regulars, and we've been crashing their little party about once a month now."

"Hi! You're Drea, right?" The presumed Rose, who had been tucked up under Titan's arm and snuggled into the corner cushions, sprang up and all but hurled herself across the table. Drea found herself being squeezed around her middle by a brunette with shoulder-length hair and all the exuberance of an eager-to-please puppy. When the woman pulled back, she smiled brilliantly, as if she had some secret penchant for adopting lost things. "I'm Rose, though you probably figured that out already. Titan's my . . ." She pursed her lips and glanced back at Titan, who seemed to communicate some wordless warning before skipping his eyes to Drea and nodding his greeting. "Well, we'll go with boyfriend for now. Have you been here before? The food will literally make you cry, it's so flippin' good. I hope you're hungry!"

"Starved," Drea conceded before her ravenous stomach could out her. "Do you guys really rent out this place? How is that even possible?"

Rose averted her gaze beneath sweeping lashes and merely shrugged. Around the table, which was actually a combination of six giant gold platters pressed together and surrounded by cushions and various ice buckets, knowing eyes became absorbed in their drinks. "We love Amira, and we're big supporters of her business. So, that kind of comes with some perks."

"That's one way to downplay it," Drea breathed out through a smile.

Rose tucked her arm around Drea's and leaned in. "You have no idea."

She threw Drea a wink and trotted her around to the two other women in their party. Tucked in the small area where the shadows beat back the light was a woman with chestnut hair that fell to the center of her back—or it would fall there, if the man petting the thick mass of waves would pause long enough to let it settle. Drea recognized him and the rest of the men she hadn't formally met yet as the ones who'd gone into the lab with Ty after he'd gotten her and the man they'd rescued out of there.

She'd not thought a single one of them capable of the soft affection this man now lavished on the woman who—Drea squinted—looked exactly like Rose.

"I take it you two are twins?" Drea remarked.

The woman paused in her silent conversation and lifted identical bright eyes to greet her. With a friendly wave, she said, "Yup. I'm Tammy, Rose's older sister by four minutes, and this is Tung."

The man next to her raised Tammy's hand to his lips and dropped a reverent kiss while never taking his eyes off her or acknowledging the muttered "whatever" from Rose that had everyone else at the table chuckling into their drinks. Only when Tammy took her hand back and introduced him formally did he direct his attention to Drea. "It is a pleasure to finally meet you, Drea. Please, welcome to our family and our table. We are at your service."

"Hi. Thank you. That's very kind." Drea managed a two-finger wave to go with her stilted sentence fragments, but even that called on more mental resources than she had in the bank.

As soon as she thanked him, Tung returned his attention to Tammy's hair, even placing a small kiss to the crown of her head while the older twin conversed with Brass next to her. Drea swallowed past an emotion she couldn't name and tried not to gawk at the obvious show of adoration Tung had for Tammy. It flowed seamlessly through their interactions and conversations, like it was a living breathing thing as much as the couple was.

A curious emotion caught in her throat, and she quickly tried to clear it away.

"If you look at them too long, you'll go crossed-eyed. Steel." A blond man to her right extended a wide palm toward her. His cheerful expression exuded the type of easygoing charm common among neighbors from nineties sitcoms, and Drea adored him instantly. "And that's my better half, Bridget. She's the lead animator on *Fallen Angels Rising*."

Drea froze mid-handshake. "Wait—the video game that just launched last month? The marketing campaign for that was insane! Whoever came up with the idea to release the game in collectible special-edition boxes featuring the individual characters was genius. My roommate and I wanted the Forest Queen, but my boyfr— um, my friend who was going in on the game with us argued for the Demon Marauder, so we got that instead."

A low grunt echoed behind her, and Ty, who had been silent since they'd gotten there, grabbed a golden wine glass and one of the bottles from the ice bucket and started pouring.

Why was she hesitant to mention Malcolm by name or their relationship? It was hardly a secret, as Ty was obviously aware of the man.

For the same reason you didn't invite Malcolm to this lunch after Ty extended the invitation to him as well. Or tell him who you'd be seeing. He still thinks you're going to work today.

The woman with chin-length black hair next to Steel, Bridget, stopped a very animated conversation with Bronze, judging by the hand gestures, flung her hand high in the air front-of-the-class style, and proclaimed, "That was my idea! The firm I work for out of Boston allowed the animators to pitch some concepts to the marketing team for the launch, and that was one of mine that they ran with."

Steel wrapped an arm around Bridget's shoulders, propelling every ounce of pride he had for her into the gesture. Bridget, meanwhile, went right back to arguing with Bronze over something Drea didn't catch. What she *did* catch was the moony-eyed gaze and blinding smile that never left Steel's face as he watched her win whatever disagreement she'd been having with his brother.

Drea's head swiveled around the group assembled before her. She was fairly certain she'd get rug burn on her chin from dragging it across the lush carpet in shock. How did a restaurant like this manage enough space to allow for the prevalence of shoulders and breadth of chests these men sported and *still* have room for the food and furniture? It was a veritable assembly of gargantuan giants, broken up by a handful of women who apparently had a knack for turning goliaths into goo. The whole scene was one idyllic production that stole her breath and quite literally her wits.

"Drea."

Ty's voice tugged her back to reality, though she quickly swiped her tongue along her bottom lip to check for drool. Beside him was another man, the only one she hadn't met yet, and from the looks of him, she wasn't sure what to expect. As tall as Ty and with a chest nearly as wide as one of the golden platters beneath their drinks, the russet-haired man's dual-colored gaze pinned her to the spot. His look was all at once assessing and penetrating, as if her very measure was both being taken and summarily judged.

"This is Iron. He assisted with the lab as well."

The man bobbed his bearded chin slightly but didn't say anything more than, "Pleasure."

"Yes, I remember you," she said. "Thank you so much for everything you did."

His eyes, one hazel and one brown, flitted across her features before he lifted his glass in salute and drained it. He'd taken his final gulp when the house lights went down, and lanterns with jewel-toned light bulbs flared to life along the walls. The three women instantly dropped their drinks or, in Tammy's case, their significant other and squealed the high-pitched excitement of a thousand teenage girls.

Drea whipped her head to Ty. "What's going on?" But her words were swept away on a riotous cacophony of Arabic music pumped through speakers concealed beneath the bric-a-brac. "Oh!"

Slim arms hooked through hers and pulled her toward the

main carpeted area of the dining room. From the kitchen, servers brought out trays of Moroccan cigars, skewered shrimp, and seemingly bottomless baskets of hummus, baba ghanoush, and toasted pita. Cardamom and coriander wove through the small dining space, mingling with mint and roasted meat. Her tongue darted from her mouth, wetting her lips, as the food was placed on the platters where she'd just been.

"I hope you like to dance, Drea!" Rose, who'd nabbed her right arm, tossed her hands in the air and started swirling her hips in time to the music's pounding rhythm. To her left, Tammy mimicked her sister's movements, exuding the same wordless sensuality she'd had sitting down.

Panicked, Drea turned to Bridget, who was the only one not yet dancing. "Please tell me what's happening!" The music grew louder. Jolting percussion joined enticing flutes she had no name for, and Drea had to practically yell to be heard.

Bridget pulled Drea's ear to her lips. "Think of this as a family tradition. The first time's always the most nerve-racking, but I swear, the release is *amazing!*"

"Like a what tradition? What's nerve-racking?" Panic tinged her voice as the men before them all took their seats and turned to face the women. Ty leaned back in his chair, his powerful legs falling open, a golden goblet dangling from his fingertips. But most unnervingly, perhaps, was the unreadable expression barely visible beneath the strobing flashes of purple and red lights.

The three women ran to an ottoman in the far corner and pulled out an assortment of scarves, finger cymbals, golden chains, and—was that a *sword?* When they returned, each adorning Drea with their dazzling finds, they beamed back at her with sheer and terrifying excitement, all shouting at the same time.

"Belly dancing!"

CHAPTER 23

Ty brought the gold cup to his lips, savoring both the drink and the woman before him. Oh, he'd known the afternoon would include this particular show. A part of him had been counting on it. The women loved to dance, and his brothers loved their mates, so the indulgence was mutually adored. What Chrome *didn't* count on, however, was the effect Drea's unbound hair would have on him.

Or her unbound in general.

At first, he wasn't sure whether he could bring himself to look. Temptation, especially where Drea was concerned, had been a dangerous tripwire he'd barely managed to maneuver around. When his brothers' mates swept Drea into the din of the roaring music, however, her braid caught the air in the crosswind caused by the girls' yanking her to the makeshift stage and swept along his forearm. Her lily fragrance fanned the simmering coals of his fire within, and he nearly stumbled after her, but Iron quickly swapped Chrome's drink for a much stronger one and forced Chrome's ass into his seat.

In all his years, he'd been no stranger to torture. Skin flayed from his body, wings snapped mid-flight, acid poured down his throat while he writhed in his metallic form. None of it held a candle to the torment of watching Drea's honeyed locks gently pulled free of their braid by mischievous women who clearly enjoyed his suffering.

When the final section of hair was undone, Drea sank her fingertips into her scalp and shook out the mass. Chrome's jaw relaxed around the rim of the cup as her own jaw fell open, offering up her elongated neck like the tantalizing treat it was.

Never had he seen her hair unbound, not even in his memories. During the single night they'd shared, her hair had remained plaited and easy to wrap around his fist. But, oh, he'd imagined the freed tresses. Fantasized about the silky strands sifting through his fingers. They'd be long enough to hide the parts of her that had tormented him in his dreams but not so long as to withhold all of her secret treasures.

Treasures, he knew, were concealed by the similar honeyed silk that now whipped violently around her as the twins twirled Drea in time with the music.

His cock pounded to the beat of the *dumbek's* distinctive rhythm, further tightening his pants as Bridget divested Drea of her cardigan, revealing a tank top with straps thin enough to be a marvel of engineering. Then Steel's woman had the audacity to fasten a single gold chain around Drea's narrow waist. The links fell in a tantalizing trail over the curve of a generous hip.

Chrome shot back his whiskey, urging the burning liquor to dull his senses as fast as possible lest he have to answer for his sober actions. Chief among them being the furniture he'd destroy on his way to scooping Drea away from his family and finding the nearest hard surface to take her against, horizontal or otherwise.

A shadow to his left filled his periphery, until Brass's rust-hewn hair caught the light of the strobes. "You are in so much trouble," the angel chided.

Chrome reached for the rest of the whiskey but had the

bottle snatched from his fingers before they could curl around the neck. Iron, spirits in hand, gestured toward Chrome's cup and obliged him with several good glugs of amber courage before returning his attention to the women.

Miserable angels didn't even trust him to pour his own drink.

"She still has no idea who I am, who any of us are," Chrome lamented into his cup.

"I don't know about that. I think the girls are doing a great job of introducing themselves and making her feel right at home." Brass swiped a green olive from a platter laden with roasted eggplant and charred peppers.

Chrome swirled the liquid under his nose, subjecting the spirits to a whirlpool as tempestuous as the swirling silks and abundant laughter before him. "I guess I'm having second thoughts."

"Bullshit."

Chrome cocked a disbelieving brow at his brother. "Come the fuck again?" He could count on one hand the number of times he'd heard his brother curse over the centuries, and half of the time it had been directed at Bronze.

Brass dismissed the remark like one would any tantruming toddler. "When have you ever had a second thought in your life? You're literally wired for intelligence. You don't *have* second thoughts. Don't act for a moment like you haven't already cataloged every possible outcome of what could happen if she decided, on her own, to spend more time with you and less with that other guy."

He *had* cataloged the outcomes. All of them. Even the ones involving a shovel and a few hours of manual labor. Arm day had always been his favorite anyway.

So, why was he running from this? From her? This was the plan all along, wasn't it? To introduce her not to only him but his family. To show her the angel he'd become, rather than the memory he couldn't escape.

Rose brought out a sword from the trove of props and gingerly laid the blunted edge—which every mated male in the room had made damn sure was *actually* blunted—on the crown of Tammy's head. With all the flourish of a magician, Tungsten's soul bond spread her arms wide and twirled in a slow circle, hips languidly swaying in time with the music. To Chrome's eternal torment, Drea moved right along with her. Generous hips popped right and left while that confounded belly chain taunted him like cream to a cat. He was one torturous gyration away from rushing up from the table and snagging that damn chain with his teeth. It was bad enough that Drea had knotted her tank top beneath her breasts, exposing a torso so long and sensuous, his tongue ached to map every curve and plain of her supple flesh.

In his arms, against his tongue, there'd be no danger to her, for his beast was hers to command. Always had been, since the moment she'd pushed him aside in the records room and dashed about like one late to a party. She'd been more concerned with the lives of others over her own well-being, her own happiness.

Her own pleasure.

It was her nature, unabashedly good to a core so pure Chrome nearly came undone to bask in it.

A muted flush crept up Drea's cheeks, mingling with the vibrant hues of the lights painting her skin. *He* should be the only one to make her unravel like that. The heat in her skin should be caused by him alone. Her pleasure should be keyed to his specific stroke, not some pulsating music or a jerkoff with an agenda. With Chrome, she would be free to explore her passions.

Smoke teased his nose, and the sharp jerk of Brass's head had them both looking at Chrome's hand. Warm whiskey dribbled down the pad of his thumb, leaking over the melted edge of the golden chalice. Vapor tendrils wafted up from his skin as the heat from his angel fire softened the metal.

Casually, as if Brass did this sort of thing often, he lifted the deformed cup from Chrome's vice-like grip. "I think you know what you need to do."

Brass's words flitted through Chrome's mind but still stuck where the angel had intended them to land. The music crested its pounding crescendo, easing to a more conversational tempo. Waitstaff funneled out from the kitchen, replenishing empty trays with fresh platters of beef kofta, rice pilaf, and lamb tagine.

"Food! I'm starving!" Bridget quickly gathered the props and returned them to the ottoman while Drea broke free from the rest of the women, offering some excuse Chrome couldn't quite make out.

Not that it mattered. He was done with excuses. Done waiting.

Chrome rose from his seat with a hunter's focus, snatched up a discarded silk scarf, and stalked toward his retreating prey.

DREA SAUNTERED into the women's bathroom, swaying from the music that still thrummed down her spine long after it had ended. A pleasant exuberance lightened her step, bolstering a giddiness that couldn't help but boot out any remaining nerves at meeting Ty's family.

Holy hell, those women were wonderful. Never had she been thrust into companionship so quickly as she had been just then, and before a crowd of men—brothers, it was important to note —who seemed to delight in nothing but the women's joy.

And joyous she was.

In the restroom, Drea was surprised to find a formal sitting area opposite the sinks. Two burgundy armchairs embroidered with golden petals and ivy flanked a simple mahogany end table, upon which sat chilled bottles of water, an assortment of mints, and matching burgundy napkins with an ornate golden S stitched in the corner. Drea flopped onto one of the chairs and pitched her head back over the edge, while the tip of her finger drew lazy circles around the neck of a water bottle.

Only behind her closed eyelids did she allow herself to finally simmer in the aftershocks of what she'd just indulged in. Never had exhaustion felt so good that she had to seek solace from the rush. Though the meal was served, she didn't trust herself to come down from her euphoria in the presence of strangers.

In the presence of Ty.

Her mind still rushed with the tremors of relief she felt exploring her freedom. There had been no insistent nagging for propriety's sake, no way she needed to behave or speak or address those around her. When she was out with Malcolm on his lunch breaks over the weekends, she'd always conform to his professional demeanor, regardless of how many times he urged her to relax. That always irked her to no end. How could one possibly relax when her boyfriend's smiling picture lit up the side of the bus stop they'd just walked past? Nor could Drea explain away her beloved casual leggings when potential clients recognized Malcolm on the street, heedless of the lunch date they'd just interrupted. So long as he offered his recommendation on what the interlopers should list their house for when putting it on the market three freaking years from now, all was forgiven, at least on his part. Expected, even.

But once Rose fastened that silk scarf around Drea's hips and Bridget got to work unraveling Drea's hair, everything changed. Drea never knew what it meant to truly be off duty. To not have to dress to impress or make sure the wrong thing never slipped past her lips. Under those lights and swept away by that heart-pounding music, the only person she needed to answer to was herself.

And then there was Ty.

Though the opulent lights danced brightly across her and the girls, there was just enough of it to make out the strength of his legs, spread wide and inviting in a dangerous self-assured awareness. Every time he brought that damn cup to his lips, his eyes tracked her with a predatory flare that caused her hips to sway wider. The graceful lines of his fingers, cloaked largely in shadow, teased at her consciousness, pulling thoughts of another shadowed encounter.

Was he thinking of her, of that moment they shared in the dark?

Could she go a single hour without reliving the taste of him?

Up on that sparse carpet, surrounded by strangers as lost to the dance as she was, she knew her answer. Unabashedly.

A soft click preceded the sweep of the door opening.

"Oh, don't mind me. I'm just taking a load off for a sec. That was insanely amazing. I can't believe how much I needed that." Drea settled her neck farther onto the rim of the chair, letting whatever lingering tension was there leech from her shoulders.

When the person didn't respond and there was no further movement around the sitting area or in the restroom stalls, Drea opened her eyes and sat up.

A hulking form as familiar as her own face stood in front of the closed door. Back flat, shoulders still, hips wide but poised. Ty posed the very picture of brutal desperation. He claimed that space but didn't move, like a well-trained dog silently begging to be allowed to approach.

To approach, Drea realized with a tremulous swallow, for the promise and permission of a treat.

When he spoke, the words danced between them on a hungry breath.

"I'm inclined to say the same," he growled.

Floating on the high of warming spices and perfumed adrenaline, Drea bent her elbows and pushed off from her chair —

"No, stay there."

She froze, arms arranged awkwardly and her heart firmly lodged in her throat. Air rushed from her lungs as her chest rose and fell in time with his. Silence stretched between them. She searched those silver eyes for any sign of doubt or shame. Some blatant sign that what they were about to do was wrong, that the electricity lassoing her every thought to this man was a symptom of trauma and stress.

There was none. Only fierce determination and silent understanding stared back at her.

Then he sprang off the door like a mountain lion to its quarry. A thud shook the small space as Ty's knees hit the carpet before her.

His mouth silenced her racing thoughts with one smooth hungry kiss.

CHAPTER 24

What Chrome had planned to be tender intimacy turned into impatient need. When Drea's lips were on his, kisses were not just kisses. They were violent infernos of every sleepless night and dagger to the belly that kept him writhing long enough to relive the taste of her. But he'd been so wrong, so utterly simple to think the mere memory of her mouth would ever be enough to carry him into the future. Not when her skin was beneath his hands again as his thumbs traced the delicate curve of her jaw.

The kiss deepened before it had even grown roots, bypassing all notions of gentle play and idle banter. When her mouth reached for his with a fervor to match his own, his cock roared in time with his fire. Each drugging pull of her lips ripped something harsh and foreign from him, tugging a peculiar sensation to just below the surface of his awareness.

Awareness. What a simple and wholly inadequate word to describe the thrumming she ignited in him. One was *aware* of the sun's smiling rays on their skin or the flowers' fragrance in the air. No, he wasn't simply aware. He *burned*.

Fiery coals raked across his lower abdominals from within,

punching his hips forward into the apex of her legs. She sucked in a startled breath against his mouth, stealing the air from his lungs. Still, their lips never separated, even when he forced himself to gentle his hands and savor the flavor he wasn't sure he'd ever taste again. The resigned thought pulled him from his frenzy, only to stoke another longing he'd feebly managed to keep at bay even in his darkest hours.

Chrome slowly swiped hungry lips over hers before gentling them into softness with a measured insistent kiss.

When he pulled away, Drea's heavy lids hooded her violet eyes, though they did nothing to dim the spark he'd proudly put there. Her chest rose and fell with perfect little pants, pushing her nipples more insistently against the thin fabric of her shirt with each inhale. Her tank top remained knotted right above her ribs, baring her long, lean stomach to him like an offering. The fire roiling within urged him to take it all, to rip the cloth free and rake his teeth over the tightly gathered nipples until everyone in the fucking restaurant knew who her pleasure belonged to.

His logical brain, however, the one most definitely *not* in control of his body but still very much aware of his otherwise important needs, yanked him back by his dumb handle and forced him to look at her. *Really* look at her.

But looking turned to savoring, and savoring turned to desperation. If he didn't find another haven for his eyes soon, that chasm of loneliness he'd worked so hard to plug up would burst wide open, condemning him to more millennia with only his memories for comfort. As his fingers toyed with the little knot of fabric, loosening it with maddeningly slow pulls, he wished there was another way to prove what she meant to him, how her precious gift of not only her body but her beautiful soul had carried him through his darkest moments.

A part of him begged for a blade to fall on or a train to leap in front of. Anything to show the lengths he'd go to repay even a modicum of what she'd given him.

But all he had was his body, and by the fucking mages, he'd make it more than enough.

"Why do you keep looking at me like that?" Drea's soft whisper didn't snap him out of his thoughts, so much as focus them.

When he finally untangled the knot of fabric, he didn't pull it down. Instead, he lifted it higher, revealing lush breasts lined in lace and long-kept memories. *Only* in his memories. "Because I almost forgot how fucking gorgeous you are."

Drea stilled beneath him, and a stunned expression stole over her features. In one panicked blink, Chrome saw how the whole thing would play out. She'd press those kiss-swollen lips together and try to regain some of her composure by sitting up higher, perhaps even tugging down her shirt to hide her embarrassment. Then her eyes would dart around the room, landing on the door, the sink, even the toilet stalls, until some distraction would loom large enough and allow her to cling to it instead of her insecurities.

Fuck. That.

Chrome swiped the silk scarf he'd tucked into his back pocket and cradled both her wrists over her bare stomach. Before she could make sense of his movements, he kissed her soundly, until the tension didn't even have a chance to stiffen her shoulders. Once he was absolutely certain he had her attention again, he pulled back.

"You should be told that every day, and often, in as many ways as there are languages, and in however many words it takes for you to believe them. You. Are. Beautiful. And if that schmuck of a boyfriend doesn't have the stones to show you what it means to cherish that kind of beauty when it comes along, then he's not done cooking yet. Send him back to his mother."

His icy words settled like frost over a field. Drea sat para-lyzed and powerless as the chilling truth accumulated on the surface of her skin before sinking into her bones. Then her lips tilted on a slight tremble, and she couldn't hold back her winsome laugh. An infinitesimal mist tinged the joy sparkling in her amethyst eyes. Joy. He'd never seen that look on her face before, not truly.

And he'd make damn sure he'd see it again.

"You don't have to say that stuff," she whispered, though her brows curled into a pleading furrow confessing just how desperate she'd been to hear the words. Her small shuddering breaths nearly broke him. Each tremble was a silent whisper that begged him to say it again lest she fall apart under another lie.

"I've told you before, Dee. I do what I like."

Her chin jerked, and her lips rose in a disbelieving smile, as if she'd never heard the words before.

You've heard them before. You just don't remember . . .

When her confusion didn't fade, he redirected her attention to her wrists, still bound softly in one of his hands.

"I'm going to prove to you just how beautiful you are."

DREA'S STOMACH MUSCLES QUIVERED, and she found herself momentarily longing for the odd anonymity of the carpeted pseudo-stage in the dining room. Under those lights and with those women, she was one of many strobing energies flitting around without an anchor. Here, under Ty's insistent eyes, trapped as she was beneath his warm weight, he gave her no quarter. There was no shadowy corner or wall of women to hide behind. That penetrating stormy stare saw everything, even the broken and chipped bits she'd tucked away so tightly, she hoped no one would think to look for them.

But he did. That fact alone sent her soul spiraling and her heart battering against her chest.

Ty pulled a bolt of delicate lavender silk from behind him and gently laid it across her wrists. A single dark eyebrow arched in silent challenge, but even his firm lips couldn't keep the mirth out of his expression.

Just where was he heading with all this? Certainly, she *knew* where that scarf was most likely to end up, but that sort of sport never usually followed such a playful smirk—if features as hard as his could ever claim to house the lighthearted gesture.

"You know," she informed him, while he loosely fastened the scarf around her wrists, "anyone could come in here."

"No, they couldn't."

The words were spoken with such finality, it was enough to make her original question seem foolish.

"Women need to pee, you know. You don't control that."

He didn't look at her but merely checked his rigging, as it were. Then he ducked his head under her bound wrists and popped up within the circle of her arms. The movement stunned her, both in its speed and his resulting proximity. She tried to rear back but was impeded by the chair. Well, that and the heated torso pressing against her bare skin.

"No one's coming in here, Dee. Not unless you want them to." Then he paused for a moment, and a prominent vein along his hairline pulsed as his jaw tightened. "*Do* you want them to? Do you want to leave?"

Did she want to leave? The question was a valid one, and since she hadn't had anything to drink yet, she supposed she had enough of her faculties to answer it honestly. Above her, molten strength smothered her senses so fully, it crowded out the miserable logic and harsh voices that had so often dictated her life. With all that noise silenced, she finally heard the truth roaring free from within, and she was determined to speak it for once.

"No, I don't want to leave." Then she playfully tugged her bound wrists against the back of his neck. "Kind of can't, anyway. Someone's got me all tied up."

A groan vibrated across her lips as Ty claimed them once more in a searing kiss. "Fuck, woman. What you do to me . . ."

Then her arms lowered, following his body as it dipped impossibly closer. His mouth hovered over her breasts, breathing heated temptation across fevered skin. A single curled finger hooked over the lace concealing one breast and peeled the fabric down. Her nipple sprang free and rebounded directly into the wetness of his velvet mouth. Drea arched her head back, slamming her eyes closed, as he tenderly lapped at her with his merciless tongue before gently tugging the sensitive bud with his teeth. Her fingers responded in kind, scoring gashes into the back of his neck with the same fervor he bestowed on her. A low rumbling chuckle against her other breast was the only response to her ministrations.

Annoying insufferable man.

The next lick sent a jolt straight to her core, settling firmly between her legs like a mountain climber staking his flag on a summit. Drea clenched her thighs reflexively, both to soothe the small hurt and spur it on. Every bit of Ty's body that melded against hers was a symbiotic explosion she couldn't explain. Another nibble, this time underneath her breast, and her leg bucked out from beneath her trembling hips. She needed to move, needed to freaking touch him anywhere other than the crisply shaven hairs dusting the base of his hairline.

"Ty, please. I want to touch you. I can make you feel good, too. Let me take care of you first." At another time, she would have regretted the pathetic tone of her plea or that she even begged at all, but there was no earthly way this man would let her do anything but exist in the here and now. "Please, Ty. I don't need—"

His scorching hand didn't dip below the waistband of her jeans. It *dove*.

"Your pleasure is my responsibility. End of fucking story."

With a thrilling nibble against her breast she could only assume he added for emphasis, pulsing tendrils of electricity raced to her core, to the very apex where his expert fingers found her tight bundle of nerves ready and waiting. His skilled touch, slick with her arousal, feathered over every drenched part of her in a teasing caress that drove her mad with wicked confusion. Each triggered breath that caught in her throat was chased by a corresponding swipe across her sex. He was a dancer, a master choreographer, one who could only break the steps because he'd mastered them.

Oh, and he'd mastered them.

"Ty, I can't— I think—"

"Just let go, Dee. I've got you. Just let go."

Another finger joined the dance and explored farther, lower, teasing her quivering channel open with slow insistent presses, until she couldn't help but ease her thighs open. The slick slide of his hand over the heat of her never lost its rhythm but was only bolstered by the addition of more. It was entirely too much and entirely not enough.

Drea whipped her head from side to side against the onslaught of his masterful orchestrations. No man had any right to touch a woman the way he did, for how would she survive? How did he possibly expect her to breathe and blink and bumble her way through such pleasurable torture when she could hardly keep a thought in her mind, let alone on her lover?

When the firm pressure of his touch intensified, so did the curling teases inside her. A rocking wave sent a jolt through her body, singing every inch of her skin with soul-searing fire. Soft desperate spasms pummeled her core, shooting unfathomable pleasure through the very lifeblood in her veins. On top of her,

Ty growled his approval, and the skin beneath her tattoo burned so hot, she nearly cried out for a different reason.

With nowhere to escape and no desire to do so, she let the ripple of bliss pulse through her. When her heart reached its crescendo and her wrist had slowed its pulsing pain to a heated whisper, she sagged against the only shoulders capable of truly supporting her.

Sweat misted over her exhausted eyelids. Soft rhythmic tugs at her wrists pulled her eyes the rest of the way closed. Silk fell away on a whisper, but she never removed her hands from around Ty's neck.

How could she? Surely, there was no possible way she could disconnect herself after some soul-deep part of her had been so irrevocably altered. That was the only explanation, the only feasible reason for why the cage around her heart had been cracked open just wide enough to fit a Ty-sized ball of hope.

With no small amount of strength, Drea finally leaned back, emboldened to voice her shattering realization. Instead, she stared into eyes not dappled with a muted gray but flashing bright with a raging storm of silver.

"What the hell is that?" Drea shrank back farther into her seat and tried to curl her legs up to her body, but instead, she succeeded in kneeing two out of the three precious commodities between Chrome's legs.

Pain lanced through his loins, only narrowly missing his already painful erection. He jerked his head back on a choked cry and threw himself off her. When his knees hit the carpet, every conceivable curse in English or otherwise landed with them. Hunched over in agony, he sucked in more oxygen than his cells could probably hold in one sitting and willed the precious stuff to repair his other precious stuff.

It didn't matter how long a male existed. Some things just fucking hurt and warranted taking a goddamn moment to breathe through the trauma. Only when he was sure his walk wouldn't be noticeably affected did he rise.

One look at Drea's horror-stricken face had him reconsidering.

She sprinted forward, shucking off the rest of the silk scarf with her hands outstretched before her. "I am *so* sorry! I didn't mean to do that. Well, who *does* mean to do that, you know?

Obviously, it was an accident, but also obviously, I doubt it makes a difference." Regret softened her eyes, and she grimaced. "I was just so shocked. How did you do that?"

He gritted his teeth through the pain. "Wrong place at the wrong time—"

"No, not that!" Exasperation turned to annoyance as she swatted his chest. "I mean, how did your eyes change color? One minute they were their usual gray, and the next . . ." Words seemed to fail her as she looked around for something to aid in her explanation. When her eyes caught on the mirror, she ran to it and extended her arms out in her best game show host presentation. "They looked like that! A mirror. Only, maybe more like one of those moving funhouse mirrors at carnivals. Like molten silver or something. I've never seen contacts do that." Then her head levered to the side. "Come to think of it, you've never told me whether you even wear contacts. I never thought to ask." She leveled him with an expectant look. "Do you? Wear contacts, that is?"

Chrome stepped closer to the mirror, silently working through every internal system. His metallic power hovered at the ready like any other sense or ability, neither present nor dormant. Then he discreetly rolled his shoulders. When no weight from his wings tugged at his scapulas, he mentally checked that A-OK box. While his wings could be called on at will and appear translucent during their transition, their manifestation never impacted his eyes. His body could be flesh or chromium, and his wings functioned just the same. A sickening dread sank in his gut.

That left his angel fire.

The low lanterns cast the sitting room in only slightly brighter hues of purple and sun-kissed orange than the rest of the restaurant. It was dim but not so dim that one couldn't notice a trick of the light if they had been paying attention.

And as always with his Drea, she'd been paying fucking attention.

The reflection that stared back at him wasn't anything to write home about, but neither did it present anything out of the ordinary as far as he could tell. His eyes boasted their usual cinder block gray and were just as tired, if not more so.

What *was* different wasn't anything Drea could see.

Beneath his breastbone burned the source of his power. The writhing kernel of energy that housed his angel fire should have been dormant and calm, though always at the ready should he need it. Instead, his power's spark churned through him like a raging river held in check by a mighty dam. Every time his fire crashed against the walls of his body, the flames recoiled at the obstruction.

Chrome pulled his gaze away from the mirror and discreetly curled his fingers toward his palm, creating a private cocoon away from Drea's viewpoint. With the flick of a thought, electric blue angel fire bloomed from his fingertips. The muted violets of the room added the appropriate amount of shadow and tint to mask the small display of power.

He tensed, and the rest of his hope froze as well.

A trickle. That was all he'd managed to produce. The flames dancing on his fingertips were no brighter than a dying coal, and even that small amount of energy still drained his fire reserve.

How was this possible? How the hell could his power roil so violently within, yet such a small sliver be let free? It was there, all of it, and yet . . . not. As if it was being blocked by a dam.

Chrome swallowed back his confusion and schooled his features against the worry threatening to show. He snuffed his fire with a casual flick of his wrist, assimilating the gesture into a chin rub.

"Yeah, it's my contacts. Probably got a funky batch this month." He gently turned Drea from his reflection and ushered her toward the door but not before tugging her clothing back into place—a fact she'd adorably overlooked. "I'll follow you out in a bit." Then he swept a kiss onto the crown of her head and urged her to rejoin the others.

Drea trotted toward the door, pausing briefly to peg him with her hesitant regard. Those violet eyes didn't miss a beat, and for a moment, he feared she wouldn't leave it alone and would start poking at things she shouldn't be busting open. Instead, resignation softened the curiosity in her inquisitive gaze, releasing some of the starch from her shoulders. She bit back whatever thoughts she had on his bullshit explanation, sparing him the need to lie to her further, and walked down the hall.

Thank fuck.

Once he'd given her a more than generous grace period, he did his own walk of anything but shame and grabbed his seat by her side at the table.

"Where did Iron and Bronze go?" Drea asked before tucking into her food. One particularly ravenous bite of marinated eggplant drew a sumptuous moan from her lips, and damn if those sinful vibrations didn't make a beeline straight to his cock. He shifted against the cushion and masked the action by grabbing the nearest cup and drinking deeply. Leave it to that woman to inadvertently ensure all his systems were still operational, even the internal ones.

Titan passed a basket of fresh pita to Tammy. "They had to head out a bit early to check on something."

"Oh, are they house-sitting?"

A knowing look passed between the angels before Titan's trim beard curled around his charming smile. "Something like that."

Axtar would need to be looked in on soon, and wasn't that the other giant fucking nightmare he needed to figure out as well? Chrome dragged a hand over his tired face, wincing at the stubble he'd let get a little too stubbly. He quickly regarded Drea, assessing for any redness or abrasions blooming across her delicate skin. Nothing stood out immediately, but the lighting was shit for that kind of perusal.

And Drea was just the kind of person to keep any discomfort like that to herself.

Just as he was making a mental note to do a more thorough examination of the woman, a soft touch rocked his arm. Tungsten's pewter gaze pegged him with concern, the same concern etched across his brothers' faces. The girls had relocated to the far end of the table and were readily absorbed in conversation, so Tung took advantage of the opportunity and dipped his head low.

"Something is different about you. Do you feel all right?"

Across from Chrome, Brass's amber eyes briefly flashed the ochre of his angel fire, burnishing his forelock with shades of sunburnt gold. "I sense your fire, but its flow is off somehow."

"I don't know," Chrome hissed in frustration. "I feel it. Holy fucking hell, do I feel it. But I can't access it, not fully."

"How so?" Steel inquired with careful regard.

"It's there, stronger than ever, but when I call on it, only scraps seem to surface. I've never had this happen before." Chrome scanned his memories, searching for the words to best describe the strange phenomenon. "It reminds me of what it was like accessing my full fire in the Empyrean. It's painful and blinding and brilliant and so much more powerful than the mountains' minerals can provide me each night. But it's just not budging. It's like my full power is—"

"Trapped." Titan whispered his suspicion, his gaze fixed on Rose. One by one, the angels drew their attention to the women. Laughing smiles and rousing toasts bled through the restaurant on a current of contentment.

Chrome didn't take his eyes from Drea, who lifted a golden cup the same color as her hair high in affirmation of whatever feminine declaration they'd just agreed to. All he could see was that black slick of tattooed seaweed smudging the space on her wrist where one's soul bond mark would appear.

His mark. The one connection that would restore his full power. The one hope he never voiced and only begged for when the nights got so lonely even his memories of her couldn't chase the chill away.

But he'd touched her skin, tasted her mouth and even other secret parts of her once upon a lifetime. No bond had ever revealed itself.

He swallowed down his agony and ripped his gaze away while his fire raged at the walls of a locked cage, no more than a trickle escaping through the grates.

Chrome dropped his head into his hands. In his small cocoon of darkness, he let his desperation consume his features.

He truly was trapped.

DREA STUFFED the ruffled clump of once-blue fabric into her suitcase. In the before times, it had been a sundress purchased with the hopes of poolside getaways and too many margaritas. Recently, however, its vibrant azure had faded to an anemic periwinkle after one too many accidental tumbles with the lighter loads. A shame, considering she'd only ever worn the thing three times: the first time was the day she purchased it because she was feeling cute, the second time on a company picnic some three years ago, and the last time was that one instance she'd been invited to a baby shower by a neighbor who wound up moving away a year and a half ago.

Now, her finest dress was no better than a jumbled mass of barely there fibers . . . and that made up the sum total of what she'd hoped would impress Malcolm on his surprise weekend escape. By tomorrow afternoon, she needed to be packed and prepared, though prepared for what, she wasn't entirely sure.

Molly joined Drea at the foot of the bed. Peering into the tiny suitcase with a sympathetic deportment, her friend gingerly plucked the balled-up sundress and took it over to her steamer station—because, of course, Molly would have a steamer station.

"Where is he taking you again? Rhode Island?"

"No, just Concord. About an hour and a half south of here. He booked a room at a hotel for the weekend."

"Very nice," Molly crooned, working the steam in hard around the dress's hemline.

Drea stared at the rest of the items she'd yet to cram into her bag. It was all so normal, so basic. T-shirts, shorts, and a toothbrush seemed about as significant to her as garbage pickup day would be to a single-family homeowner. How the hell was she supposed to follow through with her misguided *yes* to Malcolm after the mind-blowing *oh, hell yes* Ty had coaxed from her?

It had only been a matter of hours, and still, she couldn't get that damn bathroom out of her mind. Or, more specifically, what she'd done in said bathroom. And with whom.

When he dropped her home, it'd been *her* mouth that crept toward him for a parting kiss. When he insisted on walking her upstairs, it'd been *her* hand that searched for his strength instead of the banister. And when she told Ty about the weekend she'd agreed to with Malcolm, it'd been *her* shame that flooded her skin with hives and caused Ty to excuse himself from her company with all the polite indifference of a second cousin once removed.

Drea sagged on top of her bed, not even caring whether her long limbs messed up Molly's pristinely folded piles.

"Oh boy, something's eating you."

Of all the words Molly could have chosen, those had to be the absolute worst.

Because they called to mind a certain barbaric brainiac with a mouth that had feasted on hers like a death row inmate would attack their last meal. She'd been devoured before, as eager lovers tend to be, but never *savored*. Never been lapped at with a hunger so desperate it was infectious. Ty had been everywhere at once, in her mind, on her mouth, across her skin, and she'd not returned one iota of pleasure. The thought was utterly mortifying. What did he think of her? Malcolm always insisted on things being equal in the bedroom, even if she wasn't particularly in the mood. It was fair. It was right.

Right?

With Ty, not only had the rulebook been rewritten but thrown out entirely. She'd *tried* to reciprocate, tried to as soon as she saw where things were heading. His response had been so feral, so shockingly intoxicating that any of her remaining synapses had stalled out and gone on strike.

Your pleasure is my responsibility. End of fucking story.

But it wasn't the end of the story, was it? She was a cheater. A dishonest woman who volleyed between men like favorite handbags, apparently, and here she was going at it again.

"Molly, I'm such a freaking coward." A sharp tremor cut off the last word, and Drea threw her arm over her eyes to shield herself from the judgment in her best friend's inevitable glare. Molly was nothing if not a rule follower.

The mattress dipped, and Drea braced for the castigation she'd been too chickenshit to adequately give herself. The sigh that floated through the room dripped with disapproval.

Crap. She couldn't handle this. She was not woman enough to hear the words that needed hearing.

Stupid stupid stupid . . .

A small hand rested on her leg and gave it a firm shake. "Just give me a heads-up before you break it off with Malcolm, okay? If I don't have to buy the extra meat for burger night, I'd rather save the money." Then a sudden wistfulness warmed her friend's voice. "Not going to lie, though, I will miss his wine selection. Man can't toss a salad or scrub a pot worth a damn, but he knows his reds."

Wait. What?

Drea hinged up on the mattress, and Molly quickly scooped her neatly folded piles out of the disaster zone. "What are you talking about?"

Molly stared at her as if Drea had just sprouted a third eye. "What are *you* talking about? You can't sit there and honestly expect me to believe Ty hasn't convinced you it's okay to have second thoughts."

Her words would have stung if they hadn't been so fucking accurate.

"How did you—"

"Oh, please." Molly waved away the question with a pair of Drea's sleep shorts. "The man *picked you up from the hospital.* After you were almost killed, Drea." Then she leveled a look that could melt glass. "And I'm still fucking pissed I wasn't your emergency contact, but I'm not one to kick a woman when she's down. Don't think you're getting out of that one, though." She flicked a vengeful finger at Drea, promising retribution.

Drea tried to digest Molly's reaction, but her friend was far from finished.

"*Why* did Ty pick you up? Because Malcolm didn't. Couldn't. Doesn't freaking matter, really. When you care about someone, you show up. Period."

Drea sat there, mind whirling over what her friend was saying. "But you like Malcolm," she hedged.

"Oh, honey." Molly scooted next to Drea and wrapped a tender arm around her shoulders. "I like *you*. Malcolm was fine as long as you were happy, but . . ." An uncomfortable sadness tightened her best friend's smooth features. "You're a different person around Ty."

"How so?"

"Well, you're happy, for starters. The only time I've seen you smile like that around Malcolm is out of courtesy. The fool still doesn't know your favorite flower."

"It's only been three months. We're still getting to know each other." Though why Drea felt the need to defend the man, she wasn't sure.

Molly cast her a droll look. "And how long have you known Ty? Three *days?*"

"Six," Drea mumbled. "But point taken."

"No, the point is, what are you doing?" The severity of the question nearly took Drea back down to the mattress. "Do you really want to go away with Malcolm? And answer yourself honestly, for once in your life. What do *you* want?"

Molly looked at her expectantly, as if Drea could possibly pull an answer to such a monumental question out of her head without days to analyze every possible outcome. How much pain she'd cause versus how much reward she stood to gain, if any at all.

"You're thinking too much, Drea. Just answer the question."

Thinking. That had always been her problem, hadn't it? When her wheels were turning, she was a happy little hamster with a purpose and a passion. When the wheel suddenly stopped and she found herself spinning out of control with no equilibrium to steady her, where did all that thinking get her?

With Ty, she'd never had to think, at least not without his own take on things inspiring her curiosity. When her mind took her down a rabbit hole, he was there digging right along with her. A partner in not just analysis but sensation as well. His graceful body and powerful prowess taught her how to *feel*, how to live and laugh and find joy in things that had nothing to do with approval or acquisitions.

With Malcolm, she'd somehow become just another acquisition, a chip on the board to make a pretty spread.

And it had only required multiple near-death experiences to fully understand that.

"I need to make a phone call." Drea squeezed her friend back and leaped from the bed.

"Who are you breaking the news to first?"

Drea looked back at her friend and gave one fortifying nod. "Myself."

CHAPTER 26

The light streaming onto the sidewalk from inside Mills Realty didn't match the glowing opulence that was downtown Aurora. On a Thursday evening in July, food trucks peddling everything from Not Your Madre's Tacos to Bitchin' Plant-Based Barbecue lined the main thoroughfare. Twinkle lights were strung from streetlight to streetlight, creating a glittering pergola under which pedestrians walked and gathered. In front of the library, perched beneath the building's gazebo, a cover band of adorable retirees was taking requests from lawn-chair listeners—provided those requests included the Beach Boys, the Eagles, or, strangely, very specific Michael McDonald tracks.

It was the perfect backdrop to a lively summer night when couples would take off from work the next day to be with each other, and families would let their children stay up late to get the *good* ice cream at Dharma's Dairy Maid.

It was also apparently the perfect backdrop for a breakup.

Drea walked into Malcolm's real estate office and immediately missed the soft glow of the string lights outside. Though his base of operations was decked out in tasteful workplace furniture, with the obligatory potted plants and guest refreshment station, it was also equipped with one not-so-very tasteful feature: obnoxious fluorescent lighting.

The same lighting used to interrogate the guilty until proven innocent. Or maybe just the guilty in general, which was oh so freaking appropriate.

The soft chime on the door drew Malcolm from his cubicle in the back of the office space. At nine o'clock, he was the only one still there. Good. That was good. She didn't need any witnesses. Or a sentencing jury.

"Babe! What are you doing here?" Malcolm hurried over and swept her into a big hug. He wore his light gray linen suit, this time with a periwinkle tie and the same brown shoes from yesterday. His standard Thursday outfit.

Drea accepted his affection but couldn't bring herself to lean into it. Instead, she squeezed him gently and feigned interest in a particular fern with leaves stretching toward the window, as if it wanted to get the hell out of there too. She brushed her fingers along its fronds in silent solidarity.

"I . . . I wanted to talk to you before tomorrow." She cringed, wondering when her voice had gotten so small.

"Well, you caught me at a good time. I'm just wrapping up. Trying to get everything in order for these listings so that tomorrow, it's just you and me." He clapped his hands together, and the smile that lit his face would have been genuine if not for his overeager excitement. For the first time, it made her question the true intentions behind their trip. Had all his hard work and late nights really been for her, for them, or was there something else?

Didn't matter. It wouldn't involve her anyway.

"Malcolm, I have something I want to tell you, and I'd appreciate it if you'd let me get what I need to say out before you respond."

He pulled a face that wouldn't be out of place in a conversation with a five-year-old who'd just declared they were running for president. "Whoa, sound's serious. I hope you're not getting second thoughts about the trip. The hotel's great. You're going to love it. Indoor pool, heated outdoor pool, spa, even on-site ax throwing."

Drea steeled herself and forced the words she'd practiced two dozen times on the cab ride over to get in line and follow through. "Yes, this is serious. Please."

She gestured toward one of the chairs in the waiting room, while she took the one across from it. *Please let these chair legs be sturdy enough to withstand the bomb I'm about to drop. Not forever. Just long enough for me to get clear of the blast zone.*

Malcolm cocked a curious brow at the request but said nothing as he took his seat. With his charming smile, which had melted her resolve the first day she'd met him but now struck an erratic rhythm behind her ribs, he nodded his encouragement. "I'm all ears. Let's hear it."

Drea took one final fortifying breath, then let the words tumble free. "I don't want to go on the trip tomorrow."

Shock danced across his eyes, but he quickly recovered, replacing it with cool, practiced ambivalence. "Okay, where do you want to go instead?"

"No, you don't understand. I don't want to go on any trip . . . with you." A stony suspicion flitted over his face, so she stormed ahead before she lost her nerve. "I've been doing a lot of thinking lately, and I've come to realize that I'm heading toward a different place than I was when we first met."

Stunned silence slammed against her words, unsettling her determination. Malcolm was never quiet, ever. Her momentum faltered, falling mercy to his stillness.

When he finally spoke, the timbre of his voice contained an unfamiliar chill. "You're not heading toward a different place, Drea."

"Please, let me—"

"You're heading nowhere."

Icy shock froze the words in her throat. *What?*

And then he stood, yanking at the lapels of his fine suit as if dusting off a victory. "You think I didn't know?"

"Kn-know what?"

"Oh, please. You don't get to come into my place of business, bat your eyelashes, and fuck me over the way you fucked him."

Her thoughts stalled out as she tried to process his words. No. No no no . . . this was all wrong. "Malcolm, that's not—"

"True? Sure, let's talk about the truth, while we're on the subject." Malcolm pulled his phone from his pocket and pulled up a photo. "What was his name? Trey? Troy?"

Drea could hardly pull enough air into her quivering lungs as she stared at a picture of Ty leaving her apartment the day of her accident. His strong profile was turned toward the parking lot after he'd just left her front door. Another swipe and the back of Ty's head filled the screen while he held his truck door open for her. She'd been wearing her work clothes. That was the morning Ty had taken her to the lab . . .

Drea surged to her feet. "You were *spying* on me?"

Malcolm pocketed his phone and scoffed. "Not spying, waiting. I was waiting for *you*. Jesus fucking Christ, Drea, I was trying to get back to you! And every time I managed to sneak away from work, to convince a buyer to give me an hour before I got back to them on their offer, I did it for you, to get back to *you!*" Crimson crept into Malcolm's sculpted cheeks. "Imagine my surprise to find that asshole there at every fucking turn. I never even had a chance. Each time I pulled into your apartment complex, I couldn't even park my car before he was sauntering around your building," he spat.

"Did you seriously take those photos?" Indignation fueled her accusation. "Ty was only there because you broke your promise! You *promised* to pick me up from the hospital, and you never came. I almost *died*, Malcolm! And after, when I still needed to work and a way to get there, did you even bother answering your phone? No. Ty offered to drive me, and I accepted, because, again, where were you? Where was the truth of your words when it came to checking on someone you supposedly care for?"

"I was working *for you*! Busting my ass to provide *for you*!"

"I didn't need you to provide for me. I needed you to *be* there for me!"

Their vile statements were little more than a children's shouting match at that point, until his words from earlier broke through the haze of her rage. "What did you mean when you said I was heading nowhere?"

Malcolm shirked off his blazer, tossed it over the nearest cubicle wall, and pinched the bridge of his nose. "I meant the truth. You were never going to go anywhere, at least not professionally. I was the first man you'd dated longer than a month, at a time when you'd just started your fifth job in four years."

Drea swallowed around ice shards, frozen over what he'd say next.

"You were a sure thing. A gorgeous lab tech with no real career aspirations, coupled with a friend who was rarely around at night. Wrap that all into a heap of an apartment in a shitty area you never had any intention of leaving, and it's no surprise I looked good by comparison. It didn't matter that my sales were crap when we first met. My colleagues loved you, you were more than willing to accompany me to any work function, and you looked great on my arm. *We* looked great together, and coming from a guy who'd always been too charismatic for most women and not charismatic enough for most employers, it was the win I needed." Malcolm pressed his lips together and tossed her his well-honed closing sales expression. "I needed someone who would add the luster I lacked but who also wouldn't dull my shine. You were perfect." His voice dropped low, and his lip lifted in disgust. "Until you weren't."

Hot tears pricked the corners of her eyes, but over her dead body would she let them fall. Her throat trembled to hold back the sob pressing against her windpipe, struggling to break free. Every happy memory, soft smile, or tender touch played like a greatest hits reel of her nightmares. Gifts she'd held precious, moments she'd laugh about, even the intimate times that left her smiling and giddy—fucking horrors of another person's design.

She'd been soiled. Used.

Broken.

"We're done." Drea threw as much hatred into her voice as her chest would allow without her body crumpling to the floor. Before he could answer, she turned on her heel and ran out the door.

She didn't stop.

She ran down the street, dodging bikers and dogs and kids with too-big ice cream cones. She ran until the streetlights faded into the reflective paint on the bike trails. She ran until roads became sparsely populated parking lots and her hair stuck to the tears that hadn't stopped flowing.

When she finally slowed enough to plop her ass down on a park bench, her hands did the work her mind couldn't. Her phone was in her hand a moment later. Once the text message was hurled into the universe, she wondered briefly if it would even come back. Had she sent her heart's most broken plea on a boomerang that would simply return to her in the same shattered pieces? Or would her words just sink into the ether because, yet again, she thought too much and cared too deeply?

She'd had an economics professor once who preached about not building infrastructure around a commodity the market didn't want. Was that what had happened? Was she the commodity girlfriend waiting for Malcolm's infrastructure that he'd never had an interest in providing?

A faint ping sounded behind her, where one side of the municipal park jutted up against the parking lot. When she squinted at the shrubs outlining the walking trail, a large figure stepped out of the foliage holding his phone. The deep grooves of his features were hardened by the shadows dancing beneath the moon's glow. Large shoulders rose and fell with breaths as steady as the sun and just as vital.

Then his eyes, stormy gray beneath the moon, found hers and locked on tight.

Ty.

CHAPTER 27

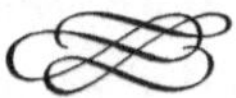

Chrome hadn't intended to make himself known to Drea. He never did. But he couldn't stand in the shadows with the words from her text burning through his palm and *not* go to her.

I need you. Please.

That final word nearly broke him. *Please.* The anguish in her plea threatened to burst the dam bottling his fire.

Chrome beat feet across the short stretch of grass between them, which may as well have been a canyon-wide chasm. One step seemed to take an hour. Two a lifetime. Powerful legs pumped in time with his heart, fueled by a raging impatience to see her, touch her.

Taste her.

They met in a clash of arms and mouths. Wild abandon fueled eager and anxious limbs. Warm wetness absorbed into his cheeks as she kissed him. *Tears.* When he tried to pull back, she only clung to him more tightly. The tiny crescents of her nails dug into his sides with an insistent urgency he'd not seen from her. Passion, yes. Hunger, yes. Never pain. Never with a need so frantic, she grasped at him with desperation instead of desire.

Chrome gentled his kiss with soothing strokes, letting her consume any and all of him. Hell, she already had. He'd flay his chest open with all the flourish of a sommelier sabering a champagne bottle if it would ease her search. Whatever she wanted of him, she could have. Gladly, with seconds.

When she surged on her toes to claim more of him, her slight weight dangled from around his neck. Her usual strength had fled along with her words.

"Drea." He uncoiled her arms and placed them securely at his sides instead. "Talk to me."

Hysteria pitched her usual husky voice into a higher register. "How are you here? I texted you, but I didn't think you'd be in the park."

Now it was his turn to temper his desperation. How much of the truth should he—could he—tell her?

Enough of it, he decided.

He dragged his hands down her back, massaging soothing strokes along her spine. "I'm always here. You need me, I'm here."

Her brow creased in adorable confusion before she swiped her sleeve across her nose. "That's not a thing."

"It is where you're concerned." Summer heat thickened the air between them, causing wisps of hair to escape her braid, reminding him how tenuous her world had become. How dangerous her life was with him in it. The realization urged more of his truths forward, whether or not he was ready for her to know them. "You remember when I asked my brothers to watch your apartment that night?"

She nodded slightly.

He cleared the gathering emotion from his throat. "I wasn't prepared to take the risk that something might happen to you, especially after the lab. So, yeah, I've been around."

Chrome waited for her to connect the dots and braced himself for the reproachful glare he was all too used to seeing.

Instead, Drea closed her eyes and dropped her forehead against his chest. "Thank you."

He blanched at the gratitude, unused to hearing it. "No need." Damn, did he like her there, though, with her head so close to his heart and her breaths warming his chest through his shirt.

"Yes, need." She reared back to look at him as, yup, those dots connected real quick. "Then I suppose you know where I was tonight."

Chrome bit back his temper. "Yeah."

"Did you . . . did you hear what happened?" She pinned him with a look of bleak sadness that did little to hide her mortification.

Like she had a goddamn fucking thing to be mortified about.

He pulled her tighter, curling his fingers into the hair at her nape so his hands wouldn't snatch up the gun in his ankle holster instead. "Piece of shit doesn't deserve the economy-brand cotton covering his bony ass, let alone a woman like you. Never did." Those were quite literally the nicest words he could say about the prick without cursing . . . Wait, had he cursed? Ah, fuck it.

Regardless, he'd deal with that bastard later. Slowly.

Drea scoffed. "A woman like me."

The derision in her tone made him see red and sparked the challenge in his blood. "Yes, a woman like you. A woman who's so fearless and selfless you'd put others' basic securities before your own, because you know that safety isn't a right but a privilege. A woman whose intelligence is so vast that those in power put you in a box of their choosing because they know that *when*, not *if*, you break free, they'd never be able to keep up." Chrome's mind spun so fast with admiration, his mouth worked double time just to make sure she heard it all. "A woman so breathtakingly beautiful, she'd force the sun to look away." He crooked a finger under her chin and brushed a tender kiss across salt-smeared lips. "A woman who, when she comes alive under the right touch, can white out the night sky with the force of her brilliance." He touched his forehead to hers and, in a revenant whisper against her heated skin, said, "I wish I could show you . . . Fuck . . . Let me show you how I see you, Dee. Just for one night."

He was done. Toast. He'd become completely unraveled with each confession she pulled out of him. His thoughts were as insistent and harried as the spontaneous passion of their first night together in another time, another place. Every admission was both an order and a plea. These private, precious truths he *must* make her know about herself mingled with the uncertainty of what would happen if she never truly believed them.

Because she didn't remember the things he did, only the lies the mortal realm had fed her.

As the silence ticked on, so did Chrome's anguish. All the while, she remained still in his arms, staring at him blankly. He had no right to press her, to shower her with his own truths when context evaded her beautiful mind.

But he would try. Mages preserve him, he would fucking try, until she either believed him or berated him. He'd deal with either but die by one.

His lips moved, poised to say just that, when one hushed word robbed him of his remaining breath and shackled him to his fate.

"Yes."

<hr>

THEY HADN'T TOUCHED AGAIN since their embrace in the park, but Chrome still felt every one of Drea's movements with a hyperawareness reserved for a predator.

Or an intelligence master.

The access card swiped across the hotel room's keypad with quick efficiency. Before he could pull on the door handle, Drea's slim hand was already there, levering it down and welcoming them in.

She moved like morning mist over a meadow, disturbing everything and nothing all at once. When her elegant finger slid along the red velvet armchair in the suite's living room, the fabric depressed under her touch before bouncing back as if it had never been unsettled. That particular chair saw its twin right next to it. Both were angled toward the gas fireplace, because mortals, like any prey animal, were usually more comfortable if they didn't have to look each other in the eye.

"You didn't have to do this." Drea stood at the entrance to the bedroom. On the carpet next to the small dinette set sat her sandals, already toed off and turned in for the night.

It was on the tip of his tongue to argue, but he'd been stunned into silence by the sheer presence of her.

And that she'd said yes.

The sconces on either side of the bedroom's doorframe were some of those flameless candle contraptions with lifelike flickering flames. The resulting light cast a shimmering golden curtain over Drea's hair, turning her honeyed tresses into a waterfall of opulent starlight, even secured back in her usual braid. The warm light teased her ivory complexion, spotlighting all her features in a sun-kissed glow and turning her violet eyes the richest shade of mocha in contrast.

It was the ultimate map of temptation. Chrome hungered to trace that tantalizing spotlight with his tongue, bestowing his devotion on every one of those delicate heavenly features. Her rounded cheekbones, the sharp curve of her jaw, the bow of her lip, that mouth . . .

"Yes, I did," he grunted. "You were promised a fancy hotel stay. I can do fancy. No reason you shouldn't still be pampered."

The Wellington Inn and Suites in downtown Aurora may not offer ax throwing—because adventure tourism could fuck right the hell off—but it had corner-room suites with Jacuzzis, a top-notch staff that made it their business to mind their own business, and a bar that stocked Chrome's favorite brand of bourbon. Plus, when an immortal angel made his fortune mining and trading precious metals over the eternally long years, last-minute luxury was par for the course. For Drea, he'd clean out every ounce of valuable rock in New England with impunity just to lavish her with whatever she wanted.

Drea glided toward him, and he had to grip the chair to keep from pouncing and devouring her. "That's not what I meant."

She searched his face with such fine assessment. He didn't know what she was looking for, but the doubting part of him feared that if she looked too close, she'd find him lacking whatever discernible quality she sought.

Or, far worse, she'd remember who he'd been and how, despite the Sealing, he'd not been able to save her from his fate. He'd not been able to—

Warm lips smoothed over the stubble of his jaw. The kisses were featherlight at first, then increased in tenderness the farther down they traveled. Chrome waited, frozen, for the torturous caress to fall on his mouth, but as soon as her gentle ministrations landed at the corner of his lips, she'd pull away and start her path along the other side of his jaw. They were slow, supple kisses meant to speak volumes with their minimalism, and speak they did.

When her heated lips finally claimed his, it wasn't with the violent rush of passion that they were both used to. Instead, Drea's tender touches kissed away the doubt and fear that had clogged his soul ever since he'd caught a glimpse of her at that lab all those months ago.

"Dee . . ."

"Shhh." Her tall frame drew up flush against his, eliciting a shiver of need that had broken free from his tightly held regard. "I meant, you didn't have to be there for me all those times, but I'm *so* glad you were." She kissed his mouth again, then the cleft at the tip of his chin. "I'm glad you made sure I wouldn't get taken out by a four-inch block of granite curb." Another kiss, this time brushing against the tendon at the side of his neck. "I'm glad you caught one of my notebook pages and refused to give it back." A hint of tongue snaked under the collar of his T-shirt. "I'm glad you didn't mind cramming your knees beneath a too-small computer desk for far longer than we both knew your body could stand."

Shit, they were moving now. That sultry voice, all smoke and sex, was pulling him across the living room until those flickering non-candles anointed them in gold as they crossed the bedroom's threshold.

"I'm glad you followed me home that night, even though that maneuver would be high on the creep meter under normal circumstances."

"S'not creepy," he grumped breathlessly, trying to remember his own goddamn name as her fingers expertly tugged his shirt over his head. "It was . . . necessary."

Wait, what were they talking about again?

"*You're* necessary. To me, you are. To me, you're everything. You've always *been* everything, but I was so absorbed in the parts others wanted me to play that I never imagined what my own starring role would look like. What would Drea want? What would make her truly happy?" Her light chuckle filled the room, as if she was free to finally bask in her epiphany. Then she trained those mesmerizing eyes on him once more. "You. *You* are what I want, Ty. *You* are what makes me happy."

Ty.

It was the name he'd given her and was the first of many lies he'd told her since. He hadn't been that male in so long, and the foolishly arrogant part of him had hoped she'd somehow remember that. Hoped his cleverness would have been enough to jog her memory and the inexplicable circumstances surrounding her existence in the mortal realm. A key on the map that would lead to answers concerning Dee, Axtar, and, most recently, the blockade on his power.

It hadn't worked, though, and every time she used the name, it twisted the dagger further into his heart.

She claimed he was necessary. Would she still think so when she uncovered the truth? *If* she uncovered the truth?

One thing was for certain: *she* was his truth. Always had been, knee jabs to the groin and all. Her smile beat back the dark in a way that sunlight never could. Even as Drea, a mortal woman, instead of Dee, the messenger mage, she never stopped fighting.

Neither would he.

"Dee, I—"

And then she lowered herself to the bed.

CHAPTER 28

Control was a great heady thing, something Drea had sorely lacked of late. The alarming clarity hadn't had the intended effect, however. Instead of mourning how she'd been manipulated or wasted time drowning in her despair, she focused on an entirely different emotion.

Anger. Turned out, being played the fool was a pretty good motivator for demonstrating how un-fool-like one could be.

That was why she'd walked into that hotel room first and kicked off her shoes like she owned the place. She'd strutted right past the immaculate kitchenette with stainless steel induction whatevers and osmosis-filtered ice cube maker. Sure, they were nice and, before this week, were things she'd have paid more attention to because Malcolm would have paid more attention to them.

Now? Not so much.

Those things weren't essential. They weren't necessary. What *was* necessary was Ty, standing shirtless and stoic like a gargoyle over a castle. Though he towered above her with a masculinity that was more than present, there was no threat about him. If she asked him to drop the keycard on the table and

221

leave her there alone for the night, she had no doubt he'd do it . . . and probably even arrange room service for her before he left.

While her mind had been too busy drifting in the whirlwind around her, he'd always been there, ready to steady her if the ride got too rough. Ty had been the safety harness her heart had secretly clung to, even when her actions weren't entirely hers to control.

Well, they sure as hell were now, and her newfound take-charge spirit was going to start by going after the man she'd been too turned around to see clearly.

Drea kissed the hard ripples of his lower abdomen and smiled when his stomach muscles twitched against her lips.

"Drea . . ." Ty moaned her name, drawing out each syllable with an almost painful reverence.

"Hush. I'm working here."

Ty's head fell back on a sigh, then he offered up an exasperated "She's working" to the ceiling tiles with all the wonderment of a Catholic grandmother who swore she just saw Jesus in her toast.

"I want to take care of you, and I can't do that if you keep squirming. Now, stay still."

"Yes, ma'am." Right on cue, the corded tendons in his forearms perked to attention as he balled his hands into fists at his side. His quivering abdominals locked up tight against her teasing touch, pleasing her to no end.

Drea couldn't resist testing his strength, mental and physical, and traced a targeted path with her breath, blowing airy kisses across tawny skin. Each muscle responded in kind, jumping and flexing despite her order to stay still. The control was thrilling. She couldn't beat back her smile, even as she unfastened the tense denim holding back his turgid flesh. Before she let his jeans and underwear fall away altogether, she cupped him firmly. Ty hissed against the pressure, arching into her touch. That delectable tendon along his throat strained against his strength, and Drea nearly toppled over from her hungry fascination.

Ty was there, above her, before her, trusting her to take this next step.

As soon as the fabric fell away, so did her inhibitions. Any lingering kernels of doubt were shredded by desire. A carnal craving twisted her stomach, and her mouth fell upon him with eager wanting.

"Holy shit! Holy . . . Goddamn." Ty pitched forward but quickly corrected his stance. "It's so . . . Fuck."

Her thoughts exactly. Words like immense, marble, and carved batted around her mind, but they did little justice to the thickness she lapped at. Long, slow strokes of her tongue played across silken steel, eliciting tiny throbs between her legs. This act was a sacred and powerful one, because something other than possession passed through Ty's whimpers and moans. Oh, it was true: she was his as much as he was hers, but taking him on her tongue fueled a rush of emotion so powerful, she nearly came undone under its onslaught.

She *wanted* to taste him, to consume him so fully that there would be no difference between his essence and hers. Whatever unearthly power that radiated off his glorious form, she wanted that, as well. Couldn't imagine a future where he wasn't beside her, *inside* her.

He'd already captured her completely, so it was only fair to set her own traps as well.

His growl was her only warning before he pulled himself free. He hadn't even opened his eyes yet, but he'd found her shoulders by instinct and settled his weight there. Rattling breaths sawed out of his great sculpted chest, doing intriguing things to his pectorals. Restraint bunched his biceps into finely carved granite, though she couldn't determine whether it was to hold himself in check or prevent her from pouncing further.

Because pounce she definitely would.

But there was something more in the way he'd looked at her before she'd even touched him. Some overwhelming emotion he seemed to wrestle with. Strain thinned his lips, bulging his muscles more fully. His eyes had softened with something akin to tenderness. It wasn't the look of pain or remorse but genuine affection. For her.

He had chosen her, despite everything, proverbial warts and all.

Her throat closed around the intensity of it, and she quickly blinked away the emotion that threatened to burst through her skin.

While the weight of the world rested on her shoulders, literally, she reached behind her and undid her long braid. Once the tresses were free, she strategically draped them over the hands covering her. Ty's lower lip fell open, and the breath he sucked in summoned every goosebump on her skin. Then she slid back to the mattress in silent invitation.

His hands fell away, and his words left him in a pleading rush. "Are you sure? I need you to be absolutely sure."

Whatever massive bellows controlled the breadth of his chest evened out to a pace more sustainable with life. Healthy looked good on him, as did everything, a fact her overheated skin and clenching thighs chose to hammer home. Then that gunmetal gaze speared her with a look so feral, she could have sworn silver sparks swirled with his intentions.

Drea cast away her clothing until the only thing covering her was his heated regard.

Her wordless answer said it all as his knees hit the mattress.

THE BED CAUGHT Chrome's weight as well as his sanity. Good. Better something else be responsible for that part of him, because the naked goddess offering herself to him was born of his deepest fantasies.

There could be no other explanation, and thank the mages for it. The sight of her pert breasts hovering far too close, teasing him with a heavenly vision he'd no right to look upon, further cemented his downfall into madness. Which he gave absolutely zero fucks about.

His mouth fused against hers in a swift attack. Passion and pain flooded from his body in heart-wrenching torrents. If fate did play a part in their union, it was surely showing up for one last hurrah. Fine. He would take it, take all of it, as hard as she'd let him and as thoroughly as she needed.

His hands explored her body, familiarizing himself with every curve, dip, and secret hollow. There would be nothing unmapped, nothing uncharted. He needed enough of her to last him the rest of his days, however long that might be, knowing full well it'd never be enough.

Ferocious growls erupted from his heated kisses as he found her den of trimmed curls and the pleading nub of her arousal beneath. Tongues made way for moans, and then his skilled fingers got to work circling her clitoris with the exact pressure and stroke he needed. Not her need, but his. Every gasp of pleasure he ripped from her body was another keepsake he'd lock away to fortify his miserable existence when she was gone. He couldn't stay. That had already been determined, for how could he torment her, torment *himself* with living a life fabricated on half lies and lost memories? He wouldn't. She was not his soul bond. Nor would he let her go without giving her everything first.

Insistent gasps racked her body. Ty just worked harder, pumping and playing with her while her breasts heaved and her delicate ribs expanded with each hard-won breath.

She was a marvel no being could create again. Her beauty

was too ethereal, her heart too magnanimous for the rock of dirt she'd been relegated to because of him.

"I love the way you look when you're about to fall apart. It's the vision I hold to each night before—"

"Before you take yourself in hand?"

He stopped, stymied, then renewed his efforts with more vigor. "You fucking know it. Always."

The kiss was instinctual, vital, and demanding. Heat crept higher, skin scorched between them, and teeth scraped against slick lips. She cried out as her hands clutched the back of his head before dropping lower, where her nails scored his back in pleasurable pain. His cock bounced between them, and he growled through the rush of wetness her climax anointed his fingers with. It was everything he remembered and nothing he would ever forget. He'd tattoo her marks on his back and bottle up her flavor. It would never be enough. Never.

Chrome gritted his teeth through the gathering storm. Within, his angel fire roared its own furious release, crashing against the confines of its cage. Trapped power pummeled his body, warring with a growing arousal that yearned to scream its release in her, on her. His cock, hard as a pike and just as unyielding, lay painfully against her trembling thigh, but he bit the torment back down. He would *not* take what she wouldn't give.

Then her shaky hand gripped him. Firmly.

A hooded violet gaze that he'd imagined so many times in his dreams stared back at him. The sly smile tilting Drea's lips was different though, a tempting mix of one both replete and unfulfilled.

It happened so fast. First, he was on top of her, kissing away her tremors. Next, a long leg hauled over him, and with a sensuous twist of her hips, he was dumped flat on his back. The maneuver took him off guard, which happened all of never in a life as long-lived as his. A tight pulse around his cock had him yanking his head up until his chin touched his chest.

She never let him go.

And then she swept his weeping crown over her slick entrance. Chrome just lay there and watched, heart stuck in his throat as Drea slowly lowered herself down every inch of him. When their bodies were finally flush, Chrome threw his head back in the best kind of anguish.

He had been slayed, his body no better than a flying beast tossed on the rocks of a far-flung cliff. Perfection had claimed him in the form of a golden-haired mortal who'd stolen his soul before he'd known he possessed one.

His cock jerked within her, and the little minx tightened her intimate haven in response, squeezing him impossibly tighter. He grunted, and his balls drew up higher. Muscles clenched and hands fought for every last bit of softness she offered. They moved together, finding their rhythm among the waves. Generous hips slammed down on his thighs, wrenching a husky cry from her slender throat. God, he could listen to that forever. Set it as his ringtone, doorbell, didn't matter. There would never *not* be a time when the sound of her pleasure wouldn't be the sweetest thing to his ears. Never one to be outdone, he answered in kind, lifting her so far up his length that she nearly unsheathed him before he surged forward with pistoning force.

Passion, torture, loss, destiny, they all came together in a tumult of writhing bodies and frantic whimpers. Fire hammered against his body, threatening to shatter every ounce of strength into molecules on the winds.

"Ty . . . I can't . . . What's . . . What's happening?"

Desperation clawed out of him. He hinged his upper body off the bed and gripped her fiercely, clutching her gasping frame to him as they both screamed through their release. He battered her with the force of a sea gale, curling his hips in steady punishing thrusts—

Blue flames of angel fire exploded around the room, engulfing their cries of passion in an inferno of power.

Chrome tucked Drea to his chest and rolled, pitching their bodies onto the floor. His back cushioned their fall before he tumbled them along the carpet. The rapid movement flattened the flames around them low enough for him to regain control and call his fire back. Only once the heat had ebbed and he sensed no other fire within the room did he throw his legs out to anchor them.

Frantic, Chrome braced his weight on his elbows and looked down at the woman beneath him. "Drea! Drea, are you all right? Can you speak? Can you breathe?"

Her superheated skin rubbed against the coarse hairs on his chest. Her breasts stayed pressed against him for a beat, then fell, then rose again in even respirations.

His trembling hands brushed away the tangled hair from her eyes. "Drea, look at me. Please, baby. I need you to look at me."

Heavy lids fluttered open, revealing violet eyes lit with drowsy strain and . . . something he didn't recognize. Drea's gaze danced over his face. Her brows dropped low, and her bottom lip fell open. Startling suspicion warred with confusion as she took in his looming naked presence over her likewise naked body.

And then his world fell away.

A muffled cry broke free, followed by a gasp of shock. She scrambled backward, wildly reaching for the bed covers, and Chrome immediately hurled himself off her. Panic seized his lungs, reminding him of what he'd inexplicably unleashed on top of her. His power, his fire, his punishing pleasure.

"Drea, are you—"

"Sentinel?"

He froze, no longer aware of his nudity or the potential damage his fire may have caused. The weight of that single word glued his bare ass to the floor.

Had she just called him . . . ?

Once solidly wrapped in the comforter, Drea lowered her head in a slight bow. When she lifted her gaze again, Chrome realized what the foreign look in her eyes had been.

Not pain. Recognition.

"Sentinel Tyrus? Is it really you?"

CHAPTER 29

"Dee."

The name broke free from Chrome's lungs on a garbled cry. Everything about her was the same. That shimmering blonde hair his fingers itched to run through. The pointed brows and sleekly angled cheeks. Lush lips that still held the color of his kiss.

Her eyes. Scorching violet windows alive with brilliant renewed awareness.

Dee.

At some point, clothes had covered limbs numb with disbelief. He didn't trust his mouth to throw out anything other than the most basic of syllables, despite the myriad of questions and worries raking claws down his frontal lobe.

How did this happen? Why? What did she remember? Did she want him to leave?

"No." Her soft exclamation punched through his brain fog. "It's a lot. It's all just . . . a lot. But no, I don't want you to leave."

He bit back a curse at his verbal gaffe. "I'm sorry. I didn't mean to say that."

"Yes you did," she asserted. "I'm glad you did, because they're the same questions I have, though I think some of the answers may be floating to the surface. It's clear as mud, though."

She sat against the headboard, her denim-clad knees tucked tight to her chest in a hug of dubious reassurance. Her eyes hadn't stopped darting from side to side as she undoubtedly worked through a barrage of her own questions and apparently even sifted out some answers. He was just about to inquire further when she leveled him with a question of her own.

"Where are your wings?"

He stilled his pacing. *Wings.* He'd never shown Drea his wings, at least not intentionally, not without cleverly explaining them away as a fleeting figment. Dee, on the other hand, knew them well. Too fucking well. Which begged the question . . . just *who* was he speaking to now? Drea or Dee?

"Would you . . . like to see them?" A test—of her sanity or his.

"Yes. I've always found them . . . comforting." Her eyes shifted away, and he hated the embarrassment that lurked there. "That's probably a strange thing to say."

"It's not. Your heart's telling you something, you say it." His booted feet retreated from the edge of the bed before he could examine her reaction too closely. If even a small part of his body gave her comfort, he'd never deny her.

A flapping swipe sliced through the bedroom. Translucent wings solidified into solid sheets of chromium, stretching toward the opposing walls. Her startled gaze tracked his wingspan. For a brief moment, he thought he sensed admiration, not worry, in her regard. It was enough to make him forget—

A punch of power spiked through his limbs, snaking bursts of angel fire around his biceps and torso and expanding out along each flight feather. Drea's eyes widened. She sat up straighter against the headboard but never took her gaze from his glowing form.

Energy sprawled around his frame, pulling his metal free of its den within him. Liquid chromium molded over skin, hardening his body into living, breathing armor. The rush of power whirled through his mind, his muscles, his very core, writhing beneath the fire that had been inexplicably walled off from him.

Until now. It was all back, not just the reserved pool of his fire fed by the mountains each night, but the unlimited range of his celestial sorcery.

His power was back. All of it.

Chrome sucked in ragged gulps of air and clenched his muscles tight. Undiluted power roared through his veins, his metal, fueling his wings and burning away any remnants of restraint that had plagued him since he fell from the Empyrean.

With a final swallow, he sought that long-dormant control and called his fire back to him. It responded with perfect recall, like an old friend remembering the moves to a secret hand-shake. The flames extinguished, and his metal receded. Chromium wings remained, however, a proud and welcome weight tugging at his shoulders.

"Wow."

Drea's gentle whisper perked his wings to attention, despite their tucked state. Chrome had forgotten his audience, lost as he was in the ecstasy of having his full angel fire back.

"My power, it's—"

"Back?"

"Yes," he breathed out, baffled at her estimation of something it'd taken him embarrassingly long to realize. "How did you know?"

"I wonder whether it has anything to do with this."

Drea unhooked her slim arm from around her legs and held up her palm for inspection. He squinted, then tensed. Not her palm. Her *wrist*.

Chrome rushed to the bed and scooped up the offered limb. He cradled the thing like a newborn kitten and peered down in search of the dark ivy-like tattoo that had always been there . . . and nearly pitched himself off the bed.

The black seaweed was gone. In its place was a golden symbol about an inch in diameter. When he turned her wrist one way, it vanished, and when he turned it another and caught the light just so, it reappeared. Once he'd steadied her arm at the correct angle, the emblem revealed itself in its perfect Empyrean splendor.

His name, written in the celestial language, stared back at him. *Tyrus.* Immortalized forever on her delicate wrist.

The mark of the soul bond.

———

THERE WAS STILLNESS, and there was the frozen state of those whose lives were irrevocably changed. Chrome hovered in the latter camp as Drea—Dee . . . fuck, his *mate*—took her arm back. After examining the thing for long minutes, she let her arm fall free and began twirling her hair effortlessly into her customary braid.

The familiar appeasement behavior mobilized his masculine need to fix everything.

"Drea, what do you remember?" He was as grown a male as they came, but he wasn't above swiping at the tear that had sprung free when he'd seen his mark on her skin.

"Dre-ah . . . Drea . . ." Her silky voice tried on the syllables for size. "I like that name very much. I think, perhaps, it even suits me."

"Everything suits you."

She gifted him with a shaky smile. "You know, I still can't believe you're here. I . . . I never thought I'd see you again."

Chrome's patience meter bottomed the hell out, but because he wouldn't be a brute who barked orders to her, he did the only desperate act he could. He held out his hand and breathed in her sweet scent of freshwater and lilies. "I feel like I'm dying here, Dee. If I don't get some answers soon, I'm liable to combust. I live and die by intel, so if you have any inkling at all, I'd sure as shit appreciate the insight."

He hoped for warm fingers to clasp his own. A congenial offering of comfort between two sometimes lovers. Instead, strong hands, despite their size, lifted his knuckles to plush lips. He stilled as she laid a gentle kiss across his skin. Their breaths hitched in time with each other's, and Chrome couldn't help what he did next. His rough hand gripped the side of her face as he kissed her. It was a slow, languid play of lips that calmed his fire and reassured his beating heart that, yes, she was here, and she was his. When he pulled away, those amethyst eyes shone with a brilliance that made everything worth it: the night they'd shared, the fall, the loneliness, the lost memories, all of it. If this was what he'd known he'd come back to at the end, he'd have Eagle Scouted the hell out of that project and been the first one to sign up.

"Sentinel—"

"Chrome. Here, now, I'm Chrome."

"And I will be Drea, I think."

Their foreheads touched, and Chrome couldn't help but cradle her face in his long-empty palms. "But you're Dee as well?"

Her long-suffering sigh separated the two of them. Chrome settled back against the headboard, legs spread wide, and welcomed her into his embrace. Once he was abso-fucking-lutely certain she wasn't going anywhere, he did the hardest thing he'd ever had to do: shut the hell up and listen.

"I believe I'm both, if that's even possible. I have my own memories, of those in the Empyrean, of the worlds I traveled and the souls I saved, but I also have hers. Drea's, I mean."

"How is any of that possible? How are you here?"

Drea relaxed against his chest, settling his soul along with her. "Water."

He blinked. "Water," he parroted.

"What do you remember from our, um, night together in the Empyrean?"

"Every-fucking-thing," he ground out.

She chuckled softly, and he was damn glad for it. He'd take that over spilled tears any day. "Do you remember Iona?" Drea asked.

Chrome settled his mind on the neglected parts of his most prominent memory. "The sea nymph?"

"Yes, from one of the water worlds. I helped her soul pass through the mist and brought her to heaven after the Veil fell."

"She was the one you scrambled to log in the repository that night." *That night.* Was it any wonder everything always came back to that night?

"Exactly. When I swore to her that I'd come back for her family when it was their time, she gifted me with that tattoo."

"The seaweed?"

Drea smiled warmly. "The sea nymphs have a gift for prophecy. Before her final ripple of life claimed her fully, she bestowed on me a promise. That, should I ever find myself in peril, water would save me." She passed a thumb over the space where her tattoo had been and where his soul bond mark now appeared. "The prophecy was made permanent the moment she passed on and the seaweed sigil was branded onto my skin."

Chrome listened to her story, doing his best to connect the still-too-far-apart dots. "I still don't understand how water saved you."

"I couldn't leave the rest of her family," she lamented. "Not all were ready to pass on and have their souls resting eternally, but some were. Some would choose to, given the threat that was coming."

That threat being Cyro's demonic armies and the certain death they all faced.

"I had to go back. To try and save who I could. I promised

Iona I would." Her voice shrank from the conviction of her words, and an unsettled memory offered an explanation.

"You left me in the middle of the night, in the messenger mages' dormitory. You did that so you could travel to the water worlds and rescue the others before—"

"Yes."

The implication of her choice was the throat punch he never saw coming. He banded his arms around her more tightly, his throat quivering around the raw emotion of the inevitable. "You were outside the gates when we enacted the Sealing."

"Yes," she whispered, ripping his heart to shreds. "I had just made it through the mist when the blast occurred. I had no idea what was going on until I felt it. I was struck so hard and screamed for hours, it seemed, and then I fell . . ." Her gaze was lost on a memory and only returned when he shuddered from his own hellish recollection. "I landed in what the mortals today call the Mariana Trench, I believe. At least, that's where I landed as best as I can figure. I'll never know for certain."

Chrome slashed his attention toward her. "The *Trench*! The deepest part of the fucking ocean? How the hell did you survive?"

While he panicked over a past he'd give his favorite firearm to change, Drea's features lit up with a serene smile common among lottery winners and those with insider trading information. She dropped a placating kiss to his harder-than-diamond jawline, and he tried—*tried*—not to lose his fucking mind.

"Water," she replied, as if that settled everything. "And I didn't know it was the Mariana Trench at the time."

"Water," he ground out.

"It was the prophecy." She beamed, which, despite her radiant joy, did all of nothing to lower his hackles. "I remember landing in the water, but I don't have any memories beyond that, not until I started living among the mortals when human habitation took me away from the water. I think that's what protected me, physically and mentally. The sea nymph's magic. It was only when I assimilated among the mortals that my memories of the Fall returned. Returned and then . . . faded." Confusion drew both their gazes to her wrist and the unanswered questions that rested there.

Unanswered because . . .

"Holy shit," Chrome breathed out. "Tung's reincarnation theory."

It was her turn to lift her brows. "Tung?"

"The prime sentinel."

Drea shot up. "He's here?"

"All the sentinels are. Once we enacted the Sealing, we were cast out just like you. Listen." He grabbed her shoulders and, for the first time since, well, a really long fucking time, he smiled. Like, teeth and all. It took a monumental amount of restraint to tamp down his excitement, but he managed and scurried his story back to the beginning. "The gates of heaven are sealed. All souls are barred entry until Cyro's armies are defeated and the sparks of the Eternal Flame that landed in this realm can be returned to the Empyrean. Since the Sealing, it is the prime sentinel's belief that the souls of the mortals who have passed on since are reborn into other mortals because they can't ascend. What if you, dearest Drea, living among the mortals as you have been, with no memories to speak of beyond the ones immediately available to you, have been reincarnated as well, repeatedly, since you fell, with no way to break the cycle?"

Drea blinked. Her fingers toyed with the end of her braid as her mind turned over all they'd learned, all that was finally clicking into place, albeit with rusty gears and stripped screws.

"And what if *this*," Chrome said, lifting her wrist between them, "blew all of that out of the fucking water, literally?"

"I-I don't understand. This mark—"

"It's the mark of the soul bond." Then he tempered his voice. "Do you know what that is?"

Slowly, Drea shook her head, and the light that had returned to Chrome's world dimmed a little.

She still doesn't know.

Resignation tamped down his momentary elation, dousing his hope and kicking sand all over the fireworks that was his short-lived joy.

Time, it seemed, would forever be both and never on his side, but in this, at least, he could be grateful. Dee was alive, and she remembered. It was more than he could have hoped for and far more than he deserved.

She, however, deserved the sky's wonders and all the finery this mortal world had to offer. He wouldn't bring himself to hope that she'd choose to walk that world alongside him, but he could show it to her regardless.

He owed her that much, even if it fucking destroyed him.

"I have someplace I'd like to take you. People I'd like to reintroduce you to."

"People . . . your brothers? The ones Drea— I mean, *I* met at the Moroccan restaurant?"

"The very ones."

She glanced down uncertainly at her wrist. "They'll be able to tell me about this mark?"

Chrome tried to school the sadness out of his smile. "Yes, and not only that but you'll be able to see it in action . . . and make some decisions for yourself."

CHAPTER 30

The smell of earth and minerals was surprisingly just as comforting to Drea as that of water. Though it probably had more to do with the angel sitting next to her than anything about the carved cavern walls around her.

Den, she reminded herself for the umpteenth time. This was not just a cavern but their den. Theirs, the sentinel angels who'd sacrificed their freedom so the souls in heaven and the mages in the Empyrean could live. The defenders of the Eternal Flame.

And she was sitting on their couch, drinking their French-pressed coffee, agonizing over what to do about the fresh golden symbol warming her skin.

Around her, a veritable army of warriors—male and female alike—swarmed about like restless herding dogs relegated to apartment living. The uneasy energy wasn't just palpable but improbable.

Of all the things she did and didn't imagine for herself, winding up the vessel of a reincarnated soul bonded to the prime sentinel's intelligence master hadn't been on the list. Not even a little bit.

Soul bond . . .

Drea cupped her mug and slid her gaze to Chrome. In a great room of large sentinels and their even larger-than-life mates, there was nowhere to hide or even sit quietly to absorb the enormity of what swirled around her. Bereft of such a haven, she simply allowed her blossoming mind to take it all in —starting with him.

She *remembered* him. Every glorious act and inch that had ever transpired between them clung to her soul like a vital fingerprint. Even as he sat beside her talking to the prime sentinel, who now went by Tung—short for Tungsten—she couldn't help but admire the way Chrome's biceps bunched and played beneath skin her body knew to be every bit as scorching as his fire.

With her memories returned, other thoughts surfaced as well. Thoughts of that night in the Empyrean. The very reason she'd left the sanctuary of his warm body to provide a different sort of sanctuary to others. She'd have told him as much, told him how his empowering strength and fearlessness despite the terrors bearing down upon them was the spark that had ignited her journey. When she'd snuck away in the middle of the night, she'd not only had the heat of his kiss still warming her lips but also his fortitude. His passion, his drive, his blissful touches and undeterred tenderness, all of it had imprinted on her so harshly, it left only one thought racing through her mind. How could she not do the same? How, by all the mages, could she not give her all as well?

So she'd left, despite the part of her pleading to stay, and by some miracle of the Eternal Flame, he'd found her still. When Drea glanced down at the tattoo on her wrist, a part of her wondered whether he always would.

Or would he simply do the same for any soul in need of help? Was this mark just another symptom of Iona's magic, like a fingerprint that was only immortalized because it happened to be the last one that remained?

Drea hadn't been well-versed in the water worlds before she'd embarked on her journey that night, a fact that her mentoring mages had never been shy about pointing out. If she had listened and studied more and not been so reckless, perhaps she'd already know more of the significance of sea nymph prophecy magic. Would Iona have known of the soul bond? Had the old sea nymph had a hand in all of this somehow?

The prime sentinel swiped a thumb across Drea's wrist before returning her hand gently to Chrome's care. "It is good to see your name written in the old symbols again, brother." Tungsten's similar stormy eyes, though more arctic silver than Chrome's gunmetal stare, lit from someplace Drea suspected had once endured cold fires for far too long as well.

"The memories have been . . . overwhelming, for sure." Chrome squeezed her hand in a gesture meant to exude the comfort she didn't feel.

Overwhelming. If he hadn't had such a secure hold on her wrist, she'd have bolted from the chair and begged any of the women to take pity on her frazzled mind and point her toward the nearest way out.

So much had changed from the quiet sanctuary of their hotel room. There, against the backdrop of ecru walls and framed photographs of mountains she'd never ski down, she'd shared a private connection with Chrome that reached beyond words and explanations. It was her own sacred haven, where desperate limbs and mouths answered more questions than words or logic ever could. It had all felt right. Natural. Essential.

Now that the real answers were here, however, splayed out on overheated skin that itched for more contact, she wasn't sure what to make of them . . . what *he* made of them.

Tung's explanations rattled on, and Drea had to force herself to anchor her awareness into the conversation. " . . . the soul bond mark is the connection of the Eternal Flame's light within two individuals. Our mortal mates all carry a spark of the Flame as well, and because you're celestial-born like us, I suspect the bond manifested a bit differently . . ."

More words floated in and out of her grasp, while her heart raced behind her ribs. Chrome held her hand but wouldn't look at her, not truly. Her stomach flipped over as she tried to get a better read on him, but all she got was stony silence broken by the occasional grunt or nod. Nothing to indicate which way his flag flew amid the torrent of information. Did he want her? This? Neither of them had spoken of commitment or what tomorrow would look like, let alone several tomorrows. What if —

Rose hooked Drea around her elbow and hauled her to her feet. "Tung, you know I love you, but brevity is not your strong suit. Why don't you stick to, um, actual strong suits, I guess." Dragging Drea behind her, Rose pecked the prime sentinel on his still-moving cheek and ushered them both toward the hallway that led to the living quarters. "The man is the literal definition of an angel, but he's got Neil deGrasse Tyson tendencies when it comes to explaining the universe. Or whatever-verse, I guess. If there's any sort of captive audience, their ass is liable to fall asleep before he gets to the point."

Drea looked over her shoulder to assess the inadvertent damage of their departure, but all she saw was Tammy settling onto Tungsten's lap and running sisterly interference. Once his mate's arms were thoroughly draped over the prime sentinel's decidedly un-shrugged shoulders, Tammy's teasing words delivered their mild-mannered blow. "She's right, my love. Now hush. Give the girl some room to breathe."

The happy couple fell out of view as Rose whipped Drea around a corner. "I know that look when I see it, you know."

"Look?" Drea asked.

"Oh, yes. It's the look of crippling self-doubt. I wore that outfit *out,* and let me tell you, despite that trash never being in style, it owned my entire ensemble for way too long."

Rose paused in front of a door with a giant handle more ornate than a Martha Stewart tablescape and nudged the entrance open. Surprisingly, the thing moved without the weight expected of the standard iron doors common throughout the rest of the den. This door was solid wood and adorned with an oil-rubbed bronze privacy door lever, complete with Victorian rose petals on the top and bottom and a small keyhole intricate enough to match any sunken treasure chest.

Like the rest of the sentinels' den, there were no windows in the cozy room, but what it lacked in natural light it made up for in other forms of opulence. Twinkle lights dripped from low-lit standing lamps on opposite ends of the room, crisscrossing the ceiling in a net of warmth that reminded Drea of the sunsets in the Empyrean. Burgundy cushions lay in fat clumps along the far wall, behind which stood floor-to-ceiling shelving that housed everything from books to scented candles to sketch pads and drawing supplies. Potted Chinese evergreens stood sentinel in the corners. Their wide, white-spattered green leaves hung low over the floor pillows, offering a canopy of evergreen shade from the soft glow above.

"This is our spot. Girls only. I know it's ridiculously juvenile, but so are the males when they want to be. After Tammy soul bonded with Tung, she said the only way she could spend any livable time down here in the den was if she had a place where she didn't have to see Bronze practicing his flex poses after a workout. One of their storage rooms was converted to our nook three days later." Rose plopped down onto the floor and yanked open a drawer to her right. The roped red licorice hung from her bottom lip a moment later, and two more of its kind found their way into Drea's hand. "Twizzlers make everything better. Now, tell me where your head's at. And pass me a pomegranate seltzer while you're at it. They're in the mini fridge behind you."

Drea hobbled around with shaky knees before locating the drinks and tossing one to Rose. She couldn't help but track the woman's wrist and the mark it bore. Rose, who Drea quickly learned was far more observant than the other women, noticed Drea's gaze. An inquisitive brow inched toward the twin's hairline, a silent command to proceed.

Drea's lips twisted around the candy, sucking down the strawberry flavor she desperately hoped would sweeten her worried words. "When Sentinel Malthoran—Titan, I mean—when his mark appeared on your wrist, were you at all worried you didn't, perhaps, deserve it?"

Rose's knowing gaze sparked above the frosty can upheld to her mouth. "We had our difficulties like any couple, trust being chief among them. Since I was new to the whole angels and demons thing, however, it wasn't a far step for me to believe in fate. At that point, what was one more dog on the pile?" White teeth bit off a hefty chunk of Twizzler before Rose pointed at Drea. "What I *didn't* believe was that, just because this man's name magically appeared on my arm and he got his celestial woo-woo juice back, I no longer had agency. I had, and still have, every right to choose who I hitch my trailer to for as many breaths as I've got left. Deserving it has nothing to do with it. I didn't deserve to grow up in a broken home or have the only family I'd kill for ripped away from me for six months. No one deserves what life throws at them, good or bad. It just is what it is." Rose leaned forward, and whatever nonchalance might have lingered in the woman promptly found somewhere else to be. "Fate may have chosen me to be part of Titan's journey, but *I* decided he should be part of mine. The best part, I might add."

Drea fell back against the cushions, wishing the darn things weren't so plush so she could properly bang her head against the wall. It had never occurred to her that she'd have a say in any of this. When it came to self-advocacy, she was wholly out of practice. Was that why her chest felt so concave? Or was something else missing that only served to magnify the feeling?

A feeling that had always been remarkably absent around Chrome.

"I just don't want him to be cornered into a mistake he had no say in. He's too righteous to refuse the bond, too honorable to see it for more than it represents. He has his full power back."

Rose snorted, though the reaction seemed rooted more in pity than derision. "No, he has his soul's other half back." Solemn eyes filled with remnants of the woman's trials met Drea's. "There's a far cry between duty and devotion. No one can make the judgment call on the belief system of either. That's a personal choice, and it is a *choice*. Once you get that part down, fate takes over from there. Trust me on that one."

Trust. There was that word again. The thing felt so heavy that, ironically, there was hardly any choice in believing Rose at all. Drea did a quick mental recap of every memory that included Chrome, past and further past. None of them ever blared warning signals except where her self-doubt was concerned. From her mentors to Malcolm, she had never been given the benefit of the doubt or even the slightest opportunity for someone to see that there was more beneath the surface than her declared scatterbrained tendencies and perceived flight risk.

Declared and perceived by everyone else, except Chrome. To him, she'd always just been Dee. Not striving-to-impress-her-superiors Dee. Or one-day-she'll-measure-up Dee. Just Dee. As she was.

He'd proven that across more lifetimes than she had any right to live, through incarnations and relationships fate had planted in front of him in some sort of celestial challenge.

A challenge he'd stood up and accepted over and over . . .

"I've got to go." Drea shoved the remaining Twizzler into her mouth and scrambled to her feet. The door wasn't even open all the way before Titan, who had a habit of never leaving Rose's side for too long, and his brick house of a chest filled the space. He barely had time to step aside before Drea ducked past him and ran down the hall toward the great room.

"He's not in there," Titan called after her.

Drea halted and spun around. "Where is he?"

A lopsided grin lifted the angel's mouth. "Someplace only you could barge into."

CHAPTER 31

The slow rise and fall of Axtar's chest was the only comfort Chrome allowed himself to indulge in. Every other time he ventured down to the sick bay, the sight of Ax's wan body had nearly caused him to upend anything that wasn't strapped down. The only thing that stopped him was knowing that, ironically, it was all the un-strapped-down shit that was most likely keeping his friend alive. Days ago, he would have sacrificed his fire just to walk in here, flick the lights on, and see the seraph smiling back at him with those bright inquisitive eyes. With Drea upstairs, however, he was inclined to adjust his stance on the matter.

He didn't need brotherly advice or devil's advocate. What he needed was a comatose captive audience who couldn't talk him out of doing what needed to be done.

Unconscious, Ax couldn't see Chrome's beast, couldn't see it writhing beneath his too-tight skin. A blessing too. Had the seraph been in full health, his commander would have no doubt gleefully pummeled Chrome's cowardly hide into the stones.

A coward. That was exactly what he fucking was. While Drea's violet eyes had dipped and swept around the den earlier in obvious panic over all that she'd learned, even landing on him a time or two with a silent plea for explanation or, worse, extraction, Chrome had bit back the urge to yank her out of there and plant her someplace with a closed door and him standing between it and her. The mates were great, as always, serving her coffee and answering questions. His brothers as well were disgustingly amicable, treating Drea like the royalty all soul bonds should be treated as. Brass actually bowed to her. *Bowed.* The sympathetic smiles and polite encouragement only made the entire situation more nightmarish, until Rose—bless that woman—gave him an out he desperately needed and swept Drea away.

It wasn't until his forehead kissed the door to the sick bay that he realized where he'd wound up and why.

"Tung was at it again, you know. The prime sentinel didn't leave a single detail out. Just fire-hosed her with every bit of information we had on the soul bond connection, the Empyrean, reincarnation, Cyro, just . . . everything." Chrome tossed a shredded piece of gauze into the wastebasket, grabbed another four-by-four from a stack, and got to work tearing the fibers apart. Fucking art imitating life. "Her world wasn't just turned upside down but torched to oblivion, and then I decided that bringing her here would somehow help clear the field? Really? All it did was shine a light on the ashes so she could see just how fucked up her options are. Lack of options, actually, if we're going for specifics."

Axtar's unconscious frame didn't move, save for the parts that told Chrome his friend was still alive. Alive and now subjected to one of Chrome's melancholy broodfests powerful enough to bring down the mountains along with his disposition.

Chrome chucked another gauze ball at the garbage can. The thing kissed the rim, then lazily floated to the floor as if remorsefully sighing its commiseration on the room's behalf.

"I can't trap her again, Ax. You should have seen her face when everything came flooding back. It was like ripping a tourniquet off a blood-starved limb, where you can't do a damn thing except hope the flesh survives. Her eyes exploded with an awareness I've never seen before, and it nearly crushed me. She's only just regained herself. How the hell can I chain her up again? I can't. I *won't*."

If he needed his brothers to make sure of that fact, he'd go that route, though he didn't relish answering to the women on that front. His why was his own. Had to be.

The seraph stayed silent, but even if Ax had been awake and well while listening to this diatribe, the seraph would have held his tongue regardless. Ax had always been an angel of not necessarily a few words but the right words, while Chrome had zero qualms about saying what needed saying.

Chrome inched the covers higher over the angel's skeletal torso, snarling at the hollow spaces between Ax's ribs that still stood out in relief. Another reminder of a problem he didn't have a diagnosis for and couldn't fucking fix.

"How is he doing?"

Drea's smoky voice penetrated his morose thoughts, and he whirled around in surprise. Her lithe form slunk inside the sick bay, but she didn't step away from the door. His heart kicked against his chest. Would there ever be a time when it *didn't* do that just at the sight of her? That blonde braid resting casually over a slim shoulder was so much more than just a memory. He knew that hair and could recall the exact patches of his skin that would pucker into goose bumps first when the soft locks grazed over him. He pressed his lips together as another memory assaulted him, one of his mouth memorizing the exact slope of her shoulder and how, when he'd press against the secret soft spot beneath her ribs, her shoulders and arms would melt away from her ears along with the fleeting tension.

Those things, those small touches and quiet obsessions, had

become so much more than simple memories. How, after all this time, had he ever survived on just the recollection of her?

A recollection she was just now coming to terms with.

"Stable." Gravel roughened his voice, but he pushed the word through like tar through a sieve.

Drea's soft amethyst gaze touched everything in the room. The light in her eyes dimmed slightly at the implications of what she was looking at. "I didn't realize you had a hospital down here, but I guess it makes sense given the circumstances."

"It's not really a hospital. Just a sick bay with slightly-more-than-basic medical and laboratory equipment. It's kind of become a need as of late, and our bodily makeup is highly specialized. We couldn't exactly waltz into Aurora Medical Center with our types of injuries."

She nodded her understanding, then paused for a moment before her words nailed him to his seat. "Or fire."

Their gazes clashed, and a heavy charge filled the otherwise sterile space.

"Yeah." Chrome stood but didn't quite know where to go. Oh, he knew where he *wanted* to go and who he wanted to take into his arms before dropping to his knees and letting every simpering plea tumble out of him in a torrent of shameless desperation.

Stay with me. I'll go anywhere you need to be. I can't live on just memories of you, not again.

Chrome's skin heated as his fire crashed against the walls of his frame, protesting his decision as much as he was. He bit it back, locking it up tight within his core, even as his celestial makeup rebelled at closing off access to his full power—a power he'd long been without until Drea freed that as well.

Then Drea took a step forward. "Tungsten told me about Axtar."

"I'll bet he did."

"You knew who he was when we were in the lab. Even in the dark, you knew."

Chrome's head nodded for him, while his mind raced to figure out where she was going with this.

She took another step forward. "You always seem to do the right thing."

"No," he bit out. "I do what needs doing."

Her chin dipped, and something he couldn't quite read tempered her expression. Chrome cursed inwardly, and a misplaced rage locked his muscles. He thought he knew all her tells and ticks. Again, he was wrong. His fire roared, threatening to burst free, to search and swarm his soul bond for any signs of discomfort, but again, he tamped it down.

Then she twisted her lips and drifted closer. "I think . . . No, I'm not doing that anymore. Not with you."

Pain a thousand times worse than any dark magic lanced through his soul, but he stood there, rooted to the ground, and let it crash into him. He steeled his features into placid indifference, never wanting her to see the impact her words had on him. A deep breath did little to calm his burning nerves, but he reminded himself for the umpteenth time that this was how it should be. Drea deserved to have a choice, regardless of the soul bond, and if her choice didn't include him, he'd find a way to—

Warm fingers encircled his right hand and slowly peeled back each of his clenched fingers until they were spread wide. Then Drea did the same to his other hand and interlaced her fingers with his.

"What I'm trying to say, but failing spectacularly at, is that, when it comes to you, I've done entirely too much thinking. I need to start feeling. No, that's not it either." Drea shook her head. "Crap, I'm terrible at this."

"You're perfect," he rushed out.

Trembling lips softened into a grateful smile. "Don't say things like that or you'll make me lose my nerve."

"I'll never *not* tell you what needs telling, Drea."

She dropped his hands and shoved at his chest. He had the good sense to force himself off-balance for her benefit. "See! That's what I'm talking about. I can't make the right decisions when I'm around you, even though every part of me feels nothing *but* right when we're together."

His mind stalled out while her feet literally picked up the pace. Her braid was a blur of blonde as she moved back and forth in front of him. "You're the prime sentinel's intelligence master. You are, by definition, the smartest being in the Empyrean, and I can't keep a thought in my head for longer than it takes to form one. You're hardwired for discipline and righteousness while I constantly have to convince those around me my choices are valid, even if those choices come to me at inopportune times."

Drea absorbed herself in worrying her fingernail, and Chrome had to hold his breath while she narrowly avoided turning from the wall in time before she got a forehead full of plasterboard.

"When Tungsten and Rose explained to me about the soul bond, I was scared but not because I didn't want you." She stopped moving long enough for Chrome's eyes to still and her shoulders to peel away from her ears. "I was scared because what if you didn't want me? This?" She held up her wrist, and the golden tattoo of his celestial name flashed under the overhead lights. "You said yourself, you do what needs doing, and you're so damn honorable that I couldn't imagine you'd ever say no to the bond, despite what you truly felt about me."

Chrome's fire flared within him, igniting a rage that threatened to scorch the great mountains around them. *Despite* what he felt about her? Too *honorable* to say no to the bond? Did this female honestly think he'd stay with her out of duty-bound *pity*? Was that where this was going?

Chrome blinked away the power from his eyes and prepared

to stalk toward her. "Listen to me. If you think, for one goddamn second, I don't—"

"Then I decided I didn't care." Drea hefted her chin and marched back to him while his mind worked over her words.

Wait. Didn't care?

"No, I don't care, Chrome." Then she grabbed his face in her palms and pressed her forehead to his. "I don't care about the whys and why-nots, because I just want to be with you. Whether it's the honorable thing on your part or the much-needed thing on mine, I simply don't care. I'm done thinking, done trying to figure out why my pulse rises when I'm near you but my mind stills. It's like all the noise clears out around you and I'm allowed to just . . . *be*. Whether it's fate or the bond, I don't know, and I honestly don't care. You're my choice every time. You've always been my choice, even when I couldn't remember why I was choosing you."

Genuine joy brightened Drea's features, and a smile he'd only ever given her under sheets and in private shadows bloomed so damn brilliantly, it rivaled any flame he could conjure. And by some twisted turn of fate, he'd been the one to put it there.

Chrome wrapped his arms around Drea and clutched her to his chest. "I've never had a choice, and by the mages, I've never been more grateful."

She tried to peel back to look at him, but he just held her still. "No, hear me out, Dee. Just let me say this."

"Okay," she whispered, her breath warming the coldest part of him.

"Since the morning I woke up in that dormitory, I've thought of nothing else but you. When I fell from the Empyrean and my power was ripped from me, it was *your* image I held in my mind through the pain of it all. When I landed within the rock, the scent of water lilies and lilacs pulled me to the surface. *Your* scent." Chrome leaned back and cupped the side of her cheek. "I clung to the memory of your soul every time the charmers snuffed one out of existence. And ever since you've been back, I've counted the days for what they were: miracles. Miracles I didn't understand, but fuck if I was to question how they came to be. All I knew was that you were alive, and that was more than enough. So, no, sweet Dee, I've never had a choice. When it comes to you, I'm all out of loyalty tests. I've always been yours." Emotion clogged his throat, and he quickly tried to clear it away. "But I will stand here as your sentinel and humbly honor whatever choice you make. I'll never take that from you."

Drea flashed the smile he'd cherished in his most private memories, except it was real, and it was for him. "I choose you. My soul bond."

His eyes fell shut. "Thank fuck."

Then he snatched her to him and claimed her mouth in a tender possession. The kiss wasn't a fiery frenzy of passion like the kind they'd shared in the hotel or the curious desperation that had followed them into the dark closet at the lab. This kiss was one of renewed promises and shared secrets. Chrome's soul exhaled its relief into his mate's embrace. He angled his head farther to deepen the kiss, eating up her soft moans and swiping away happy tears.

When he leaned in again, a gentle sigh filled the room.

One neither he nor Drea had made.

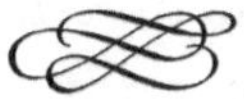

For the second time in her memory, Drea didn't want the sun to rise. The reason for that desire held her firmly against his chest while metallic wings beat around them. The body of the angel who carried her—*her* angel—was unlike that of the body she'd gotten to relearn last night. Firm muscles and velvet steel had nothing on the rigid smoothness and strength of a sentinel angel shifted into full metallic armor.

Magnificent didn't even come close to describing the experience that was Chrome, especially knowing the choices they'd both made and the commitments they'd spoken aloud. Right was too simple a word to describe their bond. For it *was* a bond, Drea had come to realize, even during the often-interrupted hours of last night.

Chrome dipped below the trees, and Drea's stomach rose into her throat. She scrambled for purchase against his neck, barely grazing his undercut before a deep chuckle vibrated against her chest.

"You're not seriously thinking I'm going to drop you, are you?"

"I'm seriously thinking I should have brought a helmet, a harness, and possibly a zipline." Drea shrunk into his shoulder before her braid could whip around and swat her in the nose for the third time.

Chrome caught it in midair and gently tucked the thing down the back of her shirt.

"My hero," she grumbled, though she couldn't help but drop a kiss onto the side of his neck.

The touch of affection caused Chrome to stumble out of his glide. He cursed softly before quickly correcting himself. "Enough, woman."

"You weren't saying that last night," she crooned.

He grunted the grunt of a thousand frustrated males and landed smoothly on the patch of trees next to Drea's apartment building. Once her legs were firmly on the ground, she stepped out of his hold, looked around at the road they stood near, and smiled as she walked over to a familiar bit of curb.

"This is where we first met."

"For the second time." He took her hand and dropped a kiss on her palm.

She melted against him. "Oh, fine. For the second time."

Dawn was about forty-five minutes from getting its act together, and though Drea would have happily lain in Chrome's bed until the mattress needed to be flipped six months from now, they both had a lot to sort through. For Drea, that meant making sure her butt was in her own bed before Molly woke up. She still had no earthly clue what to tell her best friend, but if she didn't have to start with answering the dreaded "Hey, where were you last night?" the morning would at least begin on a manageable foot.

Which was far more than she could say for Chrome and his brothers.

Axtar had begun to show signs of consciousness while Chrome and Drea were in the sick bay. It started with subtle breath noises, then wheezing, until things progressed to full-on grunts and coughing spasms.

The den had descended into madness after that.

Alarms sounded. Angels came running. At some point, Brass had escorted Drea out of the sick bay and back to the great room, where Rose and Tammy sat in silent vigil with her. Every hour or so, one of the sentinels would give them a status report, only to slink away again when none of the news was the great white ray of hope they'd all been expecting. Finally, somewhere around one o'clock in the morning, Drea was shown to Chrome's suite of rooms and crashed. He joined her a short while later, more exhausted than she'd ever seen him.

Throughout the night, Axtar would regain consciousness in short spurts, but nothing that lasted longer than a few minutes and nothing that resulted in verbal communication or prolonged awareness. But progress was progress, and given that none of them knew the full extent of his suffering, Chrome surmised that any cognition was a good sign.

Worry over the seraph led to a desperate reminder of their own missed opportunities. They lost themselves in each other after that. Clothes fell away, and pleasure replaced sorrow. Once she had him settled against the mattress, with his proud cock bared to her and his crown weeping for her touch, she took him in every way she'd longed to since her memories had returned.

Drea failed miserably at suppressing a yawn and squinted against the purple sky as it began fading from lilac to gray. "I fully plan on going back to sleep for another week or so."

"A week, huh?"

"Maybe two to be on the safe side, just to make sure my brain still remembers how to make melatonin correctly."

Chrome chuckled softly and held her to his hip as he escorted her toward the parking lot below her building. "Are you planning on being in dark spaces for prolonged periods of time?"

"You mean like an underground den?"

He shrugged. "Something like—"

Chrome went rigid and flung Drea behind him. She barely had time to get her feet under her before liquid quicksilver consumed his body, hardening his skin into a shield of chromium armor. Blue flames erupted in the metal's wake. Flaming metallic wings burst from his back, walling off Drea from the landscape around them.

"Chrome! What's happening?"

"Stay behind me."

A shiver of fear snaked up her spine. She'd never heard his voice like that, so low and menacing, like the warning hum of a predator.

Like a reaper coming to claim the dead.

Then they were moving in tandem. His right wing acted like a shield, while his left shifted like a herding dog, ensuring she stayed as close to his spine as possible. Her soul bond's fire couldn't harm her, that she remembered from Tungsten's lectures, but Chrome was acting like whatever was on the other side of his flames sure as hell could.

A shrill cry exploded through the trees. A distinctly *other* cry. Drea whirled around in time to see Chrome's angel fire blasting into a man holding an orb of electric green light. Golden eyes pierced the darkness before tendrils of blue flame crept up his throat and along his limbs, until his body was nothing more than smoldering ash.

A scream lodged in her throat. She'd seen that green light before, lining the walls of the laboratory.

Charmers.

Chrome whipped out two guns from concealed holsters and fired off round after round at targets she couldn't see. He moved like a dancer, his powerful legs finding smooth purchase before the rest of his muscles reacted.

"Stay close! Grab my phone from my back pocket. Call the

first number in my contacts." More shots fired, with each bullet leaving the chamber in a stream of angel fire. Each time they found their target, another charmer popped up.

"Where are they coming from?" she cried.

"Portal."

"A what? They can portal here?"

Drea's hands were so slick, she almost dropped the phone once she freed it from Chrome's jeans. The phone's backlight flared, and it took the longest second of her life for her eyes to adjust and find the number.

Before she hit send, Chrome's protective blue flames around her extinguished with a hiss. She ducked under the sudden burst of steam. Chrome grunted, then roared through clenched teeth, but he didn't move. His wings shuddered with strain, and his muscles tensed as if pulling against an invisible rope.

"Chrome? *Chrome!*" Drea clawed at his body, his wings, pushing and shoving any part of him to get him to move. Nothing responded to her touch save the slight muscle twitches she suspected were involuntary.

"That's enough, Drea. Put the phone down. It's over."

It was her turn to freeze. She knew that voice. More than knew it.

On unsteady toes, Drea inched above the slope of Chrome's frozen wing and peeked through the small opening in the crux of his shoulder. He still wasn't moving beyond basic bodily tremors. His eyes, however, tracked her movements with desperate ferocity. Pools of blazing silver roiled within his solid metal frame, but still, he couldn't move.

And then she saw it. The long, thin dart sticking out of his jugular vein. To her horror, the needle's tip had somehow penetrated his metallic skin.

Impossible.

"No!" Drea dropped the phone and scrambled underneath Chrome's wing until she was on his targeted side. Once there, she yanked the dart out of him and heaved it as far away as she could. It didn't land far enough.

Because it had already been emptied.

"What did you do to him?" she ground out as she turned to face their attacker.

Familiar brown loafers stepped around the trunk of a gnarled elm tree. Malcolm's suit was the same one he'd worn yesterday. Had it really only been a day since she'd seen him last? It could have been a week, given the wrinkles in the linen and the starchless sag of his shoulders. Dawn hadn't yet arrived, but even in the twilight, his five-o'clock shadow was on full display and clearly hadn't seen its daily appointment with a razor. Black hair usually slicked to precision stood mussed and disorderly. When eyes she'd know anywhere landed on her, she stumbled back against Chrome's suspended body.

"I'm upholding my end of the bargain," Malcolm offered by way of explanation.

"Bargain?" Drea shrieked. "What bargain?" Then she took in the advancing charmers who had begun to encircle her and Chrome, all of whom carried weapons both physical and magical. "Wait, you know who these guys are?" She stopped short of saying *what* they were.

"My dear, he knows far more than he's led you to believe, which was rather the point of our little experiment."

Drea jerked her head to the right, then threw her arm out to steady herself. The man who spoke lifted his arm to the sky and, with a flick of his wrist, cast an expanding dome of green magic around everybody assembled. "There, now we'll have some privacy. I do hate an audience. Unless, of course, it's my own."

The man speaking looked like all the other charmers and yet didn't. Swirling green and gold tattoos marked his pale skin like the rest of them, as did his hairless scalp and golden eyes, but that was where the similarities ended. Drea's prey drive spiked, and she fought back the urge to scream as he stepped closer toward her. His menacing frame towered not just over Chrome but the rest of the charmers by a good foot at least. Arresting eyes turned upward at the corners assessed the landscape with a curious interest, which Drea found more frightening than the flattened nub with slits that served as his nose. He advanced not with a normal gait but with the prowl of a predator, one who knew damn well that he was at the top of his food chain.

"C-Cyro," she breathed.

"The very one." The demon ruler executed a perfect bow apropos of his black-suited finery, which looked terrifyingly out of place next to his small army of weaponized hellions in a mix of cloaks and combat gear. "Now, let's get down to business." He cast a bored glance toward the brightening skyline. "I do believe this meeting is on the clock."

The mortals had it all wrong. Hell wasn't some fiery pit lorded over by a pronghorned principal supervising the torture of souls for all eternity. It was here, in a suburban apartment complex, with her ex-boyfriend standing next to the demon ruler while her soul bond was trapped in a prison of his own metal. Helplessness had become Drea's hell, and her mind couldn't scramble fast enough to figure out how she could claw out of it.

Then Malcolm stepped forward. "I darted the angel. She's all yours now. I did my part."

Drea whipped her head toward her former boyfriend. "Excuse me?"

"His part, my dear. You know, the bit he referenced earlier when he mentioned our bargain."

"Yes," Malcolm asserted, crossing his arms and facing Drea. "I deliver you, take out the meathead, and I get what I was promised."

"And what was that?" she snarled.

A cruel smile played on his lips, accentuating the hollowness in his cheeks she hadn't noticed before. "The first human ever to be gifted demon magic."

Drea faltered backward until the cool kiss of Chrome's metal touched her skin. She shook her head vehemently. "You're insane."

Cyro stepped between them. "Let's speed this up, shall we? Deadlines and all that. In short, your boy here has been my right-hand mortal for the past three months. As much as I value my own intelligence and entourage, I am also smart enough to know when to outsource, and running a laboratory with mortal-provided equipment requiring daytime operations did need me to think outside the box a bit. When I ran into our lovely friend Malcolm, who was about as down on his luck as I'd ever seen a man, he demonstrated a certain drive that turned out to be mutually beneficial."

"Cyro found me on Allen Street under the overpass." He slid his eyes toward the tree line before squaring his shoulders. "I had a needle in my arm and too few respirations to see me through until morning."

"You *what?*"

"But he was impeccably dressed, I will add. Not your average junkie's garb by a long shot." Cyro clasped his arms behind his back. "Real estate wasn't working out for him quite as well as he'd hoped, and his family made it clear they weren't paying for any more rehab stints for him because, for our dear Malcolm, the third time was most emphatically *not* the charm."

Drea shook her head in disbelief. "Drugs, Malcolm? You never told me any of that, not about your parents or anything. You said your family lived in Milwaukee and didn't like to fly. That was why you never introduced me to them."

"Technically not a lie," Malcolm added. "But they primarily don't speak to me for reasons that are now self-evident. With Cyro's magic, however, I wouldn't need my father's enterprising connections or the trust money my mother unfairly revoked. I could become the largest real estate mogul in the country, turning the Brand family name into something worth pursuing instead of something worth settling on. Every billboard, content platform, media outlet, and industry summit would be vying for my image, my expertise." He waved his hands emphatically around his head with a crazed excitement she'd never seen from him before.

An excitement born from a heroin high, she slowly realized. "You're insane. Insane!"

"No, Drea." A calm, cruel mask stole over features she'd once adored. "I'm an opportunist. One who intends to capitalize on the deal in front of me."

Drea couldn't retreat any farther back. Instead, she sank into Chrome's cold comfort and clung to his metal body like a raft in a tempest. This couldn't be happening. None of this could be happening. Her eyes shuttered closed for a moment, and a soft whimper escaped her.

"What does this have to do with me? What did you do to Chrome?"

Cyro walked closer toward her. She braced for his unwanted touch, but when he simply kept his arms clasped behind his back, she exhaled in relief and stayed silent. That golden gaze quietly assessed Chrome's frozen metallic body.

"The two millimeter gauge worked quite nicely." Then he addressed Drea over his shoulder. "You know, I wasn't sure it would work, but if it's good enough for zookeepers to take down an elephant, it's good enough for our intelligence master. The tricky part was perfecting the magic that allowed the needle to pierce his metallic skin in the first place."

Cyro swiped a thumb over the spot on Chrome's neck where the dart had been. "It closed up fast, too. Good. It's taken me a very long time to get the formula right. Though, thanks to your tireless work at my lab and the contributions of our previous patient, I think we've finally gotten the hang of metal manipulation. The key was, of course, creating a chemical compound—well, a magically infused and chemically altered compound—that mimicked the angels' own metallic talents but without their ability to actually control the stuff."

Drea's lips curled. "What. Did. You. Give. Him."

Cyro waved a hand away. "Nothing permanent, unfortunately. That infuriating fire of his is at full force and too strong for even me to extinguish or break through this close to dawn. His metal is merely frozen for a time. The one apex I had who mastered the dark magic needed to freeze the sentinels' metals in perpetuity was, unfortunately, incinerated before he could share the magic with others. So, no, your precious angel's fire will burn the compound off shortly but not before you and I have a little chat." He turned to Drea and pinned her with a boardroom smirk. "I'm here for *you*, my dear. You and that precious celestial DNA you have floating around inside your body."

A new terror heated her insides. "Me?"

"The very one. You see, before you so rudely stole my test subject, you began to learn things I didn't want you to learn. No, that's not correct. I didn't mind *you* piecing the puzzle together, you being mortal after all and thus easily dispensable. Sharing your information with the sentinels, and the prime sentinel's intelligence master specifically, however, was a direct violation of the NDA you signed. So, as the mortal idiom goes, snitches get stitches and end up in ditches. In your case, quite literally."

Ditches. The ditch her car had careened into coming home from the library . . .

"You had me run off the road and tried to kill me," she breathed.

Satisfaction stretched Cyro's grin wide before curving his mouth into a sneer. "Finally connected the dots, did you? Was that before or after you *stole* from me? I was nearly on the verge of reconfiguring that male's makeup entirely. Rhodium, we learned, is a powerful metal that is supremely resistant to corrosion and aggressive chemicals. The seraph, being celestial-born like yourself—and, yes, I knew all about your little origin story from the moment you stepped foot in my lab—had quite the unusual reaction when we began the chemical alteration process. All this time, I thought the secret to destroying the sentinels was in controlling their metal. But it turns out, I was approaching things all wrong. It wasn't the *metal* that needed manipulation but the celestial DNA."

Cyro returned his attention to Chrome and ran a finger along the angel's throat. The silver flames in Chrome's eyes flared with repressed fury, and Drea choked back a sob at the invasion on his behalf.

"I've made my own sentinel," Cyro whispered with no small amount of awe. "One who can nullify the angels' metallic warfare with magical weapons of his own. But more importantly, I've made a sentinel who is born of the Empyrean and, thus, is recognized as one of the heavenly realm's own but who is also one of mine. He was to be the start of my army. Once I manage to reopen the gates, his celestial makeup would allow him entrance, bypassing the sentinels and the mortal realm entirely and allow my charmers to finally advance on the Empyrean, destroying the light from a world that is only hospitable to those not born in the shadows." He hissed the last words while vengeful scorn twisted his features.

Then Cyro leveled Drea with a look of vile contempt. "And you fucking stole him out from under me," he snarled. "Just as I'll steal your beloved angel from you, *before* you come to join me. Your celestial DNA will make up for what I've lost with the seraph."

A sickening power curled around Cyro's hand, casting a green glow against Chrome's metal. Drea reared back.

"Hey!" Malcolm surged forward. "You said you wouldn't hurt her!"

A powerful blast rang through Drea's ears. Her legs crumpled, and she dropped to the ground. A sickening dizziness kept her on her knees, but as she slowly lifted her head toward Malcolm, he was no longer there. Instead, severed bloody limbs were scattered around the grass like carrion dropped from the sky.

Limbs that still wore Malcolm's suit coat and slacks.

Drea covered her mouth and screamed.

"Mortals are always so messy." Cyro sneered, then reignited his magic and turned toward Chrome.

"No, wait! A bargain! Give me a bargain, and I'll go with you willingly. Just don't hurt him. Please!" Drea didn't know where the idea came from, and quite frankly, she didn't care. Her plea was a surrender born of fate and fear. Chrome had to live, and her battered mind wouldn't accept anything less. Shakily, she rose to her hands and knees and hobbled to her feet. "A bargain, Cyro. I'm yours, but leave him and the other sentinels alone. Forever."

Cyro's eyes brightened in challenge, while Chrome's trembling only worsened. She knew her soul bond was fighting whatever they'd poisoned him with, but he still wasn't moving, and she had no idea how long until the injection wore off . . . or if Cyro was telling the truth that it even would.

"Now *that* is an interesting idea." He considered her offer a moment before a dark interest sparked within his golden eyes. "Tell me, mage, in all your travels through the realms, have you ever learned about memory magic?"

Drea shook her head stiffly, not trusting herself to speak.

"It's something I've been working on with the seraph while he was in my care and, I'm proud to say, something I've become quite adept at. So, little mage, if it's a bargain you want, here is what I propose."

Breaths came short and staggered, but it was enough to keep the oxygen flowing. As long as she could breathe, she could think, and if she could think, she could figure out a way to make this advantageous for her and Chrome. She had to.

She'd only just found her soul bond. It would tear her apart to lose him again.

"I will not harm the angel, nor will I go after the other sentinels, as you have requested, *if* you come with me willingly and consent to anything I ask of you. But"—Cyro threw a finger in the air—"before that is done, I will require a bit of insurance. Namely, the angel's memories."

The world stopped spinning, and Drea fell back against the anchor of Chrome's frozen body. "Why? Why would you take that from him, from us?"

"Because *you* have stolen from *me*," he ground out. "Therefore, your angel will have no memories of you or any encounter involving you. That means he won't remember this interaction or anything discussed here. His mind will quite literally repel all thoughts of you. The magic will cast a net of repulsion, triggering anyone in his world to forget you as well." Then he stepped in front of her and, with a chilling casualness, lifted her braid from the back of her shirt where Chrome had tucked it in. "If you reveal yourself to him in any way, the memory magic will be unleashed, wiping everything from his mind permanently, until he is nothing but an empty vessel. That is the way of it. Such magic requires a balance, I have learned. Annoying in testing, but effective in practice."

Testing. Had he tested it with Axtar?

Drea's head slammed back against Chrome's hard shoulder as the remainder of her strength left her. She reached for Chrome's hand, but when cold lifeless metal met her palm, her tears erupted and formed their own tracks to her soul bond. Droplets of salty sorrow painted the silver skin she desperately wished would turn to flesh one last time.

Please . . .

When nothing happened, she swallowed down a pain she'd

never heal from. "I need time. Give me some time. A month. Give me a month in the mortal realm. I've made friends here and have commitments. I can't just abandon them. Please, give me a month among the mortals, and I'll go with you, but *only* if Chrome and the others remain unharmed. I won't say anything about our bargain."

He considered her, and it was the longest moment of Drea's life. "Fine. One month and then I'll come for you."

Breath whooshed out of her, and she extended a trembling hand to Cyro to shake on their arrangement—

"But first, I'll take my collateral."

Cyro tossed Drea to the ground and fisted his hands in front of Chrome. Magic roared forth, circling his arms in green arcs of swirling power. Then he punched his magic against Chrome's forehead. Screams erupted. Hers, his, everyone and everything around Drea shrieked in defiance as shadows enveloped the glowing dome until, finally, everything dissolved into the quiet of the dawn.

Drea lay on the cool grass, knees clutched to her chest. As adrenaline rocked her back and forth and she did her best not to fall apart entirely, she caught a glimpse of Chrome's tattoo on her wrist.

And the black band of Cyro's bargain that now rested above it.

Cyro and the charmers were truly gone.

But so was her soul bond.

CHAPTER 34

Chrome stood in front of the sick bay's mirror, racking the slide on his favorite 9mm subcompact luger for the fourth time, and blanched at what stared back. Somewhere over the past month, his five-o'clock shadow had become an around-the-clock nightmare, progressing far past casual stubble and well into couldn't-give-a-shit-to-shave territory. The bags under his eyes and beard he could handle.

It was his fire that made him want to crawl out of his skin.

A bold mass of power swirled behind eyes he no longer recognized. Flames punched against his ribs so often, he couldn't take half a dozen steps before crushing a fist against his sternum to force the energy back down. The moment he left the den each day, an uneasy awareness nearly crippled his senses. On one particular patrol with Steel and Titan the week prior, his attention had been dragged inexplicably in so many directions, his brothers had to pull him from duty. The day before that, in the armory's shooting range, his every shot went wild until, finally, he punched the button to retract the paper shooting target and, with the zeal of a tantruming kinder-gartener, popped it full of holes at point-blank range just to prove he still could. When the gunfire echoes died down, he ripped his ear protection away and stared numbly at the bullet-riddled sagging silhouette.

Something about him wasn't just off but monumentally altered. Sleep was elusive, food unsatisfying, and fuck if he knew what the hell was causing it. More than once, he'd caught himself scratching at his skin as if whatever answer he was searching for could be found just under the surface, waiting to claw free.

His body was rebelling, and he hadn't a fucking clue why, which was how he wound up in the sick bay again, counting his ammo rounds and wondering whether tonight would be the night Titan would yank him off charmer patrol for good.

Chrome holstered his gun behind his back, flicked the faucet on to glacially cold, and splashed the frigid water on his face.

"It won't be long before you'll be in the bed beside me."

Chrome jerked a paper towel to his mug but couldn't hide the smile pulling at his lips. It was the only one happening these days. "Not sure that's the threat you think it is. It's quiet down here. I don't have to worry about hearing Bronze's mouth." He tried to heft levity he didn't truly feel into his joke, but even that only flared up the ache in his chest. "Besides, I'm pretty shitty company."

"So I've noticed." The bed creaked, and Chrome turned to help Axtar sit up farther against the pillow. Two weeks ago and after approximately one thousand years shaved off Chrome's life, the seraph had finally regained full consciousness. Unfortunately, relief did not come without frustration and weariness. Ax had very few memories of his time in captivity, and the ones he did have would wake him, screaming and kicking, in the middle of the night. In those moments of panicked ferocity, despite the seraph's emaciation, it would take at least three of the angels to hold him down lest the seraph rake his own skin off.

Funny thing about that raid and recovery mission. Whenever Chrome pounded the memory pavement and thought about Ax's extraction from that underground lab, he came away with a hazy experience that made sense on paper but still seemed riddled with questions. The lab had been under the sentinels' reconnaissance for months, that much he was sure of, but the actual infiltration was a sluggish recall clouded in dulled senses. The cell Axtar had been held in was always clear, its iron bars and putrid smells of waste as ripe as ever in his mind. He remembered the slight weight of his friend's body over his shoulder and the rage that fueled his fire when he beat back the sea of charmers to get Ax out of there.

But there had been *more*. The pockets of shadowy holes surrounding the raid never made sense or why he'd been in there alone to begin with. Below the surface, some reason poked at his cerebellum. It was like a scab, one he kept picking at, but no matter how hard he scratched, he could never find the healthy pink skin beneath.

"You are not yourself," Axtar remarked.

Chrome scoffed. "Yeah, well, we can work on cracking that nut once we've cracked yours."

The seraph gave a soft chuckle that rolled over into a rasping cough, which had been more prevalent of late, though less debilitating than it sounded. The brief spell added color to his cheeks, however, which were beginning to lose some of their angled harshness. "We are always a work in progress, I fear." A haunted spell cast a pall on the seraph's umber eyes before he blinked it away, reminding Chrome that their reunion came with just as much sorrow as serenity.

Not wishing for either of them to descend into dark places, Chrome quickly changed the subject. "Your skin looks much better," he acknowledged, gesturing toward his friend's arms. "The bruises aren't as prevalent. That's a great sign."

He didn't need to add how it would be even greater if they

knew how exactly those bruises got there in the first place, but whenever he or the others tried to broach the topic, Ax would insist he needed rest and, politely as ever, kick them all out.

The seraph held out his forearms and examined them. "Yes, so it seems." Then he drew his gaze to the weapons strapped to Chrome's body. "Going out on patrol again tonight?"

"Yeah, we need to keep—"

"Searching."

Chrome stilled under Axtar's inquisitive stare. Yes, he would be searching. For what, he had no fucking clue.

As if sensing Chrome's fogginess, Axtar cleared his throat. "There is one memory that has been resurfacing lately. One that I can't explain but one that I'd like to explore further."

Chrome chose his words carefully. "What do you remember?"

White eyebrows dipped over an uncertain expression. "A name."

"A name?"

"Yes. Just a name but one I feel compelled to . . . use." The seraph stared down at the tattooed talisman on his wrist. "Rhode."

Chrome rolled the name over in his mind for any meaning he could think of. "I've never heard its like."

"Good. Then perhaps it is how I am meant to start anew in this world. As Rhode."

The seraph lifted his chin a fraction, and a chilling determination filled the room. Chrome's fire roiled beneath his chest, causing him to quickly about-face toward the door. He needed air and answers, but only one of them would find him. For now, his friend was alive, and that would have to be enough.

He clenched the door handle. "I wish I could start over with you," he whispered and let himself out.

DREA'S PHONE buzzed a quiet rhythm on top of her comforter, and the sound was as numb as she felt. She waited for the thing to run its standard four cycles before it ceased dancing and the call went to voice mail. Drea didn't have to look down at the screen to know it was Molly trying to reach out. Drea had regrettably sent her best friend to voice mail jail twice already. The third time would have repercussions, no doubt, but Drea couldn't bring herself to care about that or much of anything these days.

Outside her bedroom window, blazing orange rays had already begun snuggling into the treetops. Soon, they'd be entirely below the horizon, closing out her month-long reprieve before whatever torment Cyro had planned for her became her new reality.

However, it had only taken a week for her to realize that, whatever the demon ruler threw at her, whatever he made her do, it wouldn't matter.

She was already dead.

Swift reminders of that fact came each time her traitorous mind chose a different memory of Chrome to relive.

They weren't enough, though, not by a long shot. Even her dreams didn't entirely get the details right. On those occasions, which were most nights, she'd wake in a panic, wondering whether she'd forgotten some vital part of him. When he teased her, did his smile quirk to the left or the right? Had she ever learned what he smelled like fresh from the shower, or would peppermint and cedar always cause her breath to hitch instead?

And what she feared the most, beyond anything Cyro could do to her, was forgetting the precise heat of his skin when enmeshed with hers and how her bond not only flared its acknowledgment on her wrist but also in her heart.

She could live with Chrome forgetting her. She *needed* him to forget her.

What she couldn't fathom was what would happen if *she* forgot *him*.

Insistent scratching at the front door pulled her away from the waning light's threat. A bang shook the apartment, followed by consecutive thuds of bags hitting the floor. Drea didn't even bother to square her shoulders and steel against what she knew was coming. What did it matter?

"We. Do not. Weaponize. *Affection!*" Molly stormed into Drea's bedroom and almost did a spit take at the bags packed on the floor by the closet. "Just what the heck is going on? No, don't answer that." She held her hand up in a gesture of exasperation. "Because the Drea I know wouldn't *ignore* her best friend. You don't feel like talking? That's fine . . . for other people, but not us. Woman the hell up. You do not get to throw silence in my face like a javelin and think that's some sort of pseudo-sisterly way of protecting me from what you're going through." Then she eyed the bags like a bomb technician eyeing a trip wire. "Please tell me this isn't what I think it is."

Drea's eyes swept the carpet at Molly's feet. "I need to go away for a while."

The indignation that had stormed in on the back of Molly's temper quickly left her friend's eyes and gentled her expression. Slowly, and with a forced calm that Drea knew would come with a cost later, Molly sank down onto the edge of the bed. "You've already been gone."

The words smacked Drea in the gut. Despite her private pep talks on dealing with Molly's ire, she was in no way prepared for the real thing.

"You're a ghost, Drea. For the past several weeks, the only time you've actually gotten any food into you was when I made sure you had leftovers in the fridge . . . *with* the heating instructions written on the containers. You hardly get out of bed, and every text I get from you is monosyllabic at best."

"I'm aware," Drea whispered.

"Are you? Because you're barely human. You're too thin, and every time I try to have a conversation about it, you seem to look right through me, like you're just doing the courtesy of looking in my direction without actually listening to me. When I dropped my cast iron pan on my foot two nights ago and screamed bloody murder, you didn't even flinch. I could use an air horn for an alarm clock and I'm pretty sure you wouldn't even realize it was morning. This isn't you. None of this is you, Drea. You're like a dull shell of my best friend, and now you're telling me you're leaving? I don't buy it. Not over some *man.*" Molly slashed her eyes toward the carpet and sneered. "Malcolm never deserved you. It's a good thing he left town, because if he was still around, I'm pretty sure I'd kill him for this."

No need. He's already dead.

The lie about exactly *which* male had left her had been surprisingly easy to spin, because Chrome—Ty, as Molly knew him—no longer existed in her roommate's world. Not long after Drea had returned following Cyro's bargain, she'd tried to test his warning that even Molly, who wasn't a part of Chrome's world and had no significant celestial connections, wouldn't remember him. At first, Drea dropped subtle hints, things about her reference partner at the library, how many brothers he had. Each clue was met with a queer expression and a barrage of questions Drea couldn't answer.

Molly truly didn't remember him.

Once the depression firmly set in, Drea had to switch tactics and instead made Molly believe that Malcolm, not Chrome, had left her. She'd kept up the ruse rather nicely and wondered whether the lies came so easily because of how her time in Cyro's care was fast approaching. Desperation brewed deceit, it seemed. The overnight bags were the finishing touches, as they were merely stuffed with spare blankets and pillows to complete the effect.

Let Molly think Drea was nursing a broken heart over a

lover who'd dumped her. It was the kindest gift she could leave, and as close to a clean break as her mind could conjure.

"It's over," Drea said. "And I've decided I need a change of scenery. Get out of town for a bit. I have an old work friend from one of the hospitals I used to work at. She's in New Mexico now, and we've been chatting here and there. Turns out, she's got a spare room and invited me to stay for as long as I'd like. I'm flying out tomorrow. Figured I'd trade in sugar maples for sagebrush and see how I liked it." Drea hoped the brightness in her smile outshone the mist gathering in her eyes. "I was going to tell you, but I didn't want you to—"

"Be angry with you."

Drea simply nodded through her heartache. Neither the truth nor the lie surrounding her departure could thaw the icy shards destroying her soul. Futility only made the fight worse. What was one more nail in the coffin to firmly wall off the final vestiges of everything beloved and familiar?

Molly's arms were around her before the first tear fell. "I wish I could help more than I have. I wish I had the words or the skills to pull you out of the muck myself, but I know there's no amount of me willing you back that's going to make it all better. If you need New Mexico right now instead of New Hampshire to forget that prick, then I'll send you off to the airport with endless love and my recipe for the best damned grilled nopales you've ever put in your mouth."

Drea snorted as she hugged Molly tighter. "I love you." *Please don't forget me.*

"I know. Same. Always the same."

When they both finally pulled away, Drea tried to wipe off the tears that had landed on Molly's shoulders but only succeeded in spreading the wetness. Then a thought occurred to her. "Will you do something for me before I leave tomorrow?"

"Anything."

"Can you drop me off at Gillickin Lake right now? New

Mexico may have plenty of cacti, but it won't have the lakes surrounding the White Mountains. I'd love to see it at sunset one final time before I head out."

"Of course."

Drea trailed Molly out of their apartment, gliding in a fog so thick her feet hardly touched the floor. She hadn't lied to her best friend when she'd told her she wanted to see the sunset over the water one last time.

Because once the night blanketed the sky, she'd never see the sun or water ever again.

CHAPTER 35

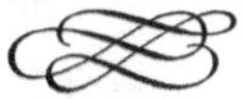

Chrome glided above the great elms blanketing the lush landscape of the White Mountains, doing his best to clear the cobwebs that threatened to entangle his mind. Spidering snares of dread and confusion pinged behind his eyes. If it weren't for the rote movements of flying, he'd no doubt be picking tree bark from his teeth. Thankfully, Titan, Brass, and Iron had already left to patrol Aurora's manufacturing district and hadn't questioned him when he said he'd catch up in a few.

He didn't miss the grim expressions of concern they did a piss-poor job of hiding.

Count me among the concerned parties as well, fellas. Misery loves company.

Chrome banked hard, then came up to circle one of the lakes near the mountain under which the majority of their den was located. Twilight was ending soon, and the final rays of sun backlit the growing mist floating along the lake's undisturbed surface. Already, the temperatures had begun to drop in the evening, with autumn threatening to pull rank over summer's short-term lease on the region. Soon, the fading days would swallow up the final vestiges of heat from the water, leaving it uninhabitable to all except wildlife and those Polar Plunge mortals.

As if humans needed another reason to prove why they didn't belong at the top of the food chain.

The smooth glass of the lake stretched out beneath him, and he'd never been more tempted to splash down and shatter the surface into a million violent ripples. His chaos craved chaos, and he was damn near out of his mind with agitation. Chrome dropped low and squinted against the setting sun, hoping the stuff would just go ahead and blind him already.

Heat surged within his muscles, pumping and priming them as if readying to go off to war. Chrome cracked his jaw and ticked his neck to the side, doing his best to swallow down the ever-present disturbance.

A disturbance that inexplicably worsened as night drew near.

Time was running out. He didn't know how or why he knew it, but he did. The harried rush of impending darkness threatened to douse his fire whenever it burned to near bursting. Chrome was an agitated mess of worry and warrior, not knowing whether to throw a punch or drop to his knees in desperation.

He circled the treetops again, faster this time, wondering just how long he could sustain the mania crawling under his skin.

Something is wrong. Something is—

An expanding wave rippled along the water's surface. Chrome cast his celestial senses about, searching for the animal that made it. White-tailed deer were common in this part of the mountains. So were moose and black bears. None ever wandered to the lake this close to sundown.

Chrome banked to the left and hovered behind a thick copse of balsam firs. He silently pulled a bough of needles to the side . . . and almost snapped the branch in his hand.

Small footprints tracked a neat line in the sand, bisecting the final tangerine rays of twilight. Once the steps reached the water's edge, they disappeared under flowing lavender skirts that billowed out across the glassy surface. Chrome's breath hitched. He gripped the tree branch so tightly, bark crumbled to the forest floor.

A woman with flowing blonde hair inched farther into the calm lake, her hands drawing lazy circles in the water at her sides. She was uncommonly tall, so much so that her sundress seemed to climb up her toned body, desperately reaching to cling and cover what it could manage. His interest, and other parts of him, were piqued, drawing him further out of hiding. Lips he imagined would curve into the most devastating smile were turned down at the corners, while waves of honey rested unbound over sagging shoulders.

Her face wasn't just downcast but distraught.

No, destroyed.

What was she doing there? And waist-high in what he knew was unpleasantly cold water? The approaching autumn had seen to the water's chill, especially at this time of day, mere minutes from the sun going down. Then, as she stepped farther into the lake, with the slight waves lapping at her trim waist and just below her breasts, his confusion turned to concern.

Inexplicable fear gripped him by the throat. A pang speared his temples as a faint image of another woman, one who also wore lavender robes and secret smiles, floated around his murky memory. As soon as he reached for the image, it danced away again, and his angel fire crackled a mournful cry deep within his muscles.

Chrome growled through gritted teeth and beat his head against the tree trunk. When he looked up, blonde tendrils spidered across the surface of the water before submerging entirely, leaving only outstretched hands above the surface.

"*No!*" The cry left him before he realized what he was seeing.

He bolted through the treetops and careened toward the spot near the shore where she'd last surfaced. Wind whipped across his heated skin, biting at every exposed scrap of him, so he flew harder, faster, with no mercy or care. Fire fueled his speed.

He had to get to her. Fractured mind or not, he couldn't bring himself to witness a drowning. He was a fucking sentinel. That part of him, at least, still remained.

But a deeper part of him, one ingrained so keenly into the soul of the intelligence master, warned that he would not survive whatever waited for him below.

All thoughts left him as soon as his boots hit the water.

It was sheer vanity that had Drea yanking on her paltry-periwinkle-by-day-yet-lavender-by-night dress before Molly loaded her into the car and deposited her at Gillickin Lake. She had no idea what drew her to it this evening or why she'd spent an extra minute she didn't have studying herself in the mirror and smoothing down the last of the garment's stubborn wrinkles.

In another time, one where wishes were granted and choices didn't require a pound of flesh, she'd have thought herself beautiful in the dress.

Beautiful in someone else's eyes, as well as her own.

Drea thought of those eyes as she waded farther into the chilly lake. Icy pinpricks tickled the skin along her legs, and she had to suck in deep breaths to steady herself when the water rose above her belly button. Stormy gunmetal irises painted a shimmering mosaic on the backs of her eyelids, and she hoped the images were strong enough to carry with her on the next leg of her journey.

In the silent car ride, she'd made a promise to herself that she wouldn't forget him. She'd cling to those blazing silver eyes when the torture was at its worst or when she was commanded to do the unspeakable.

When the years had dragged on and all she had were memories painted onto her skin and soul.

Drea lifted her chin and stared down the sun that had just winked out behind the forest. Her final sunset. Instinctually, she took a step toward it—

A flash of silver skirted over the tree line to her left, and her heart sank. There, above the trees, hovered a brutal specter with wings so large even the shadows stayed away. A vicious angel whose power radiated across the mountains . . . and he was staring right at her.

When she'd given up everything to keep him from remembering her.

To keep him alive.

"No," she croaked through vocal cords numb from disuse. "No!" Drea waved her hands as if to shoo him away but only succeeded in drawing further attention to her splash radius. "Leave! You have to leave! Don't look at me! Don't—"

Her foot slipped on a stone beneath the water, and she tossed her hands into the air. Cold current swallowed her up, and the slick lake bed gave little purchase under her bare feet. Beneath the water, murky shadows she'd dismissed earlier turned corporeal, forming tight chains around her ankles. She stretched her chin high, attempting to grab a final lungful of air, but only jerked against the shadows' hold. Her arms were the last to descend, and then . . . everything went still.

Once Chrome's tattooed name on her wrist was fully submerged, a pulse of energy coursed through her. The pressure in her lungs eased, and a weightless calm enveloped her.

Not energy. *Magic.*

When she finally opened her eyes, the urge to gasp for breath had fled. Around her, lake bed grasses stretched midfloat, and young trout gaped wide-mouthed and frozen between the rocks. Her dress and hair, however, wafted unhindered among the small waves of current.

What the . . . ?

Before her, bobbing among the driftwood, was an amalgamation of shadows she'd recognize anywhere.

The winged shadows from her dreams. But as Drea's eyes adjusted to the water, she followed the lines of the shadows dancing in front of her and froze. They weren't wings but weeds. Seaweed. The very same kind that had adorned her wrist until a little over a month ago, before the soul bond mark appeared.

The shadows morphed into limbs that were thick, yet elegant and startlingly familiar. Weeds torqued and tightened until the silhouette gave way to the squat and buxom form of the last soul Drea had escorted into the safety of the Empyrean.

Iona.

"How? No . . . no, that's impossible. You should be safe behind the gates." Her words were lost among the waves. Drea lurched forward, arms outstretched, trying to grasp the sea nymph before Drea had to surface and Cyro claimed her for good. But when her fingers swiped through the pine-green tendril of Iona's hair, she caught nothing. Iona's wrinkled smile beamed through the water as the current rippled softly around them. Drea reached out again, this time trying for the old sea nymph's gnarled hand. Again, her hand swiped clean through. On the third try, Drea's wrist began to pulse and warm with a familiar heat, one that, even surrounded by cool water, she instinctively recognized.

The heat of the soul bond but . . . *more.*

Startled, Drea clutched her wrist to her chest with all the speed the water would allow. That was when she finally took in the female before her. Sagging eyelids partially covered pearlescent eyes that had long ago lost their sight but still noticed everything somehow. Robes the color of the richest loam and slickened like a seal's skin swallowed Iona's weathered frame. Everything about the female, from her conch necklace to the pearls adorning her ears, was exactly as she'd looked the day Drea had escorted her soul to the Empyrean.

"You're not real," she whispered, more to herself than the specter before her. The sea nymph smiled, gesturing toward Drea's wrist, and a mantle of understanding settled around Drea's shoulders. "You're a memory. *My* memory." She looked down at her wrist and ran her fingers over Chrome's mark, carefully avoiding the garish black brand of Cyro's bargain. "The prophecy."

And then she heard it, recalling every word Iona spoke with her final breaths as loudly in her mind as if the female in front of her had spoken them now.

Should you ever find yourself in peril, star child, water will save you. Accept this prophecy with my deepest gratitude, for it will live on and in you regardless of time or memory, whether your skin carries the mark or your soul absorbs it. Memory has no magic where prophecy is concerned. Should one attempt to alter it, a steep reversal shall take its course. This is my eternal gift to you, for the eternity of peace you have bestowed upon me and my kin.

Another image appeared, but before she could dissect what she was seeing, a heart-wrenching snap rang out and searing pain scorched down her arm. Drea screamed, and an unknown light blinded her, but any cries were lost to the lake, which had once again awakened around her. She flailed against the pain, kicking and arching as shadows gave way to darkness.

A blur of silver moved above the water's surface. Something grabbed her arm and yanked her free of the water. Air rushed into her lungs as hands forcibly patted her upper back.

"Breathe, Drea! Breathe! C'mon, baby girl, breathe for me."

Her coughing petered out, and every muscle in her body stilled. The pats on her back turned to worried rubs, and the

rubs turned to urgent caresses as large hands spun her around . .
.

And she stared into stormy quicksilver eyes she never thought she'd see again.

Eyes that recognized her.

Water streamed down the planes of the angel's cheeks until it gathered in neat drops on an unruly beard that seemed as out of place on the man's chin as a jaguar in the Arctic.

She loved every morsel.

"Chrome . . ." He'd spoken her name. Not only that, but he'd come for her, somehow, someway. He *remembered* her.

Drea threw her hands around his neck as he enfolded her impossibly closer. Then his silver wings—those wonderfully monstrous and powerful wings—curled around her, blocking out the night. "I can't believe it. I-I thought I'd never see you again."

She was a blubbering mass of sodden synthetics. Her dress was utterly ruined and clung to every place it shouldn't. As more unintelligible words tumbled out of her, however, Chrome simply stroked her spine and held her close until her breath and tears were all used up. Only once the hysteria calmed and she was able to get more than one word out per exhale did he pull back to examine her well-being.

Then she was met with a panicked force that rivaled her own.

"Do you have *any* idea what it was like to know you existed in the world and not know who you were or how to get to you?" Wild eyes lit by fire and crazed by madness bore through to parts of her she never thought she'd feel again. "I saw and heard *everything*, Drea. Every fucking vitriolic word that bastard spewed at you, and I was powerless to get to you. How are you here?" Then he cast his eyes to the barren space in the sky where the sun had been.

Night had fallen. Time was up.

Chrome's wings tensed around her shoulders, and his hands quickly slid to the guns in his chest holster.

"Cyro's not coming," she said quickly, grabbing his hands. "He'll never find me, actually, because he no longer knows I exist." Drea answered Chrome's questioning gaze by lifting her wrist for his examination. Cyro's inked bargain no longer marred her skin. All that remained was the golden silhouette of Chrome's mark. As it always should have been.

He shook his head in disbelief. "I don't follow. Please start talking before I start shooting."

"Iona's prophecy!" She beamed. "She always said that water would save me, and it did. That's why I was drawn to the lake before the month was up, though I had no idea why. When I went under, I saw her. Well, I saw the memory of her through the prophetic magic and was reminded of her final words to me about the prophecy." Drea took a deep breath and recited the words that had saved her. "'Memory has no magic where prophecy is concerned. Should one attempt to alter it, a steep reversal shall take its course.'"

A slow dawning awakened Chrome's features. "Reversal. As in . . ."

Drea drew forward and planted a kiss in the center of Chrome's chest. Right over his heart. "The last thing I saw before you pulled me out wasn't a memory but a vision. It was you and me standing in the water just as we are now, holding each other and gazing at the sunrise coming over the lake."

"But the sun just finished setting," he remarked.

"Exactly. What I saw was *tomorrow*. It was *tomorrow's* sunrise, and the only way I would be around to see it is if Cyro never came for me. Iona's prophetic magic showed me tomorrow, because Cyro's memory magic must have been reversed. And if it was reversed, he would have no memory of me or anything associated with me. We'd be giant annoying gaps in his mind just as he'd done to you and the others." She smiled up at him with muscles stiff from misuse. "We're free."

"Free . . ." Chrome tested the word, donning an unreadable expression. He grunted softly before scooping her up in a flourish of soaked skirts and marching them toward the beach. "No, we're not."

"We're not?"

"And I never want to be." He settled her bare feet onto the cool sand but never let her out of his embrace. Then he lifted her wrist to his lips and pressed a fervent kiss to his mark. Every touch was a balm to her ravaged soul, and she wouldn't take a single caress for granted ever again. "Dee, from the moment you stormed into the repository, my heart was yours. Even without Iona's prophecy, I would have found a way back to you because I cannot exist in a world where my soul cries out for its better half and you don't answer." He kissed her firmly and fiercely, robbing her of every breath and whimper until she had no choice but to melt into him and rely on his strength.

"I love you, Drea. I simply don't work without you, and to be clear, I never plan to test the extent of that theory. You're my soul and my star. Every breath I take is yours, and every beat of my heart exists only to mimic yours. So no, dearest Dee, there is no freedom for us. I will always be yours."

Drea wrapped her arms around his middle and relished every muscle and ridge that kissed her back, as she knew she would forever, just like the soul of the man who'd come for her time and time again.

"Same. Ditto. Agreed. Forever."

EPILOGUE

olly snapped the cap on her marker and hefted the small box onto the pile of its compatriots by the door of their apartment. She regarded the stack with a self-satisfied smirk. "Well, that's the last of them. Every box has been labeled to within an inch of its life. I even threw in those biodegradable packing peanuts to protect some of the more breakable items."

Drea hugged her best friend. "Seriously, I don't know what I'd do without you."

Molly snorted into her hair. "Eat like shit and run out of shampoo regularly."

"Well, that goes without saying."

They stood like that for a few more beats, neither one willing to let the other go just yet. It had been three weeks since Chrome had regained his memories, and there had been no sign of Cyro. With the lab destroyed, Axtar—who now preferred to go by Rhode—finally up and walking around, and Chrome and Drea catching up on everything in between, Drea couldn't deny the calling for a new adventure.

Only, this time, there was no one around to label her flighty or frenetic.

"I still can't believe you're moving out," Molly mumbled into Drea's hair. "It's going to be so weird without you. Who am I going to pick up after?"

"You're hardly home anyway. The restaurant keeps you so busy. Trust me, you won't even notice I'm gone."

"Hardly."

With a final squeeze, Drea released Molly and did one last sweep around the space. "Do you know what you're going to do with my room?"

"Not sure yet. Probably just leave it the way it is for now, you know, in case things don't work out with your new *roommate*."

Drea rolled her eyes but couldn't help the flush of heat that crept up her neck. "I don't see that being a problem."

"Me neither," she said smugly, "though I haven't looked over any lease agreement for your new arrangement, so I can't be certain."

A warm chuckle bubbled through Drea. Her *arrangement* with Chrome was the furthest possible thing from an agreement. It was a necessity, a promise of a new beginning, and ironically enough, it came with a very lucrative employment opportunity. Apparently, when one dealt in precious metals as long as immortal fallen angels did, nest eggs weren't so much eggs as full herds of golden geese. It also made them out to be very generous employers, with Drea being their first-ever full-time employee.

Given Drea's prior laboratory experience, as well as her knowledge of Rhode's working labs—though she hadn't known they were his at the time—the sentinels asked if she'd be open to overseeing his care as he began his long road to recovery. He still didn't speak much about his time underground or what led him there, but because Drea had kept meticulous private notes on her findings during her time at the lab, she was the only one who might be able to decipher what had been done to him and how to help him navigate the new world he now inhabited.

She'd protested at first, stating how she was the furthest thing from a nurse or a doctor. The most patient care experience she had was when Molly went away for a weekend and trusted Drea to tend to her best friend's beloved succulent, Noami.

They held a funeral for the poor flora the following Monday and sat shiva the rest of the week. Who knew one could over-water a plant?

Chrome had been the first to shoot down her objections. "We're a bit beyond standard medical practice, babe. We learn on the job and answer to ourselves. The rest, we research and figure out as we go. It's no different than anything you've done your entire existence. Survival's survival, and it's our job to make sure no one has to go it alone."

Between the promise of autonomy and aid and moving in with Chrome to live among the sentinels, her life had finally felt *right*.

Except for leaving Molly.

The door to the apartment swung open. Chrome's gargantuan shoulders led the charge, followed by the more subdued but no less impressive Brass and Titan. Chrome stared at the pile of boxes by the door. "This the last of them? Because I've got tons more room in the truck if there's anything else you want to bring. I've got eight feet of length in the truck bed, and we haven't even filled up half of it yet."

"Oh, I forgot something! Be right back." Molly scurried to her room on feet that shouldn't have been so quick given the decaf chai tea they'd both enjoyed that morning.

"I'll take these down in the meantime." Titan grabbed the top half of the boxes and headed downstairs, while Brass loaded up on the other half.

Chrome and Drea agreed it was best not to tell Molly the

truth, at least in terms of their celestial natures. To Molly, Chrome—who gently explained his new naming preference, something about it being an old family name—was just an amazing boyfriend who loved Drea the way she deserved and came from really good breeding stock, as did his brothers.

Like Drea was one to argue that particular point.

A minute later, Molly returned with another box, this one larger and more cumbersome than the others, though no less immaculately packed up. Sealing tape gleamed in perfect neat rows along every cross-section, and the words *Dutch Oven* were scrawled along each side of the box in pristine bubble letters.

Actual bubble letters.

Drea quirked a brow. "I'm not stupid enough to ask what that is, because you've done such a wonderful job of clearly labeling the thing, but why are you giving it to me?"

Molly puffed out her cheeks, held her breath for a three count, as she often did when she needed to choose her phrases carefully, and exhaled a barrage of words with a force that would have knocked over an NFL offensive lineman. "Because this thing is enameled cast iron, has excellent heat retention, boasts a nine-and-a-half-quart capacity, and will easily feed all of those giant men who keep hovering around you. Also"—she sucked in a breath—"I've included a dozen recipe cards, all scalable for size, and none of them involve tomatoes, mushrooms, or eggplant, which I know you hate, so there's no reason for you not to make them and pleasevisitoften!"

Drea, Chrome, and Brass all blinked in unison. The sentinels exchanged apprehensive looks, as if they weren't sure what to acknowledge out of that string of sentences, but Drea merely stared at the woman who was like a sister and let each wave of emotion slam into her.

"I love you, Molly," she whispered.

Molly's lower lip quivered. "I love you, too."

"And I'll be over for lunch tomorrow. No burgers. Tacos?"

"With barbacoa." She sniffed insistently.

"Perfect."

Molly held out the box, but just as Drea was about to take it, Brass stepped forward and lifted it from her friend's hands. "Allow me."

The auburn-haired angel carefully hefted the box onto his shoulder, cradling the rest of the stacked boxes beneath his other arm. Molly's hands were frozen in front of her as she locked eyes with him. Then he dipped his head in her direction, breaking the spell, and marched downstairs.

Before Drea could turn back to her friend, Molly was already down the hall and shutting herself in her bedroom.

Chrome eyed the exchange but wisely kept his own council.

"I'll have to unpack that later, I suppose." Drea sighed.

Then the warmth of Chrome's body melted into her as he pulled her against his chest and brought her into the circle of his arms. "Ha ha, very punny."

"Punny?"

He shrugged. "I thought it was cute."

Drea kissed the dimple in his chin, which had become far more prominent since he'd gone back to shaving regularly. "I think *you're* cute."

A growl rumbled through his broad chest, and she sighed as the vibrations passed through her, calming any lingering nerves she may have had about the move.

"Kittens are cute," he clarified. "*I'm* terrifying."

"Terrifyingly cute," she teased.

He rolled his eyes but never eased his hold on her. "Thoughts, Dee. I want to hear 'em. You ready for this?"

Ah, yes. The elephant in the room. Was she ready for this? *This* being the close of one book and the beginning of another. She'd been turning that question over in her mind on repeat, wondering whether the change was coming too swiftly after all she'd been through.

It hadn't taken her long to settle on the truth.

"The moment you snatched my notebook paper off the street and didn't look at me like I was some kind of never-let-out-of-her-cage egghead, and I learned you weren't a troglodyte chest-thumper, something sturdy formed between us. A part of me suspected it, but I never had the wherewithal to fully examine it until now. It wasn't just the soul bond but the fulfillment of my soul. Learning who I am again, helping Rhode—" She glanced up and rested her chin on his chest. "Loving you, it all feels right."

"Damn right, it does." He kissed her softly and swiftly. When he pulled back, a look of pride and contentment stared back at her, tinged with something extra she'd learned to anticipate and crave. "And making up for lost time has jumped to the top of my agenda. In all ways."

She pulled him to her mouth and kissed him with the fervor of one caged for so long who was now promised the world. "I love you."

Chrome's eyes flashed the stormy silver of his angel fire. "That is my greatest gift and one I'll happily spend eternity repaying you for. I can think of no better debt to live in service of."

Drea snuggled close against him. "An eternity of service doesn't sound so bad when you put it like that."

He brushed warm lips across her brow and smiled into her hairline.

"And, apparently," she added, "it comes with free food prepared by yours truly, if Molly has anything to say about it."

"Sounds like love to me."

WITH MOLLY'S best friend finally settled, she's free to set her sights on what she's always wanted: her own restaurant. But when the staff quit unexpectedly, the one man she hasn't stopped thinking about offers himself up for dish duty. And to make the threat of this workplace romance even worse, her new hire drops a confounding bomb like no other: He's a fallen angel battling an ancient curse . . . and she's the only one who can break it. Find out what happens when Molly faces the ultimate choice: let the curse remain and risk her heart, or reverse the curse and risk her soul. Start reading Molly and Brass's story in *Angel's Temper!*

CAN WE KEEP IN TOUCH? Are you curious to see what happens when Drea moves in with Chrome, and goes from having one roommate to eight, plus mates? Old anxieties still plague her as she starts her new role as caregiver for Rhode. And if that wasn't enough, she has to learn how to navigate living among a rowdy band of fallen angels, along with a very distracting soul-bonded boss who insists workplace romances are all the rage. Claim your BONUS EPILOGUE when you sign up to my news-letter to find out just how persuasive Chrome can be. Enjoy!

THANK you so much for reading *Angel's Light!* If you loved seeing Chrome and Drea's relationship grow, let your friends know. Help other readers fall in love with this couple, and all those hunky angels, by leaving a review.

SCAN THE QR code to start reading *Angel's Temper* and the BONUS EPILOGUE today!

ACKNOWLEDGMENTS

I will never take for granted how easy it is to put a smile on someone's face with nothing more than words. Cynthia St. Aubin and Kerrigan Byrne have done that for me many times over. I'm a better writer because of those words, and can't wait to have many more not-so-straight-laced Zoom sessions with you ladies.

Although I'd like to think that this book was written in a vacuum, it sure as hell wasn't. Every time I agonized over a scene or character, my wonderful husband, Ben, was there to take the verbal pounding and be my sounding board. He's the fated to my mate, and the reason I write so many hunky heroes with beards. So, yeah, I think I'll keep him. ;-)

ABOUT THE AUTHOR

Aimee Robinson is a lover of romance novels in all forms. Her absolute favorites, though, are the ones that offer a little bit of something *extra*: time travel, guardian angels, good old-fashioned meddlesome grandmothers with a supernatural secret to hide, you name it.

She believes romance novels should transport you from the humdrum to the swoonworthy, preferably while being curled up on the couch with chocolate and tea (or a martini . . . or both!). Aimee's overactive imagination lends itself to fun tales with emotional adventures, sexy snark, and happily ever afters.

When not writing or reading, Aimee enjoys spending time with her husband and keeping up with her two young sons.

www.ingramcontent.com/pod-product-compliance
Lightning Source LLC
Chambersburg PA
CBHW061319190726
48288CB00002B/576